THEN

Also by Julie Myerson

FICTION
Sleepwalking
The Touch
Me and The Fat Man
Laura Blundy
Something Might Happen
The Story of You
Out of Breath

NON-FICTION
Home
Not A Games Person
The Lost Child

Julie Myerson

THEN

JONATHAN CAPE
LONDON

Published by Jonathan Cape 2011

2 4 6 8 10 9 7 5 3 1

First published in Great Britain in 2011 by
Jonathan Cape
Random House, 20 Vauxhall Bridge Road,
London SW1V 2SA

www.rbooks.co.uk

Addresses for companies within The Random House Group Limited can be found at:
www.randomhouse.co.uk/offices.htm

The Random House Group Limited Reg. No. 954009

A CIP catalogue record for this book is available from the British Library

ISBN 9780224093750 (cased edition)
ISBN 9780224096171 (trade paperback edition)

The Random House Group Limited supports The Forest Stewardship
Council (FSC), the leading international forest certification organisation.
All our titles that are printed on Greenpeace approved FSC certified paper carry the
FSC logo. Our paper procurement policy can be found
at http://www.rbooks.co.uk/environment

Typeset in Fournier MT by Palimpsest Book Production Limited,
Falkirk, Stirlingshire

Printed and bound in Great Britain by
CPI Mackays, Chatham, Kent, ME5 8TD

For Helen 1924–2010

Sometime in the middle of summer, the temperature drops so low that animals bite off their own tails and small birds come falling down out of the sky.

People are eating the birds. We see some lads crowded round a brazier on Houndsditch, fighting over a handful of scorched sparrows. Laughing and shouting as they pull flesh from bone and cram it in their mouths. The rest is chucked in the snow. Dogs are waiting.

It isn't the first time we've seen the birds die. Back in March, or was it April, the streets were full of them. Only now there are bigger things too. Rats and squirrels. Foxes. Cats curled up and frozen to rooftops. Even a stupid pony, leaning up against the old wheelie bins, its eyeballs white, its breath turned to ice in its throat.

And then, one dark afternoon, making my way back along Camomile Street, I step over a puddle and see a pale face staring up at me. A tiny child, no more than one or two years old – I can see the stubby bottom teeth – frozen under the ice. She must have fallen in and knocked the back of her head. The eyes are bright blue and astonished, the lips parted as if on the edge of crying out.

I take a breath and walk away fast.

All I want is to get back to the building, but on the corner of Houndsditch and Bishopsgate a man steps out from the blackest part of the shadows and grabs me.

I hear myself cry out, but just as I am about to struggle, I look down and see what's there: two gloved hands holding on to mine. The leather shabby and cracked, a sharp rip in the thumb, as if someone has used a knife on it.

Graham, I say.

Every time I see him I have to recognise him all over again. All that black hair. The staring eyes. He is hardly any taller than I am. I know that I am not afraid of him. I think that he used to be a lawyer. He would hike up mountains in his spare time, or so he says.

Graham. He stares at me now and he shakes his head. I ask him what he wants.

What do you mean, what do I want?

Why are you following me?

I'm not following you. I came to look for you. And you're lucky someone else didn't find you first.

What? I say. Who would have found me?

He takes a breath. His fingers tight on my wrists.

Look. It's almost dark. What the hell are you doing out here on your own?

On my own? I try to think what the answer to the question might be. Nothing comes. I am glad when he lets go of me. Now his eyes are softer.

Seriously, he says. Why did you run away like that? We looked everywhere for you. We didn't know where you'd gone.

Neither did I, I tell him, and for a moment or two the words do feel true. But then the face of the child comes back at me, and with it confusion.

Graham is frowning.

I was worried about you, he says. We all were.

Ted and Sophy wouldn't worry, I say, and he doesn't contradict me.

You can't just disappear like that, he says.

Disappear? I stare at him. For a second or two, splinters of light seem to flash around the corners of his eyes. When I blink, they are gone.

He sighs.

You don't remember a thing, do you? You've no idea what happened.

I hug myself.

Maybe, I say.

Really? You remember what you did?

Did?

I feel my stomach twist.

The little incident. With the kid. This morning.

The kid. The sound of that word makes my two hands clench into fists.

Leave me alone, I tell him. I don't want to talk about it.

Don't want to talk about what?

Graham, I say, I never touched him.

Snow is falling now, a pillow of cold feathers shaken down. I look at his face again, the face of this man whose name I have forgotten again – where are the clues? In his eyes? Recognition, it comes and goes. I'm still staring when he mistakes my look for something else and pulls me to him. Working his hands, the gloves off now, inside my coat.

No, I say, because I know what's coming.

Come on –

I tell him not to do it, but he doesn't listen. He does it anyway. His fingers on me, making me shiver.

I want to go now, I say.

What? he says.

3

I want to go back to the building.

Shh. I feel the wetness of his lips on the side of my ear. What's the hurry? Just let me hold you a moment.

Why?

Because I want to.

But I don't want to.

I keep myself stiff and unhelpful in his arms. But then, as he hugs me closer to him, the hot smell of his skin loosens a memory.

Am I your wife? I ask him.

A pause. His laughter in my hair.

My wife? Ha. That's a good one. Not exactly, no.

But have we . . . I mean, do we . . . ?

He laughs again, not quite the same laugh.

I'm glad I'm so memorable, he says.

He is still for a long moment. Dusk wrapping itself around us. He's right, it's dark. I tilt my head back and there's the big cold face of the moon, the only light you'll find right now in the whole city. I think about the building. Its wide, dark spaces.

So what happened? I ask him at last. Did something happen to him?

Happen to who?

To the kid, of course.

He takes a little breath.

His name's Matthew.

Matthew. The name drops into my head. The fact that there's already a Matthew-shaped space for it tells me I knew it. Some quick, dark pictures go through my mind: the kid's chopped brown hair and surly face. His brown tracksuit bottoms. His fat and grubby hands. The sudden change when he enters a room.

4

And yes, he continues. Something did happen to him.

Something? I breathe, try to keep myself steady.

Oh, I say. What was it?

He bites his lip, hesitates.

I'm sure you didn't mean to do it, he says.

We live on what was once Bishopsgate, between Wormwood Street and the old Liverpool Street train station. Thirty-five storeys that once contained lawyers and bankers. There are more buildings still standing in this part of the city, Graham says, than anywhere else. It's the way they're built. Structures of glass and steel. Windows that go from ceiling to floor. Men used to go up in cages to clean them, but they aren't clean now, even though the sun still shines in most days. Dust and silence. A hundred or a thousand empty desks. No one will ever work here again.

I walked in one bright loud morning, the air ringing with stillness. I don't know how long ago it was. I remember the bang of the door shutting behind me. I know that I stood for a moment, waiting. I didn't know what I was waiting for, but the waiting felt right. And I couldn't remember why I'd come, but I knew I had a good reason. The good reason settled around me, warm and solid and certain.

I'm here, I told the silence. I'm here.

I let myself walk around. Acting as if she owns the place, someone might have said – and maybe they did say it and maybe I did own it, for I recognised everything. Everything. Nothing was strange to me, nothing was new. The lifts, dead and defunct since the power left the city. I knew those lifts. And just along from them, a door – heavy, with a big steel handle. I'd touched it before, that handle. I pushed it and found myself in a dark and grainy stairwell. As I knew I would. The door sighed shut behind me. I smiled. I began to climb the stairs.

On the second or maybe it was the third floor I found them, the two of them. Sitting in a slumped and gloomy silence right against a wall – a boy and a girl, teenagers, with bony starving frames and anxious faces. They were very shocked to see me – in fact the girl looked terrified. She gasped and even the boy shrank back as I opened the door.

What's wrong with you? the girl said. Your hands and face – what happened?

I looked down at my hands. I couldn't remember where the blood had come from. I touched my face and wasn't surprised to find it sticky. Every part of me was shaky and bruised. As I stood there, something liquid slid down my leg.

I don't know, I said. It's nothing.

Did someone attack you?

I'll be OK, I said.

The boy asked me how I got in.

Got in?

How did you find the entrance? We thought that no one could see it. From the street.

Oh well, I said. I'm sure they can't. I think someone might have brought me here.

This seemed to frighten them even more.

Someone? said the girl who was called Sophy.

In my head I tried to wade backwards.

I think there was a man, I said.

And where is he now? said the girl.

I hope he's not coming back, said the boy, who told me his name was Ted.

Where is he now? I thought about this. The thought hurt. I pushed it away.

It's OK, I said. He's not.

Not what?

I don't think he is. Coming back.

We walked around the building. We went up the stairs. We had little juice left in our hearts and bones but we got as far as the sixteenth floor. Panting and dizzy. Sophy wanted to keep on going – the higher we go, the safer we are, she said – but Ted said no, sixteen was far enough. He told us he'd been here before, in this building.

How come? Sophy said, frowning at him.

He thought for a second.

I worked here.

She laughed.

But you're only about fifteen. You're nothing like old enough to have worked here.

Ted seemed to think about this. I saw that his face was unhappy.

I think it was work experience.

I realised I felt sorry for him. Confusion could tip you up just like that.

It doesn't matter, I told him. You're here now.

We crossed a landing and found ourselves in an office. Dust over everything. Pigeons had been in and there were streaks on the backs of chairs, on desks. A high-pitched noise in a filing cabinet turned out to be a nest of mice, grey-skinned and hairless. In the corner of the office was a bundle of clothes and inside them was a man.

The man's head was on his knees. His hair was long and

matted and his beard was black. At first we thought he was dead, but after a moment he lifted his head and started rolling a cigarette.

Ted stared at the cigarette. The man saw him staring and, after taking a suck himself, he held it out. Ted looked amazed. But he went over and took it. He had a puff, then handed it back, but the man held up his hand as if to say keep it.

Ted looked even more amazed.

Cheers, mate, he said.

With the cigarette in one hand, he put himself down at one of the dead screens. Touched the mouse. In his eyes was the look boys get when they are near computers.

Hey, maybe we can go on Facebook? he said.

For the first time, the man in the corner made a noise. It was laughter. The man was Graham.

Later that day we found the kid. Down in the old basement kitchen, a solid and sullen-looking boy, maybe thirteen years old. He was sitting up on the shiny metal counter and using a blunt knife to hack into a can of beans, the orange kind that you used to have on toast.

Sophy ignored the boy and rushed over to the cans and started picking them up as if they were little babies. There was sweetcorn, the one with the giant on it. Tuna. Peas. Chopped tomatoes. She nursed six or seven of them in her arms at once, before putting them down again.

On the table by the counter was a stack of white sliced bread that someone had ripped open and left. The slices were blue, green and grey. There was a freezer too. Sophy went over and pulled up the lid, but the smell was rank and she banged it shut very fast. The smell of rotting flesh lingered. She looked at the kid, who was still stabbing the can.

Isn't there an opener? she said.

He said nothing.

She went over and looked in a cupboard. Several packets of something, maybe crackers or biscuits, had spilled over a shelf. She snatched one up and tried to cram it in her mouth but as soon as it touched her fingers, it was dust. The kid was watching her.

There's some that are OK, he said. Over there in the other cupboard.

How long have you been here? Ted asked the kid. How did you get in?

The kid stayed where he was. He didn't answer and he didn't look at Ted. He swung his legs against the counter so his boots scuffed and banged. He put down the blunt knife and felt around in a drawer for a sharper one. Then he began attacking the can of beans again. The blade kept on slipping. Soon there was blood on both his hands.

Stop it! Sophy cried. What are you doing? Can't you see you're hurting yourself?

I asked you a question, Ted said. How did you come here?

The kid wiped his hands on his tracksuit bottoms. He looked at me.

With her, he said.

What?

I came with her.

At his words, I froze. I shook my head.

He did not, I said.

Keeping his eyes on me, the kid stabbed the knife into the can again.

9

But I brought you here, he said. After I found you. After the men had hurt you. You don't remember?

Ted was looking at me.

I thought you said it was a man who brought you?

A bright hot flush went through me.

It was, I told him in a steady voice, though my heart was beating crazily. I don't know this boy. He's just a kid. I've no idea who he is.

The kid gave up on the can and dropped it on the floor. It hit the concrete with a dull sound.

She's lying, he said, but he said it as if that was the end of the subject, and he did not look at me.

I've never seen him in my life before, I told Ted and Sophy. And I don't like the look of him either.

You could see Ted trying to decide what to think. In the end, he sighed.

If you want to stay here with us, he told the kid, you've got to join the team.

The kid stared at him.

What team?

I mean you've got to do what we say.

The kid looked at him then and he nodded. He looked younger suddenly, and solemn. There was something else, too, on his face – was it sadness, or was he sulking? I felt excited.

And now I have hurt him. Is it so surprising? That I've hurt the bloody kid? I have no memory of whatever it is I am supposed to have done, but that doesn't stop everyone else shaking their heads and knowing it. And now here they all are, waiting for me to say I am sorry.

Am I sorry? Am I? I try to think about what sorry might

feel like and whether or not it's in my mind right now. Sorry. No, I do not think that sorry will come.

I do not like the kid and I never have, but still I can't think what he might have done to make me want to hurt him. I am not a violent person, and I don't think I would ever lash out at a child for no reason.

Look at him, now, lying there. Ted and Sophy have made a pile out of some of the coats and blankets and laid him on it. He doesn't look good. He looks like someone has picked him up and dropped him from a great height.

What's he called? I ask them, more out of politeness than anything else.

Graham looks at me.

You know what he's called. I told you just an hour ago.

I shrug.

I always just call him the kid, I say.

He's Matthew, Sophy tells me in a voice that sounds like she wants to catch me out. Matt. We call him Matt.

Matt. I say the word to myself and then I say it again. An angry word. I pull my big brown cardigan up to my chin.

I think I'll just call him the kid, I say.

They all watch me. Ted – pale and skinny and heartbreaking the way some teenage boys are – watches me. He can make you feel guilty in three seconds flat, Ted can. And Sophy, the blonde and mouthy one, kneeling right next to the kid now and holding on to his hand the way girls like to do with people who are lying down. She keeps on glancing up at me, to check I've seen her.

And there's a nasty ripening bruise on the kid's head. And maybe a cut as well, because someone has got a cloth off one of the old tea trolleys and ripped it to make a bandage. The edges are black and blood has also leaked into his hair, one of his ears. His eyes are closed, his face full of shadows. I peer at him more closely.

Are you sure he's not dead?

Sophy gasps.

Would you even care if he was?

I look at him again. That sullen face. That lumpen, accusing presence. Would I care? It's a difficult question.

Graham is watching me.

Do you remember now, what you did?

Several different and violent possibilities are going round in my mind. I put the brakes on, reach out for one of them.

Did I hit him?

Sophy looks at Graham and claps her hand to her mouth as if to stop a laugh. I look again at the kid lying there on the coats. His bloody hair. The bruises on him. Then a new idea wells up.

He went for me first, I say.

This time Ted speaks up.

No, he says – and I notice that he blushes and keeps his eyes fixed on the floor, as if it somehow costs him to be saying it. No way. It's not true. I was there.

Graham looks at me. I hold up my hands, feeling sorry suddenly for Ted.

OK, I say. OK. Whatever. He didn't.

Graham looks at me and shakes his head.

You'll say anything, won't you? Whatever comes into your head, whatever you feel like saying, you'll just go right ahead and say it.

And I turn to him, about to deny it – but then, for a few quick, strange seconds, I see that he has on a suit, a clean shirt, his hair is sharply cut and his beard shaved. I smell coffee, hear a staticky hum that I think is electricity.

What is it now? he says when he sees me staring at him.

I don't answer. I notice his clean fingernails, the glint of a watch on his wrist, the newspaper in his hand. I shiver and take my eyes to somewhere else — as far away as possible, out of the window. Someone has lit a bonfire on a rooftop somewhere far off towards Bank. You can see the bright flames jumping into the black night sky, puncturing the darkness of the city.

I keep my eyes on the flames for a moment and then, when I look back at Graham, he's as he should be — dressed in his old dark and greasy clothes, skin parched and dirty, face all covered with hair.

The main entrance of the building — the big, grand entrance, with its turnstiles and leather sofas and dead and curling trees — is on Bishopsgate, but that stays shut and we come and go through the side entrance on Wormwood. Ted and Sophy and Graham are very afraid that someone else will find it. It's all they talk about. I can't bear listening to their worries any longer.

It won't happen, I tell them. I mean it. No one's going to come in.

Graham looks at me.

How on earth can you know a thing like that?

I hesitate, trying to collect up the words that will seem right to him. I know that the kid is watching me.

Because I feel it.

I know as soon as I say it that it's the wrong choice. Sophy rolls her eyes.

You feel it?

Yes.

But what do you feel?

I just know what's possible and what's not.

No you don't, Graham says. How can you?

Look, I tell him. It's not what's going to happen.

Now Sophy starts to laugh.

So, what? You're saying you know what's going to happen? You know the future?

You don't know who you are or where you came from, Ted points out. You've got no memory at all, even less than us. But you know what's coming?

Yes, Sophy says, and she shoves her pale hand in my face. Do you tell fortunes too? What can you see? Tell me everything. What's going to happen to me?

I don't look at Sophy's hand. I don't need to.

You'll be OK, I tell her.

I can't look at the kid, but I know that he has looked away.

This place. In the day, sun crashes through the windows. The air warms up. It can almost feel like the old world in the day. But at night, the temperature drops. At night, you hear things. Screaming and crying. Sounds that could be animals but aren't animals.

Sometimes in the morning there are bodies in the street. Terrible injuries that no one could survive. A day later the bodies are gone. We don't know who takes them. There are other bodies too, piles of them stacked in the old bus shelters, in the post office, under the canopy where the market used to be, or left out on the street to freeze.

It has been some time now, no one knows how long, but still the dead are everywhere. Some days the cold can stop a human heart in less than thirty minutes. You see people on the ground exactly where they sat down to rest, faces black and surrendered, clothes torn off in their hurry to cool down. You walk down Bishopsgate and see drifts of snow with human hands and feet sticking out of them, the fingers and toes black with frost, the nails falling off. Or part of a face – the eyes gone and the skin dark and swollen, the expression of terror otherwise perfectly preserved.

Mostly the freeze keeps the smell of death at bay. In that way, the city has become a perfect morgue. But then you find yourself turning a corner into some sheltered place where the walls and roof are still intact, the air ripe and warm, and you back straight out again, heaving.

All right, Graham says. I'd better tell you. If you really can't remember.

It's the middle of the night, a full bright moon. We are lying down quite close together on the blankets and coats by the window. At night, this is often how we are. Sometimes he puts his hands on me, sometimes not. Sometimes I want him to. Other times I don't care whether he does or not. His hands are his own – my body never feels like mine.

The blankets are the cleanest thing we have, the softest. I don't know where we got the blankets – maybe Ted and the kid found them somewhere in the city. You can still find things in shops sometimes. The coats smell of cigarettes and soap and scent, of the places and things that people used to smell of. I know the coats were already in the building. On the day it happened, the air began to burn before it froze and nobody took their coats.

I look at Graham. His face green in the moonlight.

Tell me what? I say.

What you did. To the kid.

Oh.

You pushed him down the stairs.

A quick fizz of surprise runs through me.

I did? I pushed him – what's his name again?

Matthew.

Matthew. I pushed him down these stairs?

Yup. You gave him a shove and he went flying. Ted saw it. He says he went down a whole flight of steps.

I think about this. I try to picture it – the moment. The feeling of my hand on him. The sudden lightness as he goes. But it's not anywhere in my memory. It's hopeless. I shake my head.

I just don't have it, I tell Graham.

Don't have what?

The memory. I don't have it in my head.

He thinks for a moment.

Well, I'm telling you, it's what happened. It's what you did.

I'm silent.

And is that all? I ask him then.

What do you mean, is that all?

Is that all I did?

Christ. Isn't that enough?

I didn't mean to hurt him.

Well, he says, did you see his head? He's lucky to be alive.

Alive. Dead. Graham is the only one who makes such big distinctions.

In what way lucky? I ask him.

I mean he could easily have died.

For a moment, I wonder what it would be like if the kid did

do that – if he did die. I suppose it would be simple, that we would put the body out in the snow with the rest.

I feel Graham looking at me.

I don't understand you, he says.

I shrug. I step away from the idea and also from the conversation. In my head I take a sharp fruit knife and begin to make a strip of peel. It falls in a long, loose circle. I smell its lovely acid perfume. Such a relief, to be able to stop thinking and watch it fall.

What are you thinking? Graham says, still looking at me.

I was thinking about an apple, I tell him.

He is silent a moment and then, in a slightly angry way, he laughs.

I saw a little girl, I tell him a few minutes later.

He waits.

A girl?

Yes. A baby really. On Camomile Street.

He carries on waiting, as if he expects me to tell him more. I wait too. I shut my eyes for a quick second, struggling to remember. Is there more?

Go on, he says.

What do you mean, go on?

And? What happened?

Nothing happened. She was dead, I think. Just lying in a puddle and dead. She was right under the ice.

He says nothing. He rolls away from me and he sits up. I wait, yawning, as he smoothes the foil and strikes a match. Soon there's a smell of burned sugar in the air.

There are dead people everywhere, he says at last.

Well – but this one was just a baby.

17

He doesn't say anything. His face is expressionless. For a few moments, it's him and the foil and the flame. When he turns back to me, his eyes are glittery, the skin on his face raw and tight.

There are babies everywhere, he says.

I watch as he chases the flame along the foil. And I let myself think of him, then – the lawyer on Bishopsgate. In his dark suit, hurrying along. I see sunshine, the last waves of heat over the city. I feel sick. I hold my breath. He sees my face.

What? he says. What is it?

You worked here, I tell him. In this building.

He flicks a look at me.

You know I did. I've told you that.

When did you tell me?

I don't know. Lots of times. You've just forgotten. I'd been here coming up to three years. My office wasn't on this side. It faced out towards St Paul's.

St Paul's?

The man's name throws me for a moment. Then I remember: it's a church. And then the rest of it comes back.

That he was at work. It was a Tuesday. That he still remembers every last detail of his journey in that morning – the man who sold him a newspaper, trying to eat a bacon sandwich at the same time and not wanting to have to put it down to give him change. The long queue to renew his pass for the train. The fact that for once he shelled out for a six-month instead of a three-month.

And the fact that it was an especially glorious and sunny morning. Hot, in fact. Much hotter than it should have been. That high blue sky, cloudless and soaring. The fact that he loosened his tie and took his jacket off in the street because it was so unseasonably warm. Sweat on his face. You should not have sweat on your face in February.

He went in the building, through the turnstiles, past security. People were already talking about what could have caused the rise in temperature. Some people were laughing and joking about it, saying to enjoy it while it lasted, others were worried. He didn't worry. The building was air-conditioned and anyway he was Graham and he had work to do.

He went up in the lift. He smelled coffee as he stepped into the corridor.

And then – and then.

He says that when he woke up, when he arrived back at something he could call consciousness, the air was scorched, an odour of burning fat, and the city was dark. The blue air and the sunshine had gone. There was ash and there was ice – and something else, something metallic, something that in some unholy way seemed final.

Final?

I can't explain it. It was like nothing I've ever felt. The worst sensation. Oppressive. As if something had happened that was beyond simple weather. As if the air or perhaps the whole of the sky had changed.

And yet even then, even after all that, he still failed to grasp what had happened.

Would you believe, I actually set off for London Bridge, he told me, his voice cracking with disbelief, to get a train home?

Home?

I mean, seriously, what in fuck's name was I expecting?

I wake in the night. His leg nudging mine. His hand on me. His breath in my ear.

Come on, he is muttering.

I don't bother saying anything. Instead, I lick my lips and I try to taste what is around me. The salty darkness. The silence above us and below. And then she comes flashing into my head – those blue astonished eyes, the little stubby teeth – and my heart sinks.

Come on, he is saying. I like you. I've always liked you. You're so fucking lovely. Even if we'd met in real life, I'd probably have hit on you –

In real life?

In the old life.

He leans up on one elbow and looks at me. I can tell by the way that his eyes touch my face then carry on going straight past it that he is still high.

I look away from him, listening. In the dark sometimes I can hear things. The distant sound of an office photocopier, sliding backwards and forwards, heavy and slow, dropping its pale rectangles into the tray. If I open my eyes, I know I will see shadows moving along the wall, sliding across the furniture. I don't know whose shadows they are.

I could tell you I loved you if you wanted, he is saying. Is that what you want? Would that make it better?

I look at him. I am hardly listening. I am thinking: why did I walk away from her? Why did I leave her lying there?

I lift my head then. A different sound.

Do you hear that?

Hear what?

That dog.

What dog?

There's a dog barking.

He yawns, scratches himself.

It'll be outside.

No. Listen. It's right here.

I can't hear anything, he says, and he tries again to pull me on to him and this time I don't bother struggling too hard. I can smell the burned sweetness of his breath. I rest my lips on his face. At last the barking stops.

I can tell from the loose shape of him that any moment now he'll be asleep and sure enough I am right and he is.

Most of the moon has slid away under thick dark cloud by the time I creep out of the building. It is the deadest time. Vicious cold. Enough to make even something as simple as breathing feel like a rough and complicated act.

The streets are empty. I see almost no one. Just one or two souls hurrying back towards the old synagogue. I don't know if they are women or men. They have dark hoods pulled down over their faces. As we pass each other, I see their teeth flash white and I hear the squeak of their boots, but they leave me alone and I am grateful for it.

I am on a mission, my heart is high with it. But as soon as I get to Camomile Street, my hopes crash. I realise it is hours or maybe days since I was here and nothing's the same. New snow has fallen, blurring everything.

I look around for anything I might remember, but the picture has changed completely. It might as well be a whole different street. I don't recognise a thing.

The building to my left is entirely burned out, its roof gone, walls charred, windows smashed. Near to it is a set of recent footprints. And a bright yellow stain in the snow where someone, maybe a man or maybe a dog, has pissed.

I look up and see a wall with red and blue paint on it and a faded and peeling sign that says Fresh Italy – Beautiful Food Fast, but even that means nothing. One frozen puddle in a big white landscape like this. What was I thinking? How could I ever have hoped to find her again?

The air above my head is black and silent, the odd flake of snow drifting down. I take a deep breath and walk about twenty paces to my left, then the same to the right. Then back to the left again. Then I turn and, as I wait, something changes. Lines and shapes settling, everything less distant and confused – the street around me beginning to make sense.

I go back a few paces in the original direction.

No, I think. Wrong. I slide a little the other way and test the ground with my foot. Nothing. I move along and do it again, harder. Still nothing. But the third time, there it is. The faint creak of ice. I stamp on it hard with my boot and feel it give.

It could be any puddle, I tell myself. There's no reason why it should be the right puddle.

Getting down on my knees, heart banging so hard that a taste comes up into my throat, I use my gloves to wipe all the soft fresh snow off the puddle's icy surface.

I look down. And there she is.

She is looking straight at me. I pull off my glove and rap my bare knuckles on the ice. Her eyes are blue as the bluest flower. Wide open and still. Nothing in her face moves.

I'm going to get you out, I tell her.

Pulling my glove back on, I go to look for a stone – a sharp one. And on the far side of the street, I find it – stacked in a pile along with all the other sharp stones. Left there for me.

I bring it back, heavy in my hands. Making sure to keep it away from her face, I begin to tap and chip at the ice, which is surprisingly tough. In the end I have to lift the stone right up in the air and smash it down hard.

Forgive me, I whisper. I don't want to hurt you.

The ice breaks with a pop and a hiss and I lift whole shards off, chucking them in the snow, where they fall against each other with a musical sound. Then I tear off both my gloves and plunge my two bare hands into that freezing water.

The cold is agony. At first there is nothing – my hands crash around and don't find a thing. But then my fingers close on something solid and I know that I have her. The chill of her flesh, the tangle of her hair, the rigid weight of her small body. As I brace to scoop her out, I think I even hear her sigh or gasp. Is it possible?

In my arms, she is a piece of ice. It hurts to hold her. Still, I sit back there in the snow with her slumped hard against me. Strands of her hair dripping over my wrists, her cold face against me, her blue skin that smells of old pond water, her clothes wetting mine.

I look down and see blood on my hands. And that's when I lift my head and notice her standing a few feet away – the dog. Head on one side, intent, an ear cocked up, the other flopping over.

I hold out my hand to her, but she pulls back, lifting her lip and snarling. Breath. Deep in her throat, the beginning of a growl.

Come on – I pat my leg to try to get her to come to me. Come on, come here.

Straightaway she takes a step back, her ears flat, tail tucked and curled between her legs. I snap my fingers at her and she backs still further away. I make my voice into a whisper.

Come on, I say. It's only me.

She shows her teeth.

I try to laugh.

OK, I tell her. Have it your way. Go on – off you go.

As she turns to go, I look down and see that my lap is full of water.

2

It grows colder. Every day the city alters a little more. There are icicles a metre long on Lombard Street. A young lad puts his tongue on some icy railings at Aldgate and gets stuck there for an hour or a day depending on who you want to believe. Trees that have stood on the Embankment for three hundred years split apart with a crack so loud that you see people fall to their knees, thinking they've been shot.

Familiar landmarks fall away, gone in an instant. A multi-storey car park near our building, which has withstood the weight of years, gives in and sinks to the ground in the space of an afternoon. One day the Monument is still up there, defiant and intact; the next it has crashed down across King William Street, the piece of sky it used to occupy left blue and ravished behind it.

London Bridge is still there, and so is Southwark, but Tower Bridge is long gone, plunging down through the ice to rest on the bed of the Thames. Ted says that if you're on the river on a bright day, you can look down and see it lying there, a massive shadow, darkening the water.

If you stand on the ice, you can see all the fish that have swum up towards the light and been blinded or suffocated. Some boys bring picks and shovels and hack away, determined to get at them, but the ice is so thick they soon give up and use the picks to threaten passers-by instead.

The police and the army are long gone and vandalism and

menace are commonplace. Heartlessness has become the law and no one cares any more who they hurt. An old woman is tied to some icy railings and her boots and jacket pulled off, and, even when she is half-naked, no one has the decency to release her so she can crawl to safety. Ted says she must have died hallucinating, because she tells everyone she sees a unicorn, a white beast with a single horn, heading straight for Fenchurch Street.

You'd think that Sophy has seen enough dead people by now, but when she hears about the old woman, she cries.

Meanwhile, the kid is getting better. He is much better. His cut has all but healed and his bruises have turned violet, then blue, and now a sinister mottled yellow.

He still complains of a pain in his shoulder but Graham tells him that will go away too. Graham isn't a doctor, but he has the knack of making people believe what he says. The kid certainly falls for it. He laps it up. He refuses to have anything to do with me, but that suits me fine.

You're not my friend, he says when I happen to pass him in that strange grey portion of corridor by the lifts.

Good, I say. You're not mine either.

I hope he will carry on walking past, but he doesn't. Instead, he stands still for a moment, the black holes of his eyes still on me. I try to meet his gaze. I'm not going to let myself be daunted by a stupid kid.

Why do you tell lies? he asks me then.

I try to smile.

I don't tell lies.

You do. You know you do. You told the others that we didn't even know each other. Why did you do that?

I don't know you, I tell him as firmly as I can. I don't know you and I don't want to know you either.

He shakes his head. I'm not even close to him but I know already how he'll smell. Mean and musty, of old skin and hair. The dirt that is boy.

You're evil, he says. I mean it.

I could say the same about you, I tell him without missing a beat.

There's something really wrong with you.

Ditto, I say.

He looks at me with a brief flicker of interest, as if someone has turned a switch and upped the voltage in his head. I make sure to return the gaze without wavering. I feel very alive, excited even.

Just try me, I think. I'm ready for you.

He has on a long red jersey full of ratty frayed holes, and over it a dirty brown hoodie with some kind of a logo on it – I don't know what, something to do with America or sport, I guess. He is a solid boy – wide-chested and fat-necked and big-thighed.

Where are you going? he asks me as I turn to walk away down the corridor.

I say nothing. I walk, looking straight ahead.

I don't want to turn back, but after a moment or two I can't help it. I do. He has turned around and is looking out of the window. I notice with a quick snag of pleasure that his tracksuit bottoms are wearing out at the back and soon you will be able to see his dirty grey pants showing through.

Another time, though, he comes and finds me on purpose. This time the look on his face is forced and jaunty. As if someone has put him up to it. As if he is carrying out a dare.

So how come you don't like kids? he says.

I give him what I hope is a cool look.

I do like kids. I like them very much. It's you I don't like.

He looks at me with interest.

Haven't you got any of your own, then?

I feel myself flush.

Got any what?

Kids.

I don't know, I say. I don't think so. It's none of your business, is it?

He looks at me and I look at him. There are sullen purple shadows under his eyes and I can see that his nose is running. He sniffs and wipes his nose on the sleeve of his hoodie. I watch as he inspects the sleeve.

It must be weird not to remember anything, he says.

I don't know, I say. Is it?

He gives me a hot little look.

I remember lots of stuff. I know my own name. I know that I know you, that I brought you here.

I shake my head.

What? he says. You don't think I did?

I know you didn't.

How did you get here, then?

I try to think. I can't answer the question.

He sniffs again.

And I know that we used to play together.

Play?

I try not to laugh.

Maybe your kids are dead, he says then, as he agitates one part of his clothing against another to absorb the slick of snot. Maybe that's why you had to play with me.

I wait a moment. I can feel the blood jumping into my throat.

Get lost, I tell him. I mean it. Just fuck off and leave me alone.

He looks impressed.

You shouldn't talk to a child like that.

You're not a child.

A new look of respect goes over his face. He licks his lips.

How do you know?

How do I know what?

That I'm not a child. How do you know it? And why do you always go around the building?

I stare at him.

What do you mean, go around it?

I hear you, all the time. Walking around. Up and down the stairs. Going into all the rooms. Even at night you do it.

I say nothing.

Well? he says. What is it? What are you looking for?

I feel my heart contract. I manage to take a step away from him.

Is it a person? Is there someone else here?

I shiver.

I don't know what you're talking about, I say. Any more questions?

He doesn't get it, the sarcasm.

Yes. What happened to your hands?

I can't help it. I glance down at my hands. They look like someone has scratched or bitten them. I pull my sleeves down to cover them.

He gazes at me.

Sometimes I feel so sorry for you, he says.

I move myself away before the temptation to reach out and strike him becomes too much.

Later that day, or maybe it's the day after, I walk into one of the offices on the floor above and I know that someone else has only just walked out.

I glance around me. The light is wavy. Shadows darting here and there.

Who's there? I whisper. Who is it?

Silence.

The room is a large one, a corner room. I haven't been in it before. I go over and sit in the big swivel chair, touch the cold metal of the arms, swing myself from side to side, lay a hand on the computer keys. A layer of dust comes off on my fingers. On the floor, a glass photo frame lies smashed, the photo inside long gone. I slide open a drawer – noiseless, clean, not much in it. I slide it shut again.

I wait then. I wait for a long time. I don't know what I'm waiting for.

After I've been there a while, I get up and go out into the corridor. The air feels like someone has already used it – sucked it in, breathed it out.

I stand by the lifts for a moment, shut my eyes, take a breath. I smell some things that should not be there. Apples. Ink. A blown-out candle. Blood. I think I hear voices, laughter. Far away, a siren. I know that none of this is possible.

Ted is always hungry. When we first came here, he roamed the building looking for vending machines. He smashed the glass wherever he found one and sat down and stuffed himself with M & M's, Ribena, Doritos. Now he goes out looking for food but mostly he comes back with nothing. He dreams of steaks, of sausages, of popcorn, of jacket potatoes with their insides scooped out, loaded with butter and cheddar cheese, of prawn sandwiches . . .

Sophy looks at him.

Prawn sandwiches?

You know the pink fat ones that used to be frozen, with lots of mayonnaise? I wouldn't even mind if they were in brown bread. And I think I'd eat broccoli now. Oh, and I've been thinking a lot about those crispy cheese things you used to get, do you remember, in a yellow packet with a cow on it?

He comes and stands in front of me and pulls up his T-shirt.

What? I say. What am I supposed to be looking at?

Just fucking well look!

I look. His ribs are like something you could play music on. I look away.

Well?

I don't know what teenage boys are supposed to look like, I tell him.

He glares at me.

Well – um – let me see. I think they're supposed to look more or less human.

You do look human, Ted.

I look like a freak.

It's true you haven't got much of a tummy, I say, trying not to look at the trail of small dark hairs that disappear down into his underpants.

He rolls his eyes.

I'm a fucking skeleton.

I watch as he tucks his T-shirt back into his jeans.

He makes me listen to a list of the food he used to get through in one school day.

Two fried eggs at home before I left, a mini-pizza or a BLT at break, chicken and chips at lunch and maybe a roll and butter too. Then maybe a piece of cheesecake or a doughnut when school finished and some crisps and a drink on the bus home. And then a big hot cooked dinner that my mum . . .

His voice tails off. He looks furious with himself. I notice that his ears are very dirty.

Oh Ted, I say.

He swallows back saliva.

I don't want some big emotional conversation about it, he says. I just want something proper to eat.

Another night, he comes back. His speech is thick and his breath is like old perfume.

What? he says.

You've been drinking.

He looks away. His eyes are hooded.

Not really.

I know what alcohol smells like. Where did you get hold of something to drink?

His eyes darken.

You can halt your shit right now, he says, and he tries to take a step forwards but staggers back instead.

Ted, I say. Don't speak to me like that.

Don't chat shit like you're my mum, then.

I say nothing. He sighs. Throws himself backwards into a chair. The chair has wheels. It moves under him.

Well? he says as he uses his feet to get the chair over to the desk. Don't you even want to know where I've been?

I look at him.

I don't know.

What do you mean, you don't know?

I'm not sure I want to talk to you when you're drunk.

Fuck's sake! I'm not drunk.

He puts his feet up on the desk. A white salt tidemark on his boots.

I went to a party, he says.

Oh, I say. Did you?

Yes.

He tilts his head back, shuts his eyes. Sophy comes in. She has a scarf wound around her neck and up to her chin. Her cheeks are pink and there are bright shadows under her eyes.

My throat, she says. It really hurts.

She looks at Ted.

What's wrong with him?

Ted pulls off his jumper. For a second or two the room is filled with the peppery smell of his sweat. I look at Sophy.

Ted went to a party.

She stares.

He didn't!

No. I don't think he did either.

It was on the river, Ted says. They had a fire on the ice. Some kids were skating.

Skating? Sophy says. Where did they get the skates?

Well, not real skates. They'd tied bones or something on to their boots so they could slide along. And they were roasting an animal. I think it was a cow. It was bare tasty —

Sophy's mouth falls open.

You had some?

And something that was a bit like vodka. And there was

music. And there were all these little kids paddling around in these pools around the fire where the ice had begun to melt and –

There wouldn't have been kids, I say quickly.

Why not? Ted tries to get to his feet but almost falls off the chair. Why wouldn't there be kids?

Is it still going on, do you think? I ask him.

The party? I guess it is. He hesitates, looks at me. You don't believe a single thing I say, do you?

Sophy goes over and touches Ted's shoulder.

Do you think there'll still be meat? Can we go there? Will you take us now?

It is almost the end of the night by the time we make our slow way down to London Bridge. Dawn, but you can see that it will be a dark day. The sky has a violent flush to it. The streets are silent.

We don't wake Graham, but the kid catches up with us as we leave the building, pulling on his coat. I try to tell him he can't come.

But why?

You're too young.

He looks straight at me for a second and then he laughs.

But I'm the same age as you.

Ted catches hold of my shoulder, steadying himself.

What's the problem if he comes? he says. The more of us the better.

I say nothing. I let him come. I have to. But I do my best to ignore him as he trails along behind us, a sturdy, silent, ir-ritating presence.

Look at him, I mutter to Sophy. Nothing stops him, does it?

She looks at me. Her face is tired, her cheeks hollow, eyes watering.

What do you mean, nothing stops him?

I glance back at the kid.

The way he keeps on going. He's never affected by anything.

She looks at me and takes a sharp breath.

But don't you realise, exactly the same thing is true of you?

What's true of me?

You're just like him. You're the same. You don't get cold. You don't even get tired. You seem to eat nothing and yet – I'm not saying you're fat, right? – but look at you.

I hug myself. I am warm and solid under my coat. I shrug.

We're all different, I tell her. And anyway, I don't always feel so great. I just don't go on about it like everyone else.

She gives me a long look.

What?

But she doesn't say anything. She keeps on looking.

What? I say again, sick of her eyes on me, annoyed at how her silence makes me feel I have something to prove.

But still she won't speak.

No one could say that Ted is not affected by things. I've never seen a teenage boy so skinny and so vulnerable. Even walking down the street he seems to tilt off to one side, like a young tree sent off kilter by the slightest gust of wind.

And that's when he's sober. Right now he's still a little giddy and drunk. Sophy has to hold on to his arm to keep him upright. It looks all wrong, the slight, pale girl supporting the tall boy. I think that we must make an odd little group, the four of us, with the dog following on behind.

She joined us almost as soon as we left the building and now, every time I glance around, there she is, hurrying along some

35

distance away, nose down, tail lifted, paws moving over the ice and snow.

After a few minutes, I ask Sophy if she's seen her.

Seen who?

The dog.

She turns around.

What? she says, eager to see what I see. Where? What dog?

Back there. Behind us.

She looks. So does Ted.

But where?

The dog stops exactly where she is. She holds one paw in the air. Only her nose moves, sniffing the cold air.

You really don't see her? I say to Sophy. Just over there?

Ted gives me a look.

How do you know it's a her?

I ignore him.

OK, I say. But can you see her?

I can see her, someone says.

I look around. The kid. Trying to muscle his way in. I say nothing.

Sophy begins to cough. A sound like someone tearing paper. When she finishes, her eyes are wet. She looks up. Looks straight at the dog.

I think it's in your imagination, she says.

We walk on. I don't think I've been so far from the building before. Every step we take, the sky loses a little of its bloody darkness.

There are few sounds. A soft crump as snow makes up its mind to slide off a rooftop. Someone sobbing from the dark insides of a burned-out shop, or from an alley piled high with rubbish, or an upstairs window that's had all its glass punched out.

We pass a pile of rubber tyres, partly burned, and a bright plastic sheet with a hand sticking out from under it. You can't tell if it's a man or a woman. One finger is gone where someone has sliced it off to get at the ring.

A bag of rubbish has spilled open and you can see the old containers of things people used to eat. Cardboard cereal packets, bleached by wet and cold but with the curly writing and pictures of cheery brown animals still there. Plastic cartons for milk. The squeezed-out halves of a lemon, still fresh-looking. Some yellow nylon netting that once had fruit in it.

A black metal railing still has a bicycle chained to it. The chain is rusty but the bicycle's all in one piece as if someone has just ridden up that moment and got off. But the kid kicks it as we walk past and the whole thing falls apart – all it was waiting for was a touch from his boot.

One or two people are crouching in the doorways of build-ings. It's hard to tell if they are alive or dead. We walk past a row of what were once shops. They're looted and burned inside but the names are still up there: Monsoon. Alliance & Leicester. Hugo Boss. Accessorize. Robert Dyas. Outside the one that says Robert Dyas, a child lies on his back on a flattened-out cardboard box. He's well wrapped up, with an anorak and gloves and a hat that someone has bothered to do up under his chin, but his eyes are dull and nothing at all is going on in his face. Next to him, a youngish man with wild eyes and red, matted hair is sobbing and crying and shouting for someone called Suzanne.

As we pass him I see that half his face is eaten right down to the bone. He has no gloves on and his hands are like two bunches of black bananas. Some of the fingers still have thick dark nails, others are blunted away to stumps.

There's no one around called Suzanne, but he keeps on crying and shouting the name until another voice from somewhere else tells him to shut up.

There's a weak light by the time we reach the river. I know without looking behind me that the dog has left us. The ice is the colour of milk. Up on the bridge, three or four large fires are burning and some people are shouting obscenities at one another. There's no sign of any kind of party.

Well? Sophy says, shivering and looking at Ted.

Ted stares at the frozen water. He yawns. His eyes are red. He rubs at them and then he yawns again.

I just want to crash out and sleep, he says.

Near to us is a bench. Someone has cleared the snow off it and the wood shows up damp but clean. Ted looks at it. I look at it too and something inside me jumps.

What? Sophy says. What's the matter?

I don't know, I tell her. That. Something about it – it reminds me of something.

What? The bench?

I don't know.

You've seen it before?

No, I don't think so. I don't know.

I know I have nothing to lose by sitting on it, so I do – I go over and I sit. Immediately, before I can stop him, the kid joins me. I don't want him there, but I feel him. I feel the slats of the bench adjust themselves under his bulk. Then – even less likely – his arm in its rough coat sleeve, it comes up and rests around my shoulders.

I can't believe it. He is shorter than I am, so he has to lift his arm at an angle to get it up around me. Even then it doesn't reach. I try to push him off but he won't let me. Sophy is laughing. So is Ted.

What the hell do you think you're doing? I say.

He wants to be your boyfriend! Sophy says, still laughing, the laugh turning into a cough.

You and Matt, Ted says. Look at you. You look like an old married couple, sitting there.

I look at the kid. I look at his face, the dimples in his fat cheeks like two stitches pulled up tight. For a moment, he looks like someone else, someone I ought to know. And then, for a few quick seconds, I don't recognise him at all. He's no one. And then that all changes and I do – he's the kid again.

There isn't any party. Or if there ever was one it has left no traces on that flat icy surface that is the river. No remains of a bonfire. No meat bones, no skate tracks – if Ted is to be believed about the skates, that is – nothing at all. It is true that Ted seems to have been drinking, but he could have got hold of something to drink anywhere – a looted pub where someone forgot their stash, a locked-up storeroom that no one has had any luck breaking into.

Soon, though, we smell meat. Under the bridge, two boys are hunched over a brazier. One of them has on a padded jacket that is ripped down both sides and his face is dark with either dirt or frostbite. The other has no hair at all, not even a hat to cover the white dome of his head, which is pitted with scars. Two more boys are hunched near them on the ground, silently pulling the feathers off a pile of birds. Dogs are watching them.

Black and grey smoke curls up from the brazier. You can

39

smell the fat coming off the carcasses. Sophy swallows and licks her lips.

It smells like Christmas, she says.

Yes, I say. It does.

She glances at me. I see that her lips are cracked and sore. She licks blood off them.

You don't even remember what Christmas is.

I say nothing.

Well, do you?

Christmas. It's hard. I close my eyes and see a fat girl baby sitting under a Christmas tree. A spray of tiny white lights. Something velvety. Laughter. I don't know which Christmas it is and I don't know whose baby.

Well, do you? Sophy says again.

I swallow to get the feeling away. Why does she always want to make things hard for me?

I don't know, I tell her.

Leave her alone, says the kid. What does it matter if she remembers or not?

Sophy turns around and looks at him, surprised.

She's not got anything to prove to you, he says.

Sophy holds his gaze for a moment and then she shrugs.

Anyway, she says at last. Christmas isn't like that.

Isn't like what?

It isn't something you don't know about. You either remember it or you don't.

OK, I say.

She remembers it, says the kid.

I stare at him.

How do you know if I remember it or not? I say.

But before he can answer, one of the boys spots us and starts yelling and chucking lumps of ice. The dogs start barking. It is all over. We hurry away.

That night I wake. I know it's the sound that wakes me. And the air. Colder than it has ever been. Icy cold. I sit up. My breath is sharp and rough in my chest. I look around for Graham but he isn't there. I wait. It comes again.

I hear Sophy sitting up.

What? she says. What is it now?

I turn my eyes towards where I know she is but I can't see her.

Listen, I say.

Listen to what?

That.

What?

You can't hear it?

Hear what? What am I supposed to be hearing?

I tell her to be quiet. I keep my head up, listening. At last I let out a breath.

It's OK, I tell her.

What's OK?

I think it's stopped.

What's stopped?

Nothing. Forget it.

I lie back down but I can feel that Sophy's still sitting up. Even though I can't see her, I know how she'll be — hunched on the blankets, holding on to her knees like they might fall off.

What's stopped?

I hear her teeth chattering in the cold.

I told you. It's nothing. Go to sleep.

I can't. I'm awake now.

Go to sleep.

But I told you – I'm awake.

Well, that's your problem, Sophy. I never asked you to wake up.

At last she settles back down. Silence. The air gets used to itself again. Then, just as I am getting used to it too, there it is. My eyes flick open. On the other side of the room, Sophy doesn't stir.

I hold my breath. Ease myself up to sit. Straightaway I hear her sigh.

Oh, she says, her voice rising to a wail. Why are you doing this?

I'm not doing anything.

Yes you are. It's like the thing with the dog. I think you're just doing it to scare me.

I think about this.

Why would I want to scare you?

She sucks in a little breath.

I don't know, she says. I just think you would.

I listen. The sounds have all gone now. I feel my blood settle.

Go to sleep, I tell her.

I can't now.

Don't be silly. Of course you can.

When the next bang comes, I sit up so fast that Sophy yelps. I strain to see her in the darkness. The air has changed now, the light's different – wavy, grainy. I can almost see the shape of her in it.

You really didn't hear that?

Fuck's sake. Hear *what*?

It comes again. A loud bang, then a whirring sound.

That!

I look across at Sophy. The light has altered itself around her so that I can pick her out – the curve of her cheek, the pale bounce of her hair.

Sophy.

What?

I can see you. Can you see me?

I know that she can't. I watch as she shakes her head.

Just stop it, she says. I really mean it now. I don't want to know what you can see or hear. Just stop telling me things, OK?

I look around me. The room's almost light. Alive with the sound of heavy machinery. Thunking and humming.

It's the lift, I tell her.

What?

It's moving. The lift's moving.

Now Sophy laughs.

You're dreaming, she says – I watch as she runs her hands through her hair. It's a dream, she says again. She sounds relieved.

I am about to tell her that I never dream, that all of my sleep is reliably black and empty, but, just as I am about to say it, the noise stops. All of it. It drops away. Silence again.

It's over, I tell her. It's all right. It's gone.

You said that before.

This time I know it. It won't come back.

I am right. I lie back down. The silence continues. After a moment or two, I lift my head and listen again to check. But the room is dark and soft and silent and I can no longer see Sophy.

Anyway, she says after another second or two have passed, it's not possible.

What's not possible?

The lift. It couldn't move. I thought you said there was no electricity?

Of course there isn't electricity.

Then how can it be moving?

You're right, I say. It can't.

I sleep. But I wake some minutes, or maybe it is hours, later to find the kid crouching over me. He is holding a candle and by its light I can make out the dull, worn-out weave of his old tracksuit bottoms. Also his face – intent, concentrating, wobbling a little in the light from the flame. He has pulled the covers back and is looking at my sleeping body.

I sit up, snatching the blankets to me.

What? – I stare at him, trembling, hardly able to find the right words. What's going on? What the hell are you doing?

It feels like a question I've asked him only recently. He looks at me carefully.

I just want to be with you, he says.

You what?

I want to be –

What are you talking about?

He says nothing. He does not move. He doesn't even blink. His eyes are sober and sad. A thought occurs to me.

Are you asleep? I ask him. Is that what this is?

He says nothing.

Are you sleepwalking?

He does not react.

I'm asking you, which is it – are you asleep or awake?

44

He shuts his eyes and opens them again.

Awake.

I see then – why didn't I see it before? – that there's a long gash on one side of his face. As if he's been cut with a knife.

What happened to your face? Did someone hurt you? I ask him.

He says nothing. He nods.

Who hurt you?

He takes a breath. Says nothing.

Who did it? I ask him again. Who hurt you?

He looks at me.

You don't remember?

Remember what?

You did it.

Me?

With the piece of glass, remember?

My stomach drops.

What do you mean? What are you talking about? What glass?

The glass. The piece that I gave you to keep.

He leans a little towards me and I try to pull back from him, wrapping the blanket tight around me.

You were scared, he says. It wasn't your fault. You didn't recognise me.

I don't know what you're talking about, I tell him. It's not true. Stop saying these things.

But he isn't listening. Instead he does something that bothers me even more. He sets the candle down on the floor and reaches out and puts a hand on my shoulder. Allows it to move around to the back of my neck. Moves his fingers in my hair.

You're so warm.

45

I hold my breath. I want to tell him to get off but the words are stuck too far down inside me. They won't come.

He moves his hand till it's on my breast, my hip, my leg. His plump and dirty boy's hand.

Can you feel that? he asks me.

I stare at the hand.

No, I say. I don't know.

In a moment, I tell myself. In a moment I'll make him stop.

I watch as his hand goes to cup my knee. It doesn't seem like the first time he's done it. There's confidence in the movement – energy, habit.

What about that? Can you feel it?

What?

My hand – he says it a little louder and I catch a hint of childish frustration in his voice.

I can't say anything. I can't speak. Calm and happiness are flooding through me. A line of warmth running straight through from knee to thighs and up to my heart.

I'm dreaming this, aren't I? I tell him, even though I haven't dreamed anything in so long.

He keeps his eyes on me.

You're not dreaming.

I'm not?

You're not dreaming.

Silence.

If you like, I could put my arms around you?

No, I say quickly. Then, changing my mind as fast as I made it up, OK. OK. Yes.

It is light when I wake. I am still dreaming of the kid. Graham is lying on the bed next to me. I see that he hasn't undressed.

He still has everything on – his coat, his boots, the knitted hat pulled down over his ears. When he sees that I am awake, he takes hold of my hand and presses something bright and cold and round into it.

Look. See what I went out and got you.

Still confused, still feeling the kid's warm hands on me, I struggle to look at the thing in my hand.

It's an orange, he says.

I know it's an orange.

I sit up, press it to my face, to my nose. Dimpled, glossy, it looks unreal. The citrus smell is intense.

You like it?

I take a breath.

Yes, I say. It's very nice.

Nice?

I weigh it and roll it in my hand. Its oily brightness makes my fingers look even more dead. I put it to my face again, breathe in its scent.

It's lovely. Where did you get it?

There were these crates, stuck under a tarpaulin at Old Street. Crowds of people, fighting for them. I'm sorry I could only get you the one. I suppose it's been frozen all this time – will it still be OK, do you think?

I'm sure it's fine, I say, and I drop it back on the blankets.

He looks disappointed.

Aren't you going to eat it?

Later.

He picks it up, tosses it in the air.

If you don't eat it, I will.

OK.

Even though my mouth is jumping to attention at the thought

47

of that fruit, I get up and pull on my sweater and coat. My scarf, gloves, my boots.

Oh, he says. What are you doing? Don't go.

I have to.

Why? Where are you going? You only just woke up.

I say nothing. The splash of colour in his hands pulls at my eyes. He carries on moving it from hand to hand. It is starting to annoy me. At last he sighs.

At least tell me where you're going?

A thousand possible explanations roll through my head. In the end I settle for the most truthful one.

I think I need to go and find the kid.

3

I look for him everywhere. I search the whole building. I go from floor to floor, along wide, dead and empty corridors I didn't know existed. I go into offices and meeting rooms, rooms left in a hurry, chairs tipped over, jackets, papers left behind. There are used white Styrofoam cups and white plastic spoons, some of them tipped over on the table, others knocked to the floor. There used to be pink sachets of sugar and sweeteners, but we ripped them open and poured them down our throats long ago. I look in dark store-cupboards where spiders scuttle among the polythene bags. Every place I look, he isn't in it.

I'm about to give up when I run into Sophy, who is making her slow way up the stairs with a bucket of snow held in her arms.

I'm giving Graham a break, she says. From fetching water – and straightaway she blushes.

She sets the bucket down, out of breath, and I stare at her for a moment, trying to decide what's different. She looks pale, a sketch of her usual self – drawn a bit too quickly by someone who doesn't care. She starts to cough. The tearing sound again. When she's finished, I ask her if she's seen him.

Seen who?

Him. That boy.

Which boy?

I wait. I know that she's testing me. I don't mean Ted. And certainly not Graham.

Matthew, I say, pleased with myself at getting his name.

She looks at me with interest.

But you hate Matt. Why would you want to find him?

It's private.

What do you mean, it's private?

I can't talk about it.

She looks like she's about to ask me something else but, before any words can come out, she doubles over with another fit of coughing so intense that it stops everything. When she straightens up again, I ask her if she's OK.

The look in her eyes is cold and tight.

No, she says. I'm not OK. Can't you see? I'm not at all well. In fact, I think I'm really sick.

She waits for me to say something. I can't think what to say. I don't know what I'm supposed to do about it.

She holds up her hands.

I can't stop coughing, she says. My hands hurt. I've got these bruises, look – and I feel sick all the time. I can't eat anything –

Well, I point out, we've no food anyway.

She doesn't seem to hear me.

And I haven't had a period in ages. Not in all the time we've been here. Are you still getting yours?

I consider this. The idea of bleeding without being injured. It seems unlikely.

I don't think so, I say.

You don't think so?

No, I'm not.

She hesitates, trying to decide what else she wants from me.

But – do you think they'll come back? When things are back to normal, I mean?

I stare at her. Back to normal? What exactly does she think this is? I shake my head.

You'll be fine, I tell her.

I turn to go, but this doesn't seem to satisfy her.

I don't feel fine, she says, raising her voice as I continue on down the stairs.

I say nothing. I keep my eyes on the stairwell. I think of the kid's warm hands on my neck. Surely he must be down here somewhere?

In the end he is exactly where I know he'll be – in one of the big meeting rooms on the floor above. A room I've already been into at least twice. Hunched on the dusty grey carpet, picking up beetles and arranging them in a line along the low metal window sill.

If he heard me come in, he doesn't show it. He doesn't look up. I notice with a snag of affection that there's a tide-mark of blackish dirt on his neck which his hair – always brutishly short and straight – never seems to grow to cover. I don't think I've ever seen such an unappealing hairline on a kid. Usually this thought would make my spirits sink, but this time it does exactly the opposite. It lifts me up. This time looking at him is enough. To know he's right here, in this room, close to me.

What do you want? he says at last.

Nothing.

I hear him take a little breath.

That's a lie, isn't it?

Yes.

He waits a moment, and then he twists round. The sight of his face – clever and furious – makes me catch my breath. I see that there's a smudge of something on his cheek. His eyes are red and sore.

Matt, I say – and I admit it's strange to hear myself say the name – are you OK? Have you been crying?

No.

What?

No, I haven't been crying. Can you go away now? he adds.

But I don't do it – I don't go away. Instead, I wait. I worry about what he's thinking of me, coming to him here, waiting, staying close, watching him. I worry, but not that much – certainly not enough to send myself away.

I put my hand to my face. It is burning. I watch as he carries on moving the beetles around. Deliberate, intent. The brittle slow motion of their legs, shiny blue-black shells slipping between his fingers. It's what boys do, I suppose. Play with insects.

What are you doing? he says after a few moments have passed.

What?

Why aren't you going?

I take a breath.

Please, Matt.

Please what?

Please just let me stay.

He smiles to himself. He says nothing. I ask him what he's doing.

Doing?

Yes, I say. What are you up to?

He tells me his answer as if it's a joke between the two of us. I'm playing.

*　*　*

Minutes pass.

You can come and sit down here with me, if you want, he says.

So I do – I get down there on the floor with him, both of us cross-legged on the carpet like a couple of kids. I'm still wearing my coat, but I unbutton it and unwind my scarf, take off my gloves. I sneak some sideways glances at him – his dirty face, his scrub of hair. The creases in his clothes. Thick dark lashes. Flashes of something I can't name in his eyes. He points to a beetle that is struggling over the fibres of the carpet.

You want to know what this one's called?

OK, I say.

I wait, my thoughts still churning.

He's called Arthur.

Arthur? – I start to laugh.

What's funny about that?

I don't know. You have a beetle called Arthur?

I watch the beetle tackling the carpet as if it was a mountain range. Matthew looks at me.

Is it a bad name?

Not really, I say, trying not to laugh. Not at all. It's just –

What's wrong with it?

Nothing's wrong with it.

It happens to be a name I like, he says. You know, like the king with the table?

OK, I say, though I don't know what he means about the king. I like it too.

You're just saying that.

I'm not just saying it. I like it. I really do.

I smile again. He looks at me and frowns.

What's wrong with you today?

Nothing's wrong with me.

Yes there is. Why're you acting so funny?

I'm not. I'm not acting funny.

Yes you are. You're acting like you're all – I don't know – happy or something.

I gaze at him, my heart beating wildly.

I'm not happy.

He shifts his eyes back to the carpet.

OK, but I don't like it.

Don't like what?

You being like this. It's not normal. It's weird.

I wait, thinking about this. I don't know what to tell him. I take a breath.

Matt –

What?

I try to find the words to explain what I'm feeling, but before I can say anything at all, he cuts me off. The look he gives me makes my stomach flip.

What is it? I ask him. What's the matter?

He is staring at me.

Whoa, he says. I can't believe you just said that.

I didn't say anything.

Yes you did.

What? What do you think I said?

He shakes his head, rubs at his face. Then he scratches at his thighs, bulging in their dark tracksuit bottoms. I see that he can't look at me.

For heaven's sake. What is it that you think you heard me say?

But he carries on shaking his head.

I can't say it. I just can't. It's just so raw.

Raw?

It's embarrassing!

Matthew, I say, please – stop teasing me. I mean it.

I'm not teasing you.

OK.

He looks at the carpet for the longest time. Finally, he scratches his head. He doesn't look at me. His face is red.

I will if you want me to, he says at last. I can, you know. I could. I quite like you actually. What I mean is, I don't really care. I wouldn't mind doing it. If you want me to.

I stare at him.

Wouldn't mind doing what?

He waits for one more second. Then he puts his hand up to my cheek and pulls my face towards his in the clumsiest way possible.

His fingers smell of cheese.

What? I begin to say – but he leaves me no space for another word. Because a moment later he has wrapped me in a deep, tight kiss that leaves me gasping for breath and sends my body, mind and heart rocketing skywards.

We lie together on the carpet, him and me, me and Matthew, me and the kid. For a long time I cannot think, cannot move. We hold on to each other so tightly that you'd think we'd just this second discovered the use of our arms.

But after a moment or two, he rolls away from me. The sudden lack of him feels like a draught of icy air. I turn my head and I try to see him, but at first the sun blinds me – coming in through the window, lifting the dust and turning it over and over.

My cheeks are hot. I shrug off my coat.

I'm boiling, I say, and then I frown because it's not something I'd say.

He says nothing.

What are you thinking? I ask him.

He doesn't reply. He isn't even looking at me. He is staring at the ceiling where what was an old fire sprinkler has come loose. I try to look at it too – wanting to see what he sees, feel what he feels.

I ask him if he's OK.

He thinks for a second.

Not really, he says. I suppose I'm a bit scared.

Scared? What are you scared of?

Not you, he says quickly. I'm not scared of you.

I feel a longing to take his grubby hand in mine and thread my fingers into the warm damp centre of it, but I don't do it. I am, I think. I'm scared of me.

Sun moves across the dusty carpet. The palest of shadows. The lightest of touches. I'll remember this, I think, and I shiver.

I didn't mean it by the way, he says. The bit about not caring. You know, when I said I didn't mind if I did it or not? It's not true. I did mind.

OK.

Ever since I've known you, I've thought you were so . . .

I wait, my heart thumping in a mad way.

What? I say. So what?

So pretty.

Pretty? I shut my eyes to stop a laugh.

Do you believe me? he says.

Yes.

You sound like you don't.

I feel myself smile.

I believe you, Matt.

You believe me – but what?

But nothing. I believe you.

Anyway, he says after a few moments have passed, it's this place, isn't it?

Which place?

Here. The building.

I sit up.

What do you mean?

You know what I mean.

I am silent for a moment. I hear him swallow. I put my hands to my face, over my eyes.

I don't know what you're talking about, I tell him.

He says nothing. Very gently he takes my hands from my eyes.

Matt?

Still he says nothing. Then I think I feel him squeeze my hand.

The next night, or maybe it's the one after that, I wake and I know that there is someone right there in front of me. It isn't Matthew.

Who is it? I say. Please? Who's there?

My heart is banging, the blood belting so fast around my body that I feel it in my jaw, my head, the backs of my eyes, my teeth. The room has turned very cold.

Tell me who you are, I say again.

The room gets slowly lighter so I can see everything. Desks, chairs, the outline of the window, the blankets and coats piled and forlorn on the floor. It stays like that for a few seconds and then it darkens again.

Nothing else happens.

Next time I wake, it is dawn. A sky like someone has chucked paint across it.

On the other side of the room, or maybe it's the next room, I can hear two people whispering to each other. One of them is Graham. I can't hear what they're saying. I don't want to. One of them laughs and then that same one laughs again. It's the girl, I think. It's Sophy.

Ted finds a couple of dozen packs of cigarettes in a cupboard on the eighth floor. He and the kid are sprawled across one of the desks, laughing together as they share them out.

Not the kid, I think. Matthew. He's Matthew.

When I come in the room, he looks up at me and there's something in his eyes I cannot name – surprise? interest? fun? – but then his gaze returns to the cigarettes.

Can you believe it? Ted is saying. Someone's secret stash. Or else they must be duty free or something.

Duty free? I try to remember what duty free is. It sounds reckless and fun.

It solves all our tobacco problems anyway, Ted says.

I stare at him.

What tobacco problems?

He makes a face.

Um – lack of. Need of. Craving for.

He holds a pack out to me.

Here, he says. And you can have more if you want.

He starts to build a tower with the rest of the packets.

I run a finger over the cellophane. It's cool and slippery. I shake the pack. The lightest sound.

I don't know if I've ever smoked, I say.

Seriously? – he snatches it back. OK, all the more for us, then.

What about Graham?

We'll keep some for Graham.

I look at the kid. Matthew. He smiles at me. I smile back. The skin at the back of my neck grows hot. Boiling hot.

I don't think you did, he says.

What?

Smoke. I don't think you ever did. I don't think you would know how to.

He does, though. Matthew does – he knows how to. He sits in the corridor with Ted and smokes one after another, quick and furious, sucking at the thing in his fingers until it reduces itself to a stub of falling ash.

At least we haven't got to worry about lung disease, Ted says when I tell him he'll feel ill if he smokes so much without any food in him.

Why not? I say. Why haven't you got to worry?

Because we'll all be dead soon anyway.

He looks at Matthew and then, as if he's only just heard his own words, he laughs.

I used to have all these panicky dreams, he says then. One was where all my teeth were loose. When I woke up I'd have to go to the bathroom and feel them to check they were there. Or I'd dream that people were chasing me, coming after me with weapons and stuff. Or the worst one was that I was in this very black room and there was this tiny point of light and I just knew it was evil. But now . . .

He stops talking and he stares into the distance for a moment.

What about now?

Ted looks back at the ribbon of smoke lifting off his fingers into the air.

Now I don't dream anything, he says.

Me too, I say. I never dream.

Matthew says nothing.

In the night, he comes to fetch me.

I know a place, he says. It's good. You'll need your coat.

I get up and pull on my coat and follow him. We go out on to the landing, past the lifts, and into the stairwell. He walks very fast. I struggle to keep up with him.

Wait, I say, but he doesn't seem to hear me.

On the stairs he stops and turns. His eyes are two holes in the darkness. He puts out a hand. I take it. His smaller hand. My large one. My hand in his. It's always been like this, I think. Always.

Three floors up, he says.

We walk up the stairs. The nineteenth floor is pretty much exactly the same as our floor, except for a lighter coloured carpet and more dead plants. Maybe a few more closed doors.

We go down a long corridor and he pushes a heavy metal fire door and suddenly we are out on a big corner terrace. A foot of snow on it, maybe more. A wall and a metal railing all around.

He lights a cigarette, smokes it, hard, not at all in the half-hearted and unsure way that Ted smokes. He smokes as if he half likes it and half doesn't, or else as if he needs it but wants

60

it over with as quick as possible. Then he flicks the butt over the railing. When he turns back to me, his face is thoughtful.

The moon is bright. I go over to the railing and stare at the city lying there beneath and around us. The dome of the big white church I've forgotten the name of.

Towards the Barbican, or maybe it's Holborn, a bonfire is blazing. More than a bonfire. Tall flames and thick black smoke. I feel myself shiver.

Something's on fire over there, I tell him.

He nods.

What do you think it is?

It could be anything really, he says.

I look over at the fire again. The smoke is piling up, repeating itself, moving off into the paler night sky. I shut my eyes. I can't watch it for long. I shiver again.

But things aren't still bursting into flames, are they?

He stares at me for a second.

You remember that?

He gets a plastic broom from one of the rooms off the corridor and uses it to clear a space in the snow. Then he gets two or three big pieces of cardboard, flattened-out boxes that once contained computers or office equipment, and he lays them on the concrete.

Somewhere for us to sit, he says.

I ask him what we're doing out here, but he doesn't answer. He takes off his coat and spreads it on the cardboard.

No, I tell him. Not your coat. Put it back on.

But I want it to be comfortable.

It's very comfortable, I tell him. Honestly. We don't need the –

He interrupts by reaching up and putting his grubby kid's hand over my mouth. Through his fingers, I hear myself laugh.

Shut up, he says. I promise you. We need it.

I let him pull me down. We sit there for a moment, shivering. Then he hugs me tight. A bit too tight. A bit too much the way a kid would hug.

I don't want you to be cold, he says when I try to pull away a bit.

I'm not cold, I tell him truthfully as he carries on almost squeezing the breath out of me. I'm never cold.

Same with me, he says, and his teeth bang together. Or at least, I feel it and I know it's there, like right now – it's freezing – but it never bothers me.

For the second or maybe it's the third time, I ask him why we came out here. Why didn't we just go to one of the hundreds of spare offices inside the building?

He looks at me. I watch his eyes, his face, the chubby tip of his nose.

It's better out here, he says. I like it. It's our place.

Our place?

I look around me for a second. I look at the cold metal railing and the sharp angles of the low concrete wall and the burst of stars that light up the vast blackness of the sky above us.

Yes, he says. Our special place.

I listen to the words and, for a second or two, the world seems to tip, then it rights itself again.

What? he says when he sees me looking.

I don't know what happens then. Maybe I fall asleep. And, in my sleep, I see things that are not there.

A sofa. A pair of shoes – small shoes belonging to a child,

brown and scuffed with a strap and a buckle. Other things too. A baby's highchair with a row of bright-coloured wooden beads on it, the dried remains of old food stuck to them. Some stairs. At the foot of the stairs. At the foot of the stairs . . .

I wake to find the kid watching over me, worry on his face.

You really freaked me out, he says.

I struggle to sit up.

What? What is it?

You must have been having a bad dream.

I blink at him.

I don't dream. I never dream.

Well, you said the weirdest things. While you were asleep.

I gaze at his face, the dark sky beyond it. Every part of my body feels cold. My heart is racing, my mouth dry.

What things? What did I say?

He looks as if he is about to tell me, but then something happens and he seems to change his mind.

For god's sake, Matthew. Tell me.

He thinks about it for a second and then he shakes his head.

I don't want to scare you, he says.

It isn't a new thing, Ted and the kid going out on to the streets, looking for stuff to bring back. There are still shops out there that have not been entirely emptied, boxes and tins buried for so long under ice and snow and rubble, forgotten corners in places that no one has yet thought to go.

Some trips they come back empty-handed, fed up and cold, angry, hungry. Other times, though, they bring things. Cans of Coca-Cola from a vending machine, the liquid still brown and bubbling when you snap the ring. A litre of frozen milk in its waxy container. A tube of toothpaste, barely squeezed, its mintiness so bright and clean that Sophy insists on keeping it in her pocket to lick like a sweet. A rechargeable battery, useless now, but try explaining that to Ted. A lump of Blu-Tack. Shaving foam. The melted plastic casing of a mobile phone.

One time they find a hoard of chocolate money – handfuls of coins, all different sizes, light as air, shiny and gold. We rush to prise off the foil and find a dusty white bloom on the chocolate, but the taste is startling and creamy. Sophy eats her share too fast and spends the next hour being sick.

And then one day Ted brings something else. A big fat suitcase full of children's clothes. He says he found it in a burned-out car near the river. The suitcase smells of melted plastic, and many of the clothes are charred and sour. It's a piece of trash and I don't know why he bothered to bring it back. As soon as I see it, I feel light-headed, exhausted, ill.

But some of it's not been touched by the fire, he says. Some of it's fine. Look, there's some almost brand-new stuff in here. Toys, as well.

Yeah, but it's all baby stuff, Sophy complains.

I look at the clothes. Bright little folds of lilac and pink and yellow, stretchy cotton . . .

Get rid of them, I tell Ted.

He stares at me. He picks up a small pair of trainers with a scuffed picture of a pink and violet fairy on them. Thumbelina. My skin crawls.

I mean it, I say. I'm not joking. Please do it now.

But why? What's the matter?

Oh, but so cute! Sophy pulls out a light-coloured fleece with a zip and a bit of sparkle on the pocket. She holds it against her. Why can't it just be a few sizes bigger?

For a moment it looks like she's going to thrust it at me.

64

Oh and look! She holds up a little brown plastic animal. Sylvanians. I think I used to have some of these.

She stands the tiny creature – an eyeless, earless thing, wearing a cotton neckerchief – on her hand and holds it out to me. The room wobbles.

Get it away from me, I tell her.

She stares.

But I was only saying . . .

I take a quick step backwards. My heart is racing.

The man who is there with us and whose name has dropped out of my head now, he's trying to put a hand on my shoulder. I struggle to stop him.

Hey, he says. Come on – what's the matter? She didn't mean it. She was only fooling around.

I push him off. Graham, that's it – I push him off.

Where's Matthew? I ask them. The kid, where is he?

Graham's voice comes from a long way away.

What's Matthew got to do with it?

I don't know.

He's not here, Sophy says. I think he went to get water. Why do you want him?

I don't know.

Are you OK? Ted says.

I don't know.

For a long time afterwards, when the suitcase has been got rid of and everyone else has gone from the room, I am still there, sitting by the window trying not to think about all the things I don't know.

I go around the building.

Again I hear printers and phones, desk drawers sliding open

and shut. I hear people laughing, talking. Or the silence that falls when they are all frowning at their screens.

Sometimes I see them. Parts of them anyway. An elbow or a wrist resting on a desk. The cuff of a shirt. An earlobe with a ring or pearl in it. A whiff of perfume or sweat. The staticky shadow of a person's hair.

I smell the sourness of burned coffee when a fresh jug needs to be put on. See the sticky pink rim of a coffee cup. A cardboard sandwich packet that has missed the bin and is on the floor, its tongue of cellophane hanging out. The core of an apple, dampening the sports section of the newspaper it has been placed on. Someone's dry-cleaning, picked up in the lunch hour and hung by its metal hanger from a filing cabinet. A pair of trainers, socks stuck in them, waiting to be run home in.

And sounds too. A faraway sound of hoovering. Bursts of laughter. Doors banging. A meeting ending. A trail of disgruntled voices moving off down the corridor, discussing it.

The place is alive. It hums, it moves. Sometimes it frightens me.

Do you ever think this place is haunted? I ask the kid as we stand in silence on our secret terrace and watch the sun freeze its slow way through the sky.

Yes, he says. I told you. All the time.

I glance at his face.

You told me?

He doesn't look at me. He keeps his eyes straight ahead. The sun is red and liquid, a flame without any warmth. He keeps his elbows on the railing and stares out towards the big white dome of the church. St Paul's. Its edges turning pink.

I've done bad things, I tell him.

Still he doesn't look at me. I wonder if he even heard.

Well, he says at last, who hasn't?

You haven't.

I can promise you, I have.

I say nothing. I don't want to ask him what he's done. I am afraid that he'll say that the bad thing he's done is wanting to be with me. Being my friend. Far away, somewhere in the building, I can hear a dog barking.

Can you hear that? I ask him. That dog?

But he doesn't answer and, next time I look, I'm not even sure he's there.

And then this happens.

A dull dark morning. I am three floors up, on the nineteenth floor, standing on the landing by the lifts, when the air empties itself of any last trace of warmth. An icy wind comes out of nowhere. It lifts my hair. I gasp, I turn. And there she is.

Down at the very end of the corridor. In the grey wavy light. Standing on the dull office carpet. A fair-haired child, very small, no more than one or two years old. Sucking her thumb.

She has on a dark dress and cardigan. Her hair is mussed up at the back as if she's slept on it. I can't tell if she has shoes on her feet. I can only look at her for a second or two at a time. I look and then I cannot look. I have to look away.

I stand there in the cold wind of the corridor, looking and not looking. I let my heart bounce. I hold my breath. Whole moments go by. The room slides around. It isn't upright. Sweat bursts out on my face. I think I might faint.

Then, as suddenly as it came, the dizziness passes. I breathe. I shut my eyes. That's it, I think, it's over. When I open them again, she'll be gone.

But when I open them, she isn't gone. She is still there. If anything, she is even more there than before. The cold wind ruffles her hair. I can see her sturdy little legs, her arms in their knitted sleeves. And her head has turned, her eyes are lit up. She's seen me.

She is facing straight down the corridor towards me now. She has a light-coloured rag and she holds it up to her face with one hand while she sucks on the other thumb. Very slowly, with tottering steps, she starts to move towards me.

Mummy, she says.

I stand still. But when I see that she's coming closer, I can't help it, I take a step away. This displeases her. Keeping her eyes on me, she lets her thumb fall from her mouth.

Mummy, she says again. An accusation.

I'm not your mummy, I whisper.

She stares at me and she says it again.

Mummy?

I shake my head. My blood is jumping.

I'm not your mummy, I say again.

Everything changes then. In a matter of seconds, the wind drops and the air grows even sharper, wilder, lighter.

With one furious cry, as if someone has picked her up and thrown her, she lifts off the ground and comes flying through the air towards me.

4

Graham finds me. He finds me on the floor by the lifts. He tells me he's been looking for me everywhere. He says, What happened, what happened? He says it again and again like a dad or a mad person or something. He tells me that my head is bleeding.

I stare at him, feel a twist of confusion.

My heart?

No, he says. Your head – look.

He takes hold of my hand and lifts it to show me. My hair is warm and sticky.

I ask him how he knew to look for me here, three floors up? He frowns.

You're always up here, he says. You wander around up here all the time.

I watch as he takes a piece of rag and makes me press it to the cut. When I keep on trying to take it away, he stops me.

You need to stop the bleeding, he says.

He puts the rag on my head again and puts his own hand over mine to show me to hold it there, but I pull it away, look at the rag. It's light-coloured, grubby, and smudged now with someone's blood. I sniff it.

Where did you get this?

What? he says. The cloth? I don't know. It was just here on the floor.

I push it back at him.

I don't want it.

But you need something to stop the bleeding.

I don't care, I tell him. I don't want this.

I fling it as far away down the corridor as I can. It makes no noise when it lands. I shudder. And that's when I realise – something is happening to my face. I put my hand up and find water there. I lick my fingers, taste salt.

Isn't that strange, I tell him.

What's strange?

She's crying.

He looks at me.

Not she, he says. You.

Me?

Yes. You're crying.

The morning runs on, dismal and flat and strange.

I lie on the blankets and coats in the weak sunshine and I stare at the sky, the city, the old life that lies frozen out there. When too many thoughts start to come, I turn myself over and stare at the wall. The wall is better. The sad little marks and stains where a shoe has scuffed or an insect has died. The row of dead-eyed plug sockets which used to bring power. The ghost of a rectangle where something once hung, a calendar perhaps, counting out the world in days and months and years. I watch the wall.

Sometimes people come and talk to me. But never the right person, never the one I wish would come.

Ted comes.

Do you want some of these? he says. I found two whole packets in the pocket of one of the coats. They're OK. I mean, they're not soggy or anything.

I look at what he's holding between his finger and thumb. A very fat worm. Fluorescent orange. Covered in a kind of dust. I don't know what I'm supposed to do with it.

Cheesy Wotsits, Ted says. Remember them? Smell it. I bet you ate them before.

He shoves it under my nose. I smell corn, salt, chemicals.

Hold out your hand and I'll give you some.

I'm OK, thanks.

Come on, you'll like it. It's nice –

Very gently he presses the worm against my lips.

Ted, I whisper, I said no.

I turn away, lick the taste off my lips. My stomach growls.

Graham comes. He puts a hand on my shoulder, or maybe it's my face. I ask him to please find the kid, but he tells me he's not around.

What do you mean, not around? Please get him.

He gives me a look I can't read, then he sighs.

He's probably gone out with Ted.

But why? Where've they gone?

I've no idea. For God's sake. They've probably gone out looking for food. Why is it so important?

I say nothing. I feel Graham looking at me. I know that the look is building up to something.

I want to show you something, he says. It's something I thought about showing you some time ago.

I shake my head. I'm sick of being shown things.

No thanks, I say.

But you don't know what it is yet.

I don't care. Whatever it is, I don't want it.

He puts a hand on my arm. I realise then that I feel all wrong – cold, shaky, sad.

71

I don't want it, I tell him again, thinking it will almost certainly be to do with sex. I'm not interested.

He gives me a steady look.

But it's something about you, he says. About yourself. Something you ought to know. I noticed it ages ago. I've been thinking about whether I should tell you and now I honestly think I should.

I stare at him. There's only one thing I want to know.

Can't you just find Matt? I ask him again.

He looks annoyed.

Forget Matthew. Can you please try and forget him, just for a moment? He's got nothing to do with this. I told you – it's about you. Now do you want to see it or not?

I look at him and bite my lip. I bite down hard until I taste blood.

I don't know, I tell him. It depends.

What does it depend on?

I'm worried it'll be something bad.

He hesitates.

It's good, he says. Or at least I think it is. But I have to undress you a bit, to show you.

I shake my head and pull away.

In that case, I don't want to.

I wipe my bleeding lip on my sleeve. Graham holds up his hands.

Christ, he says. Not like that, don't worry. I just have to lift your sweater a bit. Trust me, he adds. I'm a lawyer, remember?

I frown and lick my lip again.

Are lawyers supposed to be good people?

He laughs.

I don't know. Don't ask me. I was joking. I'm honestly not sure I can be the judge of that kind of thing any more.

He comes and kneels by me and pushes me back on the blankets. He pulls up my sweater, my shirt too. I shiver in the sudden cold air.

And your bottoms too, a little bit.

Do I have to?

Just so I can show you.

But I pull away.

I feel dirty, I tell him, because I'm not feeling like being undressed and especially not by Graham.

We're all dirty.

Not as dirty as I am.

I'm telling you, we're all dirty.

OK.

I let him pull them down. When my belly's exposed to the air, he puts a finger on it and traces it downwards. I shiver again.

Now, he says. You see? Look at that.

I strain to look.

Look at what?

That line. You see it?

A pale brown line extends from my navel right down into my pants. It looks like someone has drawn on me with a blunt crayon.

He keeps his finger on it until I make him move it off.

You know what this means?

That I'm going to die?

Don't be silly. Of course not that.

That I'm fat?

Now you're just guessing.

73

Well I am fat.

He smiles.

No. Do you know what the line means?

I shake my head. He looks surprised.

You really don't?

I try to think about my body. I don't know anything about it really. Sophy's right that it isn't thin, like everyone else's. I sigh.

Is it an act of God? I ask him at last.

He laughs.

Whatever makes you say that?

Isn't it what people say? When they don't understand something?

He smiles.

I don't know what people you're talking about.

You're right, I say. I don't know either.

He's still looking at the line. I see that his face is serious now.

My wife had one exactly like this. After our first, and then an even darker one after our second.

The words thud through me like a stone.

Your second?

He doesn't look at me.

Our girl, he says. After Lara.

I stare at him.

You have a wife? You have a child?

Children, he says. I have two children. And yes, a wife. Ex-wife now. You know all of this – I've told you it all before.

You've never told me –

I have. You've just forgotten. Anyway what I'm trying to tell you is, so do you.

So do I what?

Children. Babies. That's what the line means. You get it when you're pregnant. It means that you've had children. Or a child. You have them.

A moment passes and I say nothing. Then the person who is me puts her hands over her face. Her heart stays where it is but it speeds up as a bad feeling spreads into her limbs, her blood, her bones. Dread is the word that comes to her.

He tries to take my hands off my face. Her face.

Come on, he says. You knew that already. You must have. I just don't believe it's something you could have forgotten.

I'm silent.

What I mean is, please don't be upset. I really don't think I'm telling you anything you don't already know.

He lies down beside me on the coats. I let him. We lie there and watch the sun make its slow patterns on the wall. Slipping in and out of clouds.

I'm going to forget this, I tell him.

He tilts his head to look at me.

No, he says. You won't. You mustn't.

I forget everything.

Not this.

But I want to.

Why don't you want to remember things? Don't you want to know who you are? Don't you want to go back to being the person you once were?

Once were? A sour taste comes in my mouth. I swallow it down.

I don't know, I say. I don't think so.

But why not?

75

I think she was a bad person. I'm glad she's gone. When she went, it was a good thing. I don't want her to come back.

Graham is staring out of the window with a sad face. I wonder if he's thinking about his children. I ask him if he remembers them.

He looks at me.

My kids? Of course I do. I think of them all the time.

Every single day?

His face stays sad.

Yes, he says. Every single day.

I think about this. I realise I can't imagine Graham with children. I ask him what their names are.

John and Lara. John's eight, or nine now I suppose. He would have had a birthday in the summer. And Lara's five. I've told you about them before.

I don't think you have.

I have.

OK.

I wait a moment, then I ask him about his wife. He blinks.

My ex. What about her?

What's she like? What's her name?

He's silent for a moment.

I don't know what she's like. She used to be . . . well, our marriage kind of ground to a halt. It was my fault really. We tried to fix it, but . . . she was a good person.

What's she called?

Caroline. Her name was Caroline.

You don't think she's alive?

He takes a breath.

I don't know. Well, I hope so, obviously. I hope they're all together and safe.

But you don't know?

No.

That must be hard.

Yes.

Another day, or maybe it's that same day, Sophy comes and finds me.

She's coughing a lot and her eyes are too blue and raw and they shine a little too hard out of her pale face. I notice that she's wearing Graham's jacket, the one with the striped lining that I've seen him in a hundred times. It's much too big on her and she's pulled the sleeves right down over her hands so that only the knuckles show.

Her thin knuckles. Just bones. She glances at my face then back down again.

Are you OK? she says.

Me?

Graham said you fainted or something.

Oh, I say. It was nothing. Look, I'm fine.

You've got a really bad cut on your head.

It's OK.

She stops. Blushes.

Graham says . . .

I watch her face.

Yes? What does Graham say?

He says you don't think you had children.

I give her a hard look.

I haven't. I know I haven't. He was completely wrong about that.

She waits a second.

But –

But what, Sophy?

I've told you before that you had kids.

I swallow, feel my face grow hot.

No, you haven't.

She says nothing. Then she takes a breath.

He also says you see things.

See things? What things?

Things that aren't there.

My heart tightens.

Aren't where?

She stares at me for a second, shakes her head.

Aren't anywhere.

Sophy, I say. How come you've been spending so much time listening to Graham?

And then I look at her pretty face, her eyes, the pretty woman she would almost certainly have grown into. And I realise that Graham hasn't tried to sleep with me in ages.

She starts to say something else then, but it is swallowed by a coughing fit. When she's finished there's something in her hand. She wipes it on her jeans. We both look at it. A brownish smear.

Is that blood? she says.

I don't know.

But what else could it be?

I don't know.

It's blood, isn't it?

Well, it might be, I say.

The sun is low in the sky – what would in the old life have been a sweet and balmy summer evening – when I go up to the nineteenth floor and stand in the corridor. Dust hangs in the air. The carpet is lit up in some places and not in others. I know that I am alone.

I try to stand exactly where I was when I saw her – was it today or was it already yesterday? I look around me. I hold myself still. I listen. Then I say it as loudly as I dare.

Are you there?

The air thumps around me. Silence. The corridor stretches on ahead, empty. I can see nothing in it and I can hear no sound. Nothing shifts and when at last I cough, the sound breaks so hard into the stillness that I jump, frightening myself.

Come to me, I say. Come. I'm not afraid of you.

When nothing happens, I glance behind me and then I take some steps. I walk all the way down the corridor towards the spot where I think I first saw her. Was it here? I try to judge the distance. I stand where I think she was. Her stout little fists and feet. Her eyes fixed on mine. The sudden cold wind that lifted her hair.

I turn back then, and look at the spot where I was standing – the place where she'd have seen me. Looking at that empty spot, a wave of something washes over me. I don't know what it is.

All down one side of the corridor are office doors, a row of them – one or two open, most of them closed. Eight altogether. I count them now. I know exactly what will be in them – desks, chairs, computers with long-dead screens, maybe some plants as well.

Each office has a glass window, an internal window that looks straight on to the corridor, each one with its blind drawn down. I walk past these windows now. Each time I come to a door, I open it and put my head into the office. Each time, as I expect, nothing. Each one empty in the same way. A row of empty offices. Evening sun shining in. An innocent sight. My mouth is dry.

I walk up and down that corridor. I do it maybe ten or twenty times, up and down, up and down, not for any reason other than that I am alone and I can. All alone. My heart unsettled. My boots dragging repeatedly backwards and forwards over that carpet.

You walk this building like a ghost, Graham once said to me and I know that I gazed at him, unsure what exactly he was accusing me of.

I'm walking past these windows for the very last time – thinking I am finally bored of this game and will go downstairs and see what the kid is up to – when I see that something has changed. About three windows along, a blind has been lifted. I creep over and look in. And draw back sharply as her face meets mine.

A child, but not the same child. A different one this time. Older, this one – long fair hair almost down to her waist, delicate limbs, small oval face. A six- or seven-year-old beauty, except for one thing. The skin around her eyes and mouth is the wrong colour – mottled yellow in some places, blue or grey in others. Her lips are almost black.

I don't know who screams first or who screams loudest. Mine bubbles up from my chest, but before I can let it out, her hands have flown to her face and she has backed away across the carpet.

It takes less than a second for the wall to absorb her. She is there and then she isn't there. No shadow, nothing, just the brightness of the space she leaves.

80

I look down at myself to see if I am still there. I am. My heart is hammering and my legs have lost whatever it is that keeps them up and I have sunk down on the floor, but I am – I'm there, I'm here, here I am.

Matt and I are walking up Bishopsgate towards Spitalfields. I've no idea how we got here. The sky is dark and swollen, fat wet snowflakes coming down.

We go past the old market and along Fournier Street. There are three broken-down doorways, the wood splintered and caving in. Smoke coming from inside one of them. And beyond them, a church, its door burned and broken and all its windows punched out. It must have been done recently, because glass lies all over the snow – shards in all different colours, violet and yellow and pink.

Look – he bends down and picks up a piece in each colour, arranges them on the black nylon of his glove. Do you like them?

I stare at them.

They're OK.

He takes one and holds it up. Pink. The edge jagged and sharp. He holds it up to his face. Pink light shining through. He winks at me, but it doesn't work because the other eye closes a bit as well. I watch as he plays around with the pieces of glass. I feel like a person looking at colours in a dream – you could react but what's the point?

He puts the pink one back and holds out his gloved palm to me.

Here, he says. Which one?

I shake my head.

Which one do you want?

I don't want any.

Choose one.

I don't want to.

You have to. I want you to.

When I still do nothing, he picks up the pink one and holds it out to me. I try to refuse it but he won't let me. He reaches out and stuffs it in my pocket. Then he grabs my wrist and pulls me into one of the doorways.

I let him pull me against him and I notice how clumsy he is. Really, how young.

He looks into my face.

What?

I shake my head.

What's making you unhappy? he says.

I like that he talks about happy and unhappy, that he dares to name feelings, rather than saying, as Graham or Simon would do: What's the matter with you?

Simon? Who the hell's Simon? I think.

I look at him now, this boy, waiting for an answer. Snow clinging to his awkward brown hair, to the collar of his coat. His cheeks dark with cold.

I can't explain it, I say.

He reaches up and pushes the hair from my face. It flops straight back.

Well, try, he says. I don't like it when you're unhappy.

I try not to look at him.

You're just a kid, I tell him.

He doesn't argue. Instead, he puts his arms around me and he hugs me tight. My chin sits on his hair, where the snow is already melting. He hugs like a boy, I think. Too soft, too hard, too everything.

Gently, I try to remove him. But he stays. He sticks. Finally he gives in and lets go. I smell his musty boy's breath as he pulls away from me, frowning.

I don't see what's changed, he says.

Nothing's changed.

Well then.

His fingers are moving over my breastbone, straining down to get under my coat and jumper. I don't like it. I prise them off. He laughs and pushes them back in, delving down. I take them off again.

It's not a game, Matthew.

He scowls.

You want me to go? You want me to go away from you?

I say nothing. I feel myself swallow. My hands are deep in my pockets. I find something sharp. The glass. I press my thumb on it.

Is that what you want? he says.

I don't know, I tell him as I feel the wet of the blood.

He takes a step away. Two steps. His eyes are heavy. I take my hand out of my pocket, suck the blood off my thumb.

No, I say.

No what?

No, I don't want you to go.

On the corner of Brushfield Street, two carthorses have died and fallen over. A fire has been lit and a bunch of men with knives and sticks have taken charge. Two men hack the flesh off the animals, while another three or four keep the crowd at bay. One of them shouts that if people want meat they must queue up and pay for it.

But, says Sophy. Pay with what?

I swing round when I hear her voice. I see Ted standing next to her.

How did you get here?

What do you mean, how did I get here? We came with you.

I look at Matthew, but he shows no surprise. He's watching the men.

But seriously, she says again. What are they going to find to pay with?

I look at her. Sometimes I forget that she's just a stupid teenager.

They'll find something.

Yes, but what?

Everyone has something.

She swallows.

Do we have anything?

Ted glances at me.

Don't be an idiot, Soph, he says.

Some people have already moved away, seeing the knives. A woman and a girl, both of them in brown clothes and with their hair burned close to their heads, have been put off and are hurrying away in the direction of Fournier Street.

But others are queuing up. Most do it calmly, but one or two seem frantic, trying to push their way to the front. Some young lads of twelve or thirteen get cheeky and try to grab the meat before they've given the men anything, but they are kicked down in the snow and beaten.

God, says Sophy as we watch the snow turn red around their heads.

I feel Matthew behind me. He touches the small of my back and I shiver.

A young woman, her baby in a sling at her breast, seems in a bad way, zigzagging along like a drunk. She must be desperate because she lets the men put their hands up her skirts in return for a piece of the meat. But even then they only allow her the smallest scrap and they make sure to chuck it in the snow so she has to bend over to get it.

The crowd is laughing.

God, Sophy says again. Look at that. The poor woman.

We watch as she wraps the meat in a piece of cloth and makes her slow way off down Commercial Street, past a faded sign that says National Lottery Play Here. Finally she comes to a stop and sinks down against a low wall to feed her child.

She'll be all right, won't she? says Sophy.

I say nothing. But some minutes later, we pass her and she is still sitting in the exact same place, the child at her breast, and neither of them moving at all.

We are almost back at the building when there's a shout. A man is coming through the snow towards us, shouting and stumbling and waving his arms. I can't hear the words he's saying but the sound of his voice makes my stomach clench and my breath come faster.

Quick, I tell the kids. We can't let him see us go into the building.

What? says Ted. Let who see?

I glance back at him. He is a big man, dressed in a heavy coat and a hat with flaps that hide his face. I can't see his eyes or his hair. He keeps on calling to us. Waving and shouting.

Walk, I tell the kids. Don't say a thing. Just walk away right now.

I see Sophy hesitate. Looking at Ted.

For God's sake, I tell her. Just do it.

We hurry. We do everything short of break into a run. Snow and ice creak under our feet and it's very hard to move fast without sliding around. I hope the man will give up and stop following, but instead the opposite happens and he quickens his pace as we continue along Bishopsgate and then down in the direction of Threadneedle.

Every time I glance behind me he is just in sight.

Where are we going? Sophy gasps. What's happening? Why didn't we just go inside?

I don't bother answering such a stupid question, but Ted catches up with me and touches my arm.

Can you just tell me what we're running from?

Him.

Who?

I turn around. The man is still coming. Still shouting.

Sophy gives a little sob.

I want to go back to the building.

I grab her arm and pull her along with me.

You want him to know where we live? Is that what you want?

But want who to know? Ted is asking me again.

Sophy's coughing. Her face is red in some places and purple in others. I've never seen her look so ill.

Don't be such a baby, I tell her.

But I'm scared.

Shut up. There's nothing to be scared of.

I'm scared of you, she says.

We hurry on down Threadneedle, past what was once the grand old Bank of England. Here the streets are strewn with debris.

All the once-smart shops have been looted and burned. The signs that used to advertise perfume and make-up and alcohol are all broken or defaced.

A sign still says Mint Haircutting, and another, in faded red, Dry Riser, and another Bank Tejarat. Some window-boxes hang off a building with no windows. In them you can still see the frozen ghost shapes of leaves and stalks. Everywhere, burned-out cars and lorries and buses, all of them window-deep in snow.

Now and then you see the clean, splayed bones of a hand, gripping a rolled-down window or hanging out of a car door. We make our way around an office photocopier that must have fallen out of a window. It is on its side and a pair of feet poke out from under it. One foot still has half a sock on it. The toes on both are entirely black.

Under the arch which still says Dizzy's Bar, Happy Hour, Cocktails 2 for the price of 1, two dogs are snarling and tearing at something that might once have been human. It has no limbs or features, but the long strands of hair on it are dark and matted with blood.

We're nearly at Cannon Street when I stop. The street is empty. I realise I can't see or hear him any more. But something else is wrong. Something missing.

What are we doing? says Ted. Fuck's sake. Why have you made us come all this way?

I try to catch my breath.

The man.

What man? I never saw any man.

I look around me. The silence is hard and flat. Suddenly I know what's missing. It's Matthew.

Where is he? I say.

Who?

The kid. Where's he gone?

Ted shrugs.

Maybe he went back to the building.

I stare at him.

Why would he do that?

I wish we'd gone back there too, Sophy says. She has doubled over and is clutching herself. I wish she wouldn't be so dramatic.

I look at them both.

He wouldn't do that, I say. He wouldn't just go.

Ted looks very fed up.

Well, guess what. He has.

Sophy is still looking at me.

So is it OK? she says.

Is what OK?

Has he gone?

Has who gone?

She rolls her eyes.

Whoever you thought was coming after us.

I think so, yes.

She wipes at her face with a glove. I see that there are fresh tears on her cheeks.

So can we go home now? she says.

Home. It's a funny word for it.

We head up Moorgate intending to cut through Finsbury Circus and round the back of Liverpool Street Station, to avoid going back the way we came. But we've got no further than the beginning of Lothbury when there's another shout close behind us. I glance back and feel my throat go hot. He's moving much faster now.

What is it? Ted says.

It's him. Come on, he's going faster. We need to run.

Ted is staring at me.

But I can't see anyone.

Just run!

Sophy is crying again. I try to pull her along with me but already it's too late. She trips and goes down in the snow.

Get up, I tell her.

I can't.

Sophy, get up!

She stays there in the snow. He has caught up now and is reaching out with both his hands towards her. He's solidly built. So much hair – hard to see his face.

Please, I tell him, as fear pours through me. Please. We have nothing to give you.

He looks at me then.

It's OK, he says. It's me.

It's him, I hear Ted say.

I stare at him. He speaks again, his voice is soft. He says a name which I don't hear. Then I do. I hear it.

She's not here, I hear myself say. But he ignores me, says the name again. That's when I scream.

Ted grabs my arm so tight it hurts.

What the fuck's the matter with you? What are you doing? Can't you even see who it is?

I feel the man coming close, but I am ready for him. Before he can do another thing, I raise my arm in the air and I bring it down. He staggers backwards. I watch as blood jumps out of his face and into the snow.

Sophy screams. Ted is yelling something at me. And the man, I think he is yelling too. Or howling. And I say man, but in those few terrible seconds I see the truth, that he's really much younger than I thought, quite a boy really – no more than about thirteen years old.

Matthew! Sophy cries.

I stare as Ted tries to scoop the kid up in his arms but it turns out he is heavier than we thought – almost as heavy as a full-grown man – and in the end we all three have to carry him between us.

We are inside. We sit at the bottom of the cold concrete stairwell. The kid is on the floor by a fire bucket. I want to touch him but I don't think I should.

Someone else has already done all the things that need to be done. Ted has rolled up his bloody coat and put it under his head. Sophy is doing enough crying for everyone. The kid's eyes are shut and his face is torn. I don't know who did it, and then for a quick second I do and I feel a flush of shame.

I keep my eyes on him. I watch him breathe. His chest lifting and falling. A quick excited feeling rushes through me.

He'll be OK, won't he? I say to Ted.

He looks at me coldly.

I've no idea if he will or not, he says and he looks at the floor, the way men do when something bad or important happens.

What did you use? he says at last. Was it a knife?

What?

To cut him. What was it? What did you use?

I'm silent for a moment.

Glass, I tell him.

What?

A piece of glass.

In my pocket, I put my fingers on it. Feel its sharpness and its coldness. Some of the kid's blood will be on it.

Why? says Ted.

Why?

Yes. Why would you carry a piece of glass around?

Oh, I say. That was him. He gave it to me.

Who?

Matt. He made me take it.

Ted says nothing. I know he doesn't believe me. He watches me for a moment, then he lets his head slump back against the wall, shuts his eyes.

Fucking hell, he says.

It's almost evening, the sun going down, the side of the building so fiercely bright and light it could be on fire.

I tell Graham that I will sit with the kid. He looks at me as if I've offered to chop him up with an axe.

You're not going anywhere near him, he says.

Ask him, I say. Ask him what he wants. He'll say he wants to be with me.

For a moment or two, Graham looks uncertain. But then he draws back.

Don't you understand anything? he says. You did this. It wasn't anyone else. You were the one who hurt him. All of this is your fault.

I wander the building. I walk into an office on the seventeenth floor. A corner office, at the very end of the corridor – a wide and silent and satisfying space. The air outside is turning to night, evening shadows creeping over the building. The dome of the big white church with the man's name is there against the skyline. I take a breath. I think I am alone. It takes a good few minutes before I realise that he's there.

He has on a suit, open at the neck, no tie. A shirt with some kind of pattern on it. His hair is longish, messy – almost touching his shoulders. His chin dark enough to show that he hasn't shaved for a couple of days.

He half leans, half sits on the desk in front of the window and, with one hand over his eyes, the other clenched hard against his stomach, he cries.

I hold my breath.

The room seemed very still and silent when I first came in, but now the sound is everywhere. Brutal, tearing sobs – a noise that no man would let himself make unless he thought he was alone.

I did this, I think. It is me. It is all my fault.

At last, I can't bear it any longer. I say his name. I say it a couple of times, but nothing changes. He doesn't turn or look at me. He can't see me. He doesn't know I'm here.

A few more sobs and then he's still for a moment. I hear his ragged breathing calming down.

Another long moment goes by and then he lets his hands fall and he stares out of the window. I can't see his face, but beyond his head is a sight that makes my stomach twist. The twinkling, night-time lights of the city. The occasional red dot of a plane.

I watch him. He does nothing. He does not move. He gives one final sob and takes a breath. Wipes his face with both hands. I want it badly then – the sensation of his eyes on me. So I say it again, louder this time.

Matt?

He gets up. For a moment I think he must have heard, that

he's coming over to me. Will he see me now? Will he look at me? But no. Very quickly, as if he just thought of something – a new possibility that has not been in his mind before – he turns and walks out of the room.

His step is definite, almost hopeful. As he leaves, he grabs a phone and some keys off the table. They rattle for a second, before they drop into his pocket. He walks right past me – close enough that I could easily reach out and touch him with my hand, put my finger on the rough weave of his jacket, brush the stubble on his cheek.

I could, but I don't. Because that's when I understand the truth – that we're not there together. Only one of us is there, in that room. I don't know which one of us it is.

5

Sophy isn't well. The fever has decided to stay in her body. It has made its claim. Now every part of her is sore and dark and twisted.

Her face isn't her own face any more. It has hollow parts and swollen parts and dried-up parts. The corners of her eyes are raw. She doesn't look like Sophy. She doesn't look like anyone any more.

How did this happen to her? Ted wants to know, as if it is yet another thing that I should have on my conscience.

I lift my head, look at him.

What do you mean, how did it happen? She's ill. She's been ill for a while.

His face tightens.

But I thought she was getting better. Graham told me she was getting better.

Graham doesn't know everything, I tell him.

I sit with Sophy. Her skin is the colour of dead flowers and her breath is quick and harsh. You can watch her chest moving, up and down, up and down, like a little baby's. When she isn't coughing, she sleeps. The sleeps are her main thing now, the centre of her life. She only comes out of them in order to say things, and most of those things make little or no sense.

I dreamed we found this cat, she says. Inside a cab on Moorgate. And she was dead, but in her tummy –

Hush, I tell her. Don't try to talk.

In her tummy – as she speaks, I feel her hot eyelids moving under my hand – were all these kittens.

I smooth back a sticky strand of her hair.

And I wanted to take her home, but you wouldn't let me.

Really?

No! You wouldn't let me. You told me she was dead.

I'm sure she was fine, I say.

She wasn't fine.

OK, she wasn't fine.

Her eyes are on me. She gazes straight into my eyes and out the other side. It gives me a slightly sick feeling, to be looked through like that.

Where am I going? she says another time.

What do you mean, Soph? You're not going anywhere.

I'm not?

I told you. You're staying right here.

With you?

Yes, with me.

But I just went upstairs.

Upstairs?

Didn't we just go upstairs to see the children? Didn't we go up to say goodnight?

I take a breath, try to keep myself steady.

I think you're dreaming, Sophy.

I'm not dreaming.

I touch the hot skin on her hand and I see that one of her fingers is swollen up to three times its normal size and black as a ripe plum.

I'm not dreaming, she says again.

I look away quickly.

OK. You're not dreaming.

Graham comes in. He stands on the edge of the room, looking in.

Any change?

Not really.

He waits, his hand still on the door.

You're doing a great job, he says.

He is about to leave, but Sophy sees him standing there. With an effort, she pushes herself up on one arm.

What day is it? she says, her eyes on his face. How long have I been here?

He looks at me, helpless.

It's not the day, I tell her. It's the night.

Her eyes widen.

The night?

Yes. The night.

Graham looks relieved. He looks at Sophy one more time and then he glances at me and he goes.

The snow has mostly stopped but sometimes a single lonely flake comes spinning past the window. Sophy gives a little moan.

In a minute, I tell her, you'll fall asleep.

I don't want to.

You must sleep.

Don't make me.

You know I can't make you.

All right, but I'm afraid to sleep.

There's nothing to be afraid of.

Please just promise you won't go away?

I won't go away.

I don't believe you.

I'm not going anywhere, Sophy.

OK.

Are you still there?

I'm here. Look, open your eyes if you want to. You'll see. Here I am.

Oh.

But later, she sits up. Her face is alert and vivid. You would almost think she was well.

How many of you are there? she asks me.

What?

Every time I look there's another one.

What do you mean, another one?

Like, you know, like there's one more of you.

I shake my head.

I don't know what you mean, I tell her. Sometimes a fever can make you see things.

She listens to me hard, her brow furrowed, concentrating. Then shakes her head.

No, she says. No, it's not that.

OK.

She blinks at me.

There it is again! There's you and then – look – there's another one.

What other one?

The one that isn't you.

Yes, but which one's that?

The one that's her.

I feel myself stiffen.

Sophy, I say, I mean it. You have to stop talking now. You have to sleep.

If I do, you won't go away?

I just told you. Where am I going to go?

You swear that none of you will go?

I draw my coat close around my shoulders.

We're all right here, I tell her.

I also sleep then. And maybe I am in her dream because there we all are, me and her and the other one that isn't me, pulling a kitten out of an upturned cab on Moorgate.

The cat is grey, its limbs unmoving.

You need to warm it up, I say. Put it in your coat.

Sophy stuffs the cat down inside her coat. I see then that her face is the colour of bone. Calcium, dust, putty. Even her hair has no colour.

After a few minutes, she pulls the cat out and looks at it. The fur is matted and rough. The ears are flat and the head sags.

It's dead, I say. It died a long time ago.

Whatever, she says. It's mine. I'm keeping it.

Ted is there. He shows us some notes he found in the cab.

Three twenties and a fifty. Can you believe it? That's more than a hundred quid.

Just pieces of paper, I tell him.

He stuffs them into his pockets.

Ted, I say. There's no such thing as money any more. It's worth nothing. It's useless.

He gazes at me with a face that is almost as colourless as Sophy's.

It's still cash, he says.

Next time Sophy wakes, her eyes are dry and bright. There's a spot of deep pink in each cheek. She sits up.

I'm ready, she says.

I put my hand on her shoulder. Like touching bone.

Sophy? – I wave my hand in front of her face. She looks straight through it. Sophy, can you hear me?

I'll be round about eight, she says.

What?

Eight. You did say eight, didn't you?

She holds up her hand. The whole thing is black now, black right down to the wrist. She twists it, then she lets it drop.

I really feel like dancing, she says.

What's it like? she asks me a little bit later.

What's what like?

Not existing any more. What will it feel like?

I look at my hands. I touch my fingers on the cool back of my neck. Put my lips to the flat inside of my wrist, breathe it in. The smell is of nothing.

I don't know, I say.

But will it be good or bad?

I don't know, I tell her. Neither.

It is the hour before dawn. A sky threaded with orange. The light turns everything strange. Sophy isn't talking. I hold a

99

drink of water to her mouth but it's hard to get her lips to move.

Try to swallow, I say.

She tries, but begins to cough instead. After a few seconds, she pushes my hand away. After a minute or so, the blanket under her head is spattered with red.

I go out, into the corridor. The kid is there, waiting. He's been sitting there, lying there, waiting there – I don't know, even sleeping there – ever since Sophy got ill. I know he isn't doing it for her. He's doing it for me.

His face is better now. It's almost healed. The cut is a long one, a deep one, but it has knitted together well. It begins under his eye and it stops just short of his chin. Whoever did it to him managed to miss the side of his nose. I think it makes him look heroic and I told him so. When I said it, he gave me a strange look.

You don't remember anything about it, do you?

About what?

How it happened.

I hung my head.

I'm sorry, I told him. I know I was there, but . . .

He pulled me to him. Ruffled my hair.

But what?

I'm not sure I remember anything else.

He smiled. He looked like he believed me.

That's right, he said. You were there. You were definitely there.

Now I slide down the wall and sit next to him. I don't say anything. He puts an arm around my shoulders. For once, it fits exactly.

I lean my head in against him. I put my fists into my eyes. I want to punch myself. I can imagine doing it. I would do it hard. I would like it to hurt.

It has begun to get light. I go back in and shut the door and go over to where she lies. Sophy. She isn't a girl any more, but a pile of rags.

As soon as I sit down next to her, I smell it. Coffee. The air turns warm. I hear a phone ringing. I see the edge of someone sitting near us – a man, talking. His feet on the desk. Dark shoes with stitching, worn on the bottom.

The man is laughing. Laughing as he talks. It must be a person he likes. It might be a child. The laugh is kind, patient, expansive. It is right there in the laugh, how much he cares about the person.

I can't see much of him but, as he talks, I see his wetted finger move across and stab at a grain of something, pick it up off the desk. Maybe it's sugar. A grain or two spilled when he stirred his coffee. Maybe it goes in his mouth. I can't see the rest of his face. I stare. While the vision lasts, it is intense.

A moment later, I touch Sophy's dark and swollen hand.

Graham worked here, I tell her. He worked in this building. Didn't he?

Sophy doesn't react. I feel her breath come out and go in again. I decide to tell her a lie.

He loves you, I say. Graham, I mean. He really cares about you.

Her hand does not move. It is hot and hard in mine. I wish I could think of something else to tell her, something that isn't a lie. But I sit there and nothing else comes into my head.

* * *

Ted's tall, worried shape appears in the doorway. He beckons me into the corridor. He keeps his voice low.

She's going to die, isn't she?

I stare at him.

Ted, I say. She's young and strong. She's just got a bad chest infection.

He looks at me carefully.

It's not true, is it?

What's not true?

She's not OK. Look at her hands. Something really bad's happening to her. She's really ill.

I watch him. I see how young he looks, how his face is trembling.

What are you saying? I ask him.

He glances back into the room, then he looks at me. He bites his lip.

She needs a doctor, doesn't she?

I say nothing. I go back in the room. He stands there in the doorway, looking lost. I am very glad when he goes away.

She weighs nothing. A feather would upset the air more than she does.

When she's stopped coughing, I lift her as gently as I can and I turn the blanket over and smooth it back down so she has a clean place to lay her head. Straightaway she coughs up more. First, a spray of bright flecks that go everywhere. Then, a sudden, frightening quantity, as if someone has poured it from a cup.

The blanket beneath her head is soaked. I tug it out from under her and bunch it up and turn it around again.

She is trying to say something.

I hold her head. I can feel the frail bones of her skull, her heart pumping in her temples. Her skin is very cold. I stare at the blood.

What, Sophy? What?

She lifts her hands and grabs at the air.

I want my mum, she says.

Graham comes in again. He stands close to me, a little way from where Sophy lies with her eyes closed. His mouth is tense. He says nothing. After a moment or two, he reaches for my hand. He squeezes it.

What's happening? he says.

I don't know.

You want me to stay?

No, I say, my hand dry and loose in his.

You're sure?

Yes.

He lets go of my hand as gently as possible, replacing it by my side.

He leaves like a ghost. He leaves no imprint at all. I do not see him go.

A few minutes later, though, she wakes and stares straight at me. She licks her lips.

Why does the darkness taste of salt?

I flinch.

Sophy, I say. You're awake?

Yes, but why does it?

I glance at the window.

It's not really dark any more. Look, it's really quite light.

It's morning?

Nearly.

Which morning?

It's this morning.

Have we slept?

Not really.

But have we?

No.

I try to get her to turn her head and see how the first pale rays of sun are already scooting up the buildings, but she won't do it. She has other things on her mind.

Is this the house I used to live in?

Used to?

You know. With my mum and dad.

I shake my head.

That house was a long time ago, I tell her.

In the old life?

The old life. Yes.

But – you remember my house?

I shake my head again.

What? – her voice is high and impatient. I can't hear you.

No, I say.

But you came there?

To your house? No. No, Sophy, I didn't.

With an effort, she turns her head towards mine. I feel her trying to inspect my face. Her eyes are open but I don't know what she can see. When she speaks, her voice is a whisper.

But you did.

I try to meet her gaze.

I don't think so.

You don't remember me? From the old life, I mean?

I keep silent a moment.

I don't think so, I say again.

She shuts her eyes for a second.

But — you did. You knew my mum and dad.

I think you're mixing things up, I tell her.

She frowns.

But how many of you are there?

You asked me that before, I say, trying to smile. I told you, there's just me.

Only you?

I'm sorry to disappoint you.

Still, though, she keeps her eyes on me.

But — where are your kids?

Now my heart gathers itself.

What?

The ones I used to babysit. Where are they?

As soon as she says it, my legs turn cold. Ice dropping down them. I put my head in my hands. Feel sweat prick my scalp. I try to look her in the eye, but it's no good.

Sophy, I say, what are you doing? Why are you trying to frighten me?

The sun is up now. The sky has lightened. It is pink. It is properly day.

She lies twisted on the bed. Her hair is damp, whether from sweat or crying, I don't know. There is some fresh blood around her mouth. Her eyes have been closed again for a while now, and her breaths are struggling, painful to hear. Once or twice they seem to stop altogether, as if she's forgotten what she's doing. Then they start up again. As if she remembered just in time.

I try to look at her. The curve of her cheek. The slit in her earlobe where an earring once went. The tracing of veins on her temple. Freckles on her nose. A paler sweep of them under her eyes. The bruising on her forehead.

I don't know whether I'll remember all of it or none of it.

Outside, the sun goes behind a cloud and, for a brief moment, a shadow darkens her face. Then sunshine, spilling back over it. She lets out a long breath, but takes none to replace it.

Sophy?

I wait.

Sophy?

She relents, remembers. She gulps in air. She gives one little moan, soft and disappointed – a last protest. I keep my fingers on her arm.

It's all right, I say. It's all right. I'm right here.

She lets out another breath then and her eyes, which have been closed, open a little. She looks surprised, almost pleased, as if she's seen something or someone she knows. It isn't me she's looking at.

I wait for her to take another breath. I wait for a long time. I carry on waiting. Minutes later, nothing has changed and I am still waiting.

I wait there. I don't know how long it is. I wait until it no longer seems strange to me that although she is still lying there, I am completely alone.

Then I straighten her arms under the blankets, tucking them in so the bad, dark colour of her hand does not show. I wipe the blood from her mouth, smooth her damp hair.

I touch her face with the back of my hand. Already it has

begun to lose its heat. I try to close her eyes but they keep on springing back open and staring at the space in front of her. As if she doesn't want to miss anything.

She is still staring at nothing as I turn and leave the room.

Out in the corridor, Matthew is hunched against the wall in his boots and coat, his knees drawn up, his head resting on a frayed elbow. He looks about eight years old or a hundred and eight, depending on what thoughts are in your head when you look at him. On the floor next to him is an old brown blanket, an empty packet of cigarettes and a piece of something yellow that might be food.

I leave him sleeping and I pull open the heavy fire door and climb the stairs. Up the three flights and out through another fire door and on to the landing that is identical to ours in pretty much every way, except for one thing.

She is standing there.

She is standing there and my heart is thudding, even though this time I'm not surprised. I knew she'd be here, waiting for me exactly like before. One thumb is stuck in her mouth, the other holds the same piece of light-coloured rag to her nose. Blood on the rag. My own blood, I think, though I can no longer remember why it would be there.

She is clearer to me this time. Her hair is baby's hair, fine and light and staticky, roughed up at the back, not brushed in a while. She has on a dark pinafore dress, thick woollen tights, stout, buckled sandals. Her knitted cardigan – is it pink? – is buttoned on all the wrong holes, but done up to her chin, as if whoever dressed her that morning wanted to make sure she stayed warm.

The moment she sees me, her whole face bursts into life.

She throws her arms up in the air and moves her feet up and down, running on the spot.

Mummy, Mummy, Mummy! she cries.

Without even thinking, I take a couple of steps back, feel around for the door that leads to the stairs. But she is ready for me. Before I can touch the handle of the door, she whips her thumb out of her mouth.

Mummy not do that! Not go!

The command is wild. The wet thumb stays exactly where it is, in the air. I stand still. I don't know whether I want to stay or go. Neither feels possible. We both wait to see what will happen next.

The air is icy. I feel myself start to shiver, but I don't let it happen. I don't allow myself to feel anything at all. I don't shiver.

Mummy, she says.

This time it's not a question. When she goes back to the job of sucking, there is a little glint of pleasure in her eye. Her chin wobbles. She watches me.

I take a breath.

Sweetheart, I say. I'm not your mummy.

I know she's listening, because her eyes grow wider. So I continue.

Where is she? Where's your mummy? Shall I help you find her? Shall I? Shall we go and look for her together?

The effect is instant and extreme. I might as well have reached out and slapped her. Before I can say another word, her mouth drops open and her chin buckles and her eyes turn into two dark slits as the arms clamp down rigid against her sides.

She throws back her head and she screams.

* * *

In the corridor, I hear a door bang shut. Then another one. A brief scuffle and then the sound of feet running. A whoop of happiness.

It's her! It's her!

Yay!

Mummy!

Mum!

Before I can do anything, two children and a dog have found me. Wrapping themselves around my legs. Laughing. Kissing. Gripping on. Bumping against me. Saliva and fingers and hair.

I shudder and cry out, stagger backwards, try to get free of them. The dog circles my feet, barking loudly, then rushes off to do the same to the little girl, whose screams are at last subsiding into gasping sobs.

I want to do it gently but in the end it's not possible. In the end it's their fault that I have to be rough. I prise both pairs of hands off me and shove them away.

Who are you? I cry. What the hell are you doing?

They stare at me, shocked.

Mummy, says the boy at last in a small voice. You don't need to swear.

I feel my heart pounding. I put a hand to my throat.

Where did you come from? I ask him. What's going on? Who are you?

The bigger one, the girl, about nine or ten years old, claps her hand over her mouth and gasps. But the boy – round-faced, curly gingery hair, a chip on his front tooth and dirt on his cheeks – tugs on my sleeve.

Have you got anything to eat? he whines.

No. I twist my hand to get him off.

But, Mum.

Stop calling me that. I'm not your mum.

I give him a really hard look then. It works. He starts to cry.

The girl has pulled away now and is openly staring at me. I look her up and down with equal openness. She's a weedy-looking child. Her mouse-coloured hair is chopped in a bob and held back with some kind of plastic clip. Her face is thin and pale, her chin pointy. So much going on in her eyes that just looking at them makes me feel tired.

What's the matter? she says. Why won't you be nice to us?

Yes! the boy shouts. Why won't you? Can't you see you're being really horrible?

I glance over at the small girl, who is keeping herself up in a standing position by gripping on to a tuft of the dog's thick neck fur. Now and then she half hiccups, half sobs. Her eyes never leave my face.

I don't know who you are, I tell the bigger girl. I've never seen any of you before. I don't know why you keep on calling me Mummy.

She claps a hand up to her mouth again. She and the boy exchange a look of real misery.

Oh, she says. Please. Why are you doing this?

The boy has got his fingers back on me again. Worrying away at the edge of my sweater.

Yes, why are you? he says.

For the second time, I shake him off. I turn back to the girl.

Why do you think I'm your mother?

She blinks.

Because you are.

But I've never seen you before. How can I be your mother if I don't even know you?

Now she gasps and takes a step away.

Please, she says at last. I know you're just playing a funny game or something, but I really really don't like it.

I don't like it either, says the boy. But he doesn't pull away. Instead he puts his cold hand on mine. A touch like ice. I try to remove mine but he won't let me. He tilts his head back and looks up into my face.

Just please be normal, he says.

The dog is barking again. Sharp, identical, excited barks. The girl screams at it to shut up, but the animal only fixes its gaze on her and barks louder.

At last, she goes over and grabs its snout so the teeth snap shut. The dog makes a strangled sound. The boy laughs and then so does the little girl. When she releases it, the dog lets out a whine, then is quiet.

She looks at me.

We didn't mean to scare you, she says in a careful voice. We're just so very happy to see you, that's all.

We didn't think you was ever going to come, says the boy.

Were ever going to, the girl corrects him.

Were ever.

We'd almost given up, she says.

Without warning, the little girl lets go of the dog. As her legs give way, she sinks happily to the floor. The dog flops down next to her.

Why aren't you talking? the boy asks me.

Because I don't know what to say.

Why?

Because I'm shocked.

Why?

For God's sake, can you at least stop saying why?

This silences him. The girl eyes me for a quick moment. Then she marches over to the little one and scoops her up under the arms and staggers back with her hanging there.

She puts her down in front of me. The child stands there, wobbling slightly. Her face is still wet from crying. After a moment or two, she reaches both arms up into the air towards me.

Well? says the girl. What are you waiting for?

What?

Aren't you going to pick her up?

I shake my head and back slightly away. The dog yawns.

Is it because she's a bit snotty? says the boy.

No.

What, then?

I bite my lip.

Look, I just don't want to, OK? I'm not her mummy.

Immediately, the child starts to cry again – soft at first, but building to something more frantic that makes my whole body hurt. I reach down and try to pull her against my legs. It doesn't work. She cries even louder.

I wish she would shut up, I say.

The girl is staring at me.

Why don't you comfort her, then?

I shrug.

I'm not much good with babies, I say.

Get down on the floor and let her go on your lap, suggests the boy. She'll soon stop then.

I look at the girl.

Can't you do it?

She shakes her head.

It has to be you.

I don't believe her, but giving in is easier than fighting, so I do it. I put myself down there on the floor. Straightaway the little girl pushes herself against me. I put my hand on her small shoulder, her face, then I take it away again because it's wet. She nuzzles closer.

Say, There, there, Munchkin, says the boy.

Why?

Because it's what you say.

Is that her name? Munchkin?

He bursts out laughing.

Of course it isn't! Munchkin isn't a real name! Nobody would call their child Munchkin?

The girl frowns at me.

It's what you sometimes call her.

Not me, I say. I don't call her anything. I don't even know who she is.

I look down at the little girl. Her thumb has found her mouth and her breath comes in little shudders now. I feel her body relax as she settles against me. I feel mine too, relaxing.

There, there, I say. It's OK. You're OK.

I don't call her Munchkin, but at last the girl seems happy.

The boy's eyes flick from her face to mine.

I've got a wobbly tooth, look! he says, encouraged.

They all join me down there on the floor. The boy flings himself down on his stomach some little way away but I can feel him edging closer. The girl sits cross-legged, picking at her bare arms. The dog has its chin on its paws, but its eyes are open. Every now and then it sighs loudly. The little one is still snuggled against my legs.

Look, I say. I don't want to be unkind —

Then don't say it, says the girl.

What?

That's what you always tell us. If you need to start by saying that, then you shouldn't say anything at all.

Because it means you're absolutely definitely going to be unkind, mutters the boy.

I think about this. I say nothing.

But I know what you were going to say, says the boy.

Oh yes?

You were going to try and do the horrible thing of pretending you aren't our mum again.

The girl is looking at me. She pulls her knees up to her chest. Tears wobble in her eyes.

You don't like us any more, she says.

I can feel the boy watching my face.

Of course I like you.

But you don't really.

I wait, then I let it out.

I don't know you, I tell her. How can I tell if I like you if I don't even know you?

She bites her lip and hugs her knees tighter. I see that all of her fingernails are chewed right down to the quick, the ends of her fingers swollen and red and raw.

By the way, she says, if you want to know, I think you are being unkind. I think it's the very meanest thing in the world, to do this to us when we've been wanting and wanting you to come.

And I think so too, says the boy.

I look at their two pale faces, dirty hair, shadowy eyes.

But what am I supposed to do? Would you want me to lie to you?

Yes, says the boy.

The girl tells him to shut up.

Shut up yourself, he says, without conviction. His face crowds in on itself and he falls silent.

I look at the girl and see that she's crying. Her shoulders are shaking. She keeps her face turned slightly away from me and she makes a hard line with her mouth to keep out the tears. They fall anyway.

I reach out and touch her arm.

Maybe if you want I could try and help you find your real mum?

The boy gasps.

We don't want a real mum. We only want you!

Even through her tears, his sister gives him a sharp look.

Shut up, she says. Stop being a baby, Jimmy. I mean it. You're being a real pain.

Shut up yourself, he says again. He pushes his two grubby fists over his eyes. My tummy hurts, he says. Ow.

The girl pulls up her T-shirt and wipes her face. She looks at me.

He's still getting those stomach aches. Sometimes he cries all night. I think he needs to go to the doctor's.

I'm not going to the doctor's, the boy who is called Jimmy says quickly.

But there are no doctors, I tell her.

She stares at me.

The world has changed. Don't you know that? Nothing's how it used to be.

She sniffs.

I know that. Of course I know it. I just thought there might still be, like, one small hospital or something, that's still looking after people.

Well, there isn't. There's nothing like that and I don't think there will be ever again.

She looks at me and swallows.

Never? Then what will we do?

Let me have a think, I say, mainly to shut her up. I'll think of something, OK?

But what? What are you going to think of that you can't think of now?

I don't know.

You won't be able to think of anything, will you?

I'm not sure, I say.

I notice that the deep chill has left the air. It has grown softer, lighter, warmer. If you didn't know any different, you could almost think that the light flooding in through the far window was the bright sunshine of high summer.

Sunbeams move across the carpet. The dog sighs. I shift myself under the baby's soft weight. I yawn and feel my head grow heavy, but I shake myself out of it.

I can't stay here, I tell them.

Why can't you?

I just can't. I must go soon.

But why? says Jimmy, who has rolled along the carpet and is lying against my thigh now with his eyes closed. Why do you need to go?

There's a girl I was looking after, I tell him. A big girl, bigger than you.

A grown-up? he says. He opens one eye and looks at me.

Not quite a grown-up. A teenager, I suppose. And she's not well. In fact, I think she's dead.

The girl looks unmoved.

Did you kill her?

Of course I didn't kill her. But I need to go and see how she is.

But you know how she is, the girl points out.

If she's completely dead, says Jimmy, you can leave her out for the birds.

I look at him.

What do you mean? What birds?

I saw this film, right, where they put a dead person on a turret and the vultures came. It was wicked.

Don't listen to him, the girl says. It was a scary film. It was horrible. Afterwards I couldn't sleep. I wish we hadn't watched it.

But the vultures weren't bad. They were good! They were just doing what vultures are programmed to do.

The girl looks at him.

Stop talking so loudly, Jimmy.

I'm not talking loudly.

You are. You keep on shouting. You know you are. You're just showing off.

Jimmy ignores her.

What I mean is, even if you don't really think you're our mum and all that, I still really like you. I think you're lovely. I don't want you to go and see the dead girl. I want you to stay here with us.

I look down at the little one, who is now sleeping on me, the clean weight of her head against my thigh. I allow my fingers to sit in her soft hair.

So if he's Jimmy, I say to the girl, who are you?

She bites one of her fingers.

It's just a bit weird, you know, to have your own mum ask you what your name is.

I'll tell you. Do you want me to tell you? Jimmy says, but the girl puts a hand over his mouth.

I'm Iris. It's a kind of flower.

I know it's a flower, I tell her. A purple flower.

She gives me a sharp look.

They can be blue, she says. Or yellow. Quite a lot of colours really.

Well, it's a pretty name, I tell her.

She rolls her eyes.

You chose it.

The boy is leaning over even closer to me. I can feel his breath on my chin.

And I'm Jimmy.

I know that, I tell him.

He pulls back, astonished.

How? How did you know it?

Because Iris has been calling you that.

Oh.

It's James in fact, Iris says.

I look at him.

But you like to be called Jimmy?

He gives it a moment's thought.

I really like to be called Chitty.

Chitty?

Like Chitty Chitty Bang Bang.

It's a car, says Iris. A car in a children's film. And don't listen to him – he doesn't.

Yes I do!

I look at him.

OK, I say, today we'll call you Chitty. But tomorrow we'll have to see.

You shouldn't say that, Iris says. He'll want to be called a different thing every day.

I look down at the baby. She points at Iris.

Isey! she cries.

That's Katie, Iris says.

Katie points at the dog.

Dod! she says.

That's right, Iris tells her. It's a dog, isn't it? By the way, she says, turning back to me. Can you see that her cheeks are really red? Well, we need some of that stuff.

What stuff?

She looks unimpressed.

When she's teething. You used to have some stuff to put on her gums. Have you got any now?

Jimmy pulls at my sleeve again.

You know my baby tooth, the one that I chipped? Well, when it comes out and I get my grown-up tooth there, is it absolutely definite that it won't be chipped as well?

Jimmy, shush – Iris gives him an irritable look. You keep it in your handbag, she adds, turning back to me.

I'm about to tell her that no one has handbags any more, when there's another loud slam and more footsteps in the corridor and I snap my head around to see a small, fair-haired girl, maybe six or seven years old, running towards me. Before I can say anything, she throws herself at me.

Gloria, says Iris in a dull voice. At the mention of the name, the dog, who had seemed to be asleep, lets her tail beat softly on the carpet. Don't ask her anything by the way, because she doesn't speak any more.

She just gave up talking one day, says Jimmy. And that was that.

I look at Gloria's silent face and something in me tightens. I hold her away from me for a moment, at arm's length.

I've seen her before, I say.

Iris sighs.

You've seen us all before. How many times do I have to tell you?

No, I say, as Gloria looks straight back at me, cool and appraising, and I try not to shudder. This is different. It's like Katie . . .

What's like Katie?

I've seen them in the building.

We're all in the building! says Jimmy, and he jumps up as he sees that Gloria is trying to climb on my lap. I was here first! It's not fair!

You weren't, Iris says. You weren't even in her lap.

He doesn't listen. He keeps on pushing and shoving. The dog, seeing the game, stands up and starts to bark. Gloria holds on to my legs, firmly and silently keeping herself in my lap. The baby stirs, about to wake.

In the end, I push them both away.

There, I say. Well done. Neither of you can sit there. OK? Are you happy now?

Jimmy stares at me and then he laughs. So does Iris. Even Gloria's mouth twists up at one corner.

What? I say. What's so funny?

Iris and Jimmy exchange a glance.

That's what you always say. That means you're definitely our mum.

* * *

Gloria is standing there, gazing at me. Her long fair hair, which probably used to be pretty, is more like wool now, tangled and lumpy.

Has no one got a hairbrush? I say.

No, Iris says. Why would we?

I glance at her, noticing her sudden coldness.

I don't know what things you have up here, I tell her. I haven't seen where you sleep. I don't know what you have.

We don't sleep anywhere. We have nothing.

No toys or clothes?

No.

I don't even have my giraffe, says Jimmy.

It's a cuddly toy he used to like, says Iris.

But how do you manage?

She shrugs and her face makes me think of Sophy's. Almost without colour.

There's nothing to manage, is there? she says.

I don't speak. I take hold of one of the lumps in Gloria's hair and try to pull it apart with my fingers. She lets me do it for a second or two, then she shakes me off.

I could untangle it for you, I tell her.

It's no use saying anything to her, Iris says. I told you. She doesn't talk.

Why not? Why doesn't she talk?

There's something wrong with her, Jimmy says.

Iris flicks a glance at him and then at me.

She hasn't said a single thing since the . . . you know, the day.

Which day?

She gives me a tight little look.

That day.

The day the fish died! says Jimmy. The day we made the biscuits. The day you got pregnant and –

Not pregnant, Iris says. What are you talking about, Jimmy? It was the opposite of pregnant. You don't understand anything?

I do! Shut up – I do understand!

No, she says. You've got it all wrong.

Jimmy takes a breath, as if he's about to say something else, then he stops. Iris looks at me.

You don't know what we're talking about, do you? she says.

Something cold creeps through me.

No.

You're still our mum, though, Jimmy says, his voice threaded with anxiety.

Stop going on about it, Iris says to him.

Gloria is still looking at me. I keep my eyes on her. At last, she shapes her thumb and first finger into a circle and looks at me through it.

What does that mean?

Iris looks bored.

It's just something she does. It doesn't mean anything.

Gloria sits down on the floor then and thrusts her feet into my lap. Brown shoes on them, the straps undone.

She wants you to do them up, says Iris. She can't do it herself. You don't have to do it if you don't want to, though. She really ought to learn.

Gloria keeps her eyes on me. I do up the buckles on the straps, fiddling until I get the tightness right.

When I've finished, she stands up quickly and goes and sits down by the dog. Both of them looking at me.

She doesn't mean to be rude, Iris says.

Can I have a go in your lap now? Jimmy says. He stands and starts backing towards me.

In a minute, I say.

No, now!

All right.

I let him sit on me. I can smell the slight mustiness of his hair, his fingers. I had thought I would mind it, but I don't.

You shouldn't give into him like that, Iris tells me. He'll think he can make you do anything.

Jimmy says nothing. He just squashes himself harder against me.

Are you always like this? I ask Iris.

Like what?

I don't know – telling everyone what to do all the time.

For a moment she looks startled, then she sucks in her cheeks. She stops talking and chews on a fingernail.

In my lap, Jimmy twists around and looks up at my face.

You're not very nice, are you? he says in a cheerful voice.

I stare at him.

I don't know, I tell him. I don't know if I'm nice or not.

Well you're not. But I still really like you, he adds, pulling my arm tight around him.

When a few minutes have gone by, Iris chews a finger and looks at me.

Can I tell you something?

I wait.

It's about what happened.

What happened when?

On that day.

What day?

She looks impatient.

You know – the day we were talking about. The terrible day?

The day the fish – Jimmy begins.

OK, I say. What about it?

Iris glances at Jimmy, who is looking at us both with a worried face. She takes a big breath.

Well then, please don't get upset but . . . we're missing Arthur.

Arthur?

For a second, Iris shuts her eyes.

We haven't got him. We haven't seen him since – well, I'm worried we might have left him behind. At home, I mean.

Who's Arthur?

She looks amazed.

The baby, of course. Your baby!

I look down at Katie.

Not her, Iris says. Arthur's a real baby. He's the one you had just before . . . well, he's only just been born.

Like about six months ago or something, Jimmy explains.

Not six months, Iris says. Don't listen to him. It's nowhere near six. It might not even be a month. I don't know how long we've all been here. Arthur was newborn. He was tiny. He'll still be very little.

She stares at my face.

I think he must be all alone at home, she says again. I'm worried that he might not be OK.

Her mouth twists as if she's about to cry.

I look at her.

Iris, I say. I honestly don't know what you're talking about.

She shakes her head.

You don't even remember that you had a baby?

There was blood, says Jimmy, almost to himself. Lots of blood, in the kitchen. It was all over the floor.

I look at them both and feel something in me harden.

Look, I'm really sorry about the baby, I say. Whatever happened to it. But it wasn't mine. There's nothing I can do.

Iris looks shocked. She gulps down a breath, tears in her voice.

But I'm worried about him.

What am I supposed to do?

But – I don't have anyone else I can tell.

Well, too bad.

Too bad?

Can we just stop talking about this now?

That shuts her up. She says nothing after that. In my lap, I feel Jimmy's body go rigid, then soft, then rigid again as he listens to all of this.

A moment later, though, he has his hand up. His whole arm is stretched up past his ear.

Um – can I say something?

Go ahead.

He gives a little gasp.

Well, he begins, I'm not really worried about finding Arthur. I think Iris's being silly really. I don't think he's all alone in the house. Because you see we left him sleeping on that cushion on the floor and actually I think what happened is his heart just stopped and . . . and he died.

Straightaway Iris rounds on him.

Don't be such a stupid idiot! What a terrible thing to say about your own brother. Of course he didn't die. How could you possibly know anyway?

Jimmy looks at her.

Maybe the clue was that he wasn't even breathing?

Liar! howls Iris. You little liar!

Jimmy leans back against me. He shuts his eyes and puts his fingers in his ears.

I just know it, he says.

You're telling lies, Jimmy, Iris says. You're as bad as her. I hate you.

He drums his feet on the carpet.

My name's not Jimmy, it's Chitty, he says.

As if someone invisible has called to her, Gloria gets to her feet and, without looking at any of us, walks away down the corridor. The dog watches her go, ears pricked up in a hopeful and fascinated way. For a few seconds she looks like she might follow her, but then she sighs and rests her chin back down on her paws.

Where's she going? I ask Iris.

She doesn't look at me. She's still angry.

I don't know, she says. Somewhere. Away.

Is she OK?

I don't know.

She always does that, Jimmy says. She always goes away. I think she likes to go on walks around the building.

My heart flips.

Well, me too, I say. I have to go.

Iris looks at me.

Why? Why must you?

Is it because of the dead girl? Jimmy says.

He pats his leg and calls the dog to him. The dog lifts her head, thinks about it, then settles back down again.

Iris puts a hand on mine. It's colder than it should be. The chill goes through me. She licks her lips and glances at Jimmy.

Don't go, she says. I'm sorry if I was mean to you. I'm sorry I talked about Arthur. Stay here with us. I don't think we can carry on any longer without you.

We need you, Jimmy says. We've been waiting ages for you to come.

He takes hold of my other hand and plaits his fingers through mine, then squeezes a bit too hard.

Ouch, I say.

He laughs.

Why is blood warm?

I don't know, I say. Why is blood warm?

No, I was asking you!

I'm not sure. I'm going to have to think about it.

And why don't cats go on the beach? Do you think when people die they come back as animals? What kind of animal would you want to come back as?

Jimmy, I say. All these questions.

He's just trying to keep you here, Iris says.

And where do you think our dad is now? And will you still love me when I'm dead?

Seconds go by. The cold is coming back now and the light has turned bitter.

Where is your dad? I ask Iris then.

She stares at me for a second or two.

You really don't know?

How would I know?

She swallows and looks at Jimmy.

He left, she says.

You don't know where he is?

She shakes her head. I look at Jimmy, expecting him to have something to say about that, but he doesn't. He looks back at Iris as if she's in charge of this particular conversation.

His sister folds her arms and looks at me carefully.

I know you said you don't care, she says, picking her words, and that's OK. But I just want to know your opinion, right, because you're a grown-up? Do you think that a baby can survive all alone in a house without anyone to hold him and feed him and change his nappy and all that?

I think about this.

No, I tell her. I don't.

She turns away, puts her hands over her face.

Iris, I say. I can't lie to you. So many people have died. Don't you realise – almost everyone in the world is dead.

Jimmy's mouth falls open.

Seriously! Everyone? Are we like the dinosaurs, then?

But Iris is shaking her head.

He's not dead. He can't be. He's our little brother and he's only just been born. Don't tell me he's dead. I just can't bear to think about it.

Jimmy scrambles out of my lap and runs to the window, presses his face against the glass.

But if all the people out there were dead, there would be bodies.

He turns around, hands on hips, waiting.

Well, I say, there are.

He brightens.

If a dead body is really completely dead and nobody finds it, and they leave it for the birds, how fast does it turn into a skeleton?

Iris begins to cry.

Stop talking about it, she says. Please Jimmy, I mean it now. I'm sick of you saying all these stupid things. Just shut up.

I look at Iris, such a strange and stiff and serious little girl, and I feel bad for her. I reach out and try to touch her, but it's like touching ice. I pull my hand back.

You're so cold, I tell her.

She looks at her own arm and she says nothing.

How do you live up here? I ask her.

What do you mean, live?

Is it just the four of you? With no one looking after you?

Jimmy throws her an anxious glance.

Iris was doing it, he says. I said she could be in charge. But only until you came.

Iris nods.

It was supposed to be temporary.

But do you have food?

She blinks. Her face is whiter than ever.

Not really.

And no TV either, Jimmy adds quickly.

And how old are you?

Nine, Iris says. I'm nine.

I'm seven, says Jimmy. I'm the second oldest. Gloria and Katie are the little ones.

I'll be ten in November, Iris says, looking at me. Do you know what month it is now?

There aren't really months any more.

Her eyes widen.

Really? You mean – not at all?

Well, I suppose there are, but no one's counting them.

But why not?

Because it doesn't seem very important.

Jimmy gasps.

But that means there won't be any birthdays!

I suppose not.

So no one will get older. We'll be like aliens!

Don't be stupid, Iris says. Of course you'll still get older. You just won't know when or how much.

While Jimmy thinks about this, I begin to move Katie off my legs. She makes a noise like she's winding herself up, ready to cry. I stand up anyway. Cold in my bones.

I don't want you to go, Jimmy says again. Really I don't. I want you to stay here and make us some tea.

Iris looks at me.

It's all right. He knows that's impossible. He knows there isn't any tea.

She picks Katie up and balances her on her skinny hip. She holds her there with one hand, as if she was light as anything and not a real baby at all. Katie's shoes are off and her stubby woollen feet kick and swing against her.

I lean over and put my lips on the top of Katie's head. It almost doesn't surprise me when I feel nothing but the chilly air.

Me too! A kiss for me too! yells Jimmy.

I kiss him too, on his dirty face, but I barely feel that either. He wraps his arms around my waist to hug me and I have to look down and check to see if he's let go or is still there. Still looking at him, I reach out to touch Iris's bony shoulder. My hand goes straight through it.

Say goodbye to Gloria for me, I tell her, but even as the words leave my mouth they are dissolving. Who? Who is Gloria?

Iris is looking past me, beyond me.

Will you come back? she says. You won't just leave us, will you?

I turn my head to where the voice is coming from but find I can't look at her.

I'll try, I say.

Cross your heart?

I don't think I have a heart.

Everyone has one, Jimmy says. All mammals do. And reptiles and birds. It's what keeps you alive. He looks over at Iris. Do fish have hearts?

She says nothing. Straightaway he thinks of something else.

Do you want me to make the lift come? he asks me. I can if you want.

I glance at the lift. A button lights up for a second or two, flickers, then dies.

He's always messing around with the lifts, Iris says. I told him not to . . . But already her voice trails off.

No, I tell Jimmy. Not this time. This time I'll take the stairs.

He looks disappointed.

But definitely next time? You swear?

We'll see.

He kicks at the carpet.

That's what you always say when you're not going to do something and . . . But even as he speaks, his voice too is fading and then it slides away, it's gone.

As I walk away from them, I have a strong feeling that I'm walking away from an empty space, from nothing, from no one. No point in looking back, I think, because they won't be there. All I'll see will be an empty corridor, an expanse of carpet, the hard white sky through the square of window. All the same, just before I reach the stairwell, I can't help it. I turn.

And I was wrong. Because there they all are – a forlorn and unlikely little family, the four of them, with the dog weaving slowly between them. Iris is still holding the little girl balanced light as dust on her hip, the boy whose name I've already forgotten, and the fair-haired silent one – who must have come racing back at the very last minute to join them – standing right next to her, stiff and formal, like in a photograph taken by a stranger, their arms entwined, their faces pale and empty.

I lift my hand to them, but I don't think they see me. Maybe I'm too far away already, the shadows racing now to swallow me up. Or perhaps they're afraid of seeming too eager. I can imagine Iris murmuring under her breath to the little ones that if they all keep very still, the spell will stay unbroken and I might decide to come back.

Whatever the reason, no one, not even the little boy – Jimmy, was it? – waves back.

6

In the end, we do exactly as the little boy suggested with Sophy. We put her out for the birds.

Burying her is out of the question. The snow is thick and the ground like stone. And Graham refuses to carry her down to the street and shove her out for anyone to find.

But Matthew has told me about the perfect place, he says. There's this terrace, three floors up from here. A place where she can lie in peace and –

The perfect place? I stare at the kid. He returns my stare. His eyes are dull and hard.

I couldn't see why it mattered, he says when Graham has gone out of the room. I didn't think I'd ever see you again. I thought you'd gone.

I feel myself tense.

Gone?

I thought you'd left for ever. How was I to know you'd come back?

What do you mean, left for ever? I say. When? I haven't been anywhere.

He looks away, runs his fist across his face. When he looks back at me, his eyes are full of pain.

I knew you'd do this, he says.

What? Do what?

Try and lie about it. I just knew that's what you were going to do. I knew it as soon as you walked back in across the landing as if nothing had happened.

I look at his dark, angry face and I struggle to remember if anything did happen. In a brief flash, then, I see them again. The boy with the curly hair, standing there with his hands on his hips. The girl with the sad face and bitten-down nails. The silent blonde girl. And the baby. Her furious warmth against me. A snag of shame as I remember how I walked away from them.

I look at Matthew.

I went upstairs, I say.

He shakes his head and smiles to himself.

Oh yeah. Sure. Upstairs.

I was gone for a morning, I tell him. Not even a whole morning.

I try to remember what time of day Sophy died. I remember the long night and then the sun scooting up the sides of the buildings. Sunrise. I remember her speaking for the last time. The quantity of blood on the blankets, the dark crust of it around her mouth. I know there was a conversation which upset me. Thinking of it I flush.

Matthew is watching me.

You're a liar, he says. I thought I could believe every little thing you said. I never thought you'd lie to me.

I hold his gaze even though my cheeks are still burning.

Think what you like, I tell him. I'm not lying.

But he shakes his head.

I didn't think anything on the first day. I knew you'd been with Sophy and I thought maybe you needed to sleep. By the end of the second day, I was getting worried. On the fourth day, I thought something terrible had happened to you.

I stare at him.

But Matt, I wasn't gone for four days.

He looks away.

Sure, he says again, almost to himself. Of course you weren't.

Even though I know she is dead, it is still a shock to go in and see her lying there exactly as I left her on those bloodstained blankets.

Her eyes are still staring at nothing – but when you look more closely, you see that they've lost their blueness and got thick like old milk. When we uncover her, the stench is raw and something pale leaks out of her blackened wrists.

Christ, says Graham – he turns away and clutches his stomach, looks at me. You can't smell that?

I look around me. Maybe the kid is right, I think. Maybe it really has been four days. The room seems to have altered around her, adapting itself to her new state. As if the air itself had decided to die in order to keep her company.

Smell what? I say.

I can feel Matt watching me. I make sure to keep myself light and steady. I glance at Sophy. The rotting shell of her.

Outside, it is a sunny morning, not a cloud in the sky. A sky like the sky of the old life, hopeful and high. You can almost imagine that people are still going about their business down there in the street, walking and talking and laughing and taking money out of holes in the wall and carrying bags of things from place to place.

Matthew is looking at Sophy's feet.

I'll have the boots, he says.

Graham looks at him.

They won't fit you. They're tiny.

Matt's expression doesn't alter. His eyes are two black holes in his face. Sun on his dun-coloured hair. The ghost of a man's moustache on his fat upper lip. I look away quickly. Now is not the time to be thinking how beautiful he is.

I'm not going to leave them on her to rot.

Maybe it's the use of that word. Or maybe he really doesn't want the kid to have Sophy's boots – but Graham seems to flinch. Concern fills his face. He looks from me to the kid then back again.

But what for? he says.

What do you mean, what for?

What will you do with them?

The kid shrugs.

Swap them. Trade them.

He will, I think. That's what he'll do. I watch him with something that amounts to pleasure. I almost smile.

Graham's face is twisting with disapproval.

I think it's a bit sick. I really do. I think you should leave them.

But the kid is already unlacing a boot and pulling it off her foot. He doesn't do it very gently, and Sophy's thin body rocks as he works them off. Most of her is hard and stiff, but some parts still seem to move. When I look again, I see that a tooth is showing, making her look a little more like herself but also a whole lot more dead.

I get a sudden blue-white glimpse of a foot as one of her socks comes off with the first boot.

I said you should leave them, Graham says.

The kid doesn't even look at him. He's picking away at the laces of the second boot.

I feel Graham looking at me.

What? I say.

136

Come on. For God's sake.

What do you mean, come on?

You think it's OK? Him doing this?

Doing what?

Him taking her boots off her?

He looks at me with such energy and horror that I want to laugh. I look at Sophy, her boots half on, half off. Two teeth are showing now. You might even tell yourself she is smiling.

I smile back at her.

She's dead, Graham, I say. What difference does it make?

He takes a cigarette from his pocket, looks at it, as if he's about to light it.

In the old life, he says, it wasn't all that strange to be careful about the dead.

Careful?

To pay them some respect.

This isn't the old life, I tell him. And there's nothing so special about being dead any more.

I look at Matthew. I'm glad to see that he is putting the sock back on to her foot, though I notice he does it clumsily, working it up from the blackening end of her toe, and then giving up halfway through so it hangs there stupidly.

Graham sighs. He's still holding the cigarette. He looks at it for a moment as if he doesn't know what it is, then he puts it back into his pocket, unlit.

I don't think there are vultures in the City of London, though it might only be a matter of time, of course. But there are certainly gulls.

Of all the creatures of the land and the air, the gulls seem to have survived the most relentlessly. When we first came to the building, they would line their big smooth-feathered bodies up on the concrete parapet outside and train their yellow eyes on us, as if they had a job to do and we were it.

We all hated them, but Sophy hated them the most. She found an old wooden cleaning mop and used the handle to bang on the big glass windows to try to scare them off. But it never had any effect. They would lift off, make one lazy circle in the air and then settle back down, a terrible satisfaction on their faces.

Lately, though, they've become pests, swooping down on people as they walk the streets. At Fenchurch Street we saw a young child have his eye taken out. And I heard that a newborn baby was snatched from its mother's arms and ripped to pieces in the air above her so that she got showered with his blood. She fainted and the gull then went for her too, not stopping till her face was a bloody indistinct mess.

They are out there now, screaming and laughing in the heavy air as we roll Sophy out of her bloodstained blanket and on to the snowy terrace and then step back to look at her.

Because of the fever, she stripped herself down well and truly at the end. All she has on now is a dirty pink T-shirt, specked all over with her blood and gone slack at the neck to reveal the pale jag of her collarbone. And a pair of men's pyjama bottoms whose string is frayed and the edges ripped, so that you can see the top of her once-white pants and, if you look harder, the beginning of her little triangle of hair. I notice that Matt does look harder, and I'm relieved when Graham leans forward and pulls the T-shirt down to cover her.

I've brought her cardigan with me – the grey and ratty old thing that she said she had at school and which she didn't like to let out of her sight. I am about to bend down to lay it on her when I stop.

What's the matter? Graham says.

I hesitate.

You think I should put it on her face?

He presses his lips together, looks away.

I go over and lay the thing on her chest, but it doesn't look right. It makes her look like she's just having a nap. So I pull it up to cover her slightly open mouth, the barely closed eyes.

Goodbye, Sophy.

The face that we've seen for so many days and nights and hours disappears for ever under the grey wool.

Above our heads, the gulls are swooping and diving. It has started snowing again. Big fat flakes coming down.

Shoo! Graham waves his arms in the air. Get off! Go on, go away!

Matt finds a piece of brick and chucks it hard at them, but it thuds down hard in the snow and makes no difference.

He turns to Graham.

We could set fire to her? he says.

What?

Matt scratches his head. Snowflakes clinging to his hair.

To stop them eating her.

Graham looks confused.

I don't think so, he says.

I have matches, says Matt. He pats his pocket. It rattles.

I don't think so, Graham says again.

A thought comes to me then. A strong thought, but slippery and hard to pin down. Then I understand what it is. A memory of the boy upstairs. Talking about the birds.

I turn to Matt.

We want them to eat her, I tell him. That's the whole point of putting her out here.

He stares at me for a second and then he smiles. It feels like warm water splashed on my face.

I go over to the railings and stand close to where Matthew's standing. I point out the great white dome, topped with snow and wreathed in morning sunshine.

Look at that, I say to Graham. Isn't it something? That's called St Paul's.

The look he gives me is cold.

You think I don't know that? Everyone knows that. Even you would once have known that.

I can see that Matt is on the verge of laughing, but he checks himself just in time.

That night, as Sophy lies up there all alone on her terrace, the weather really does change. A storm breaks over the city. Ice and hail. It rattles through the sky, along the river, over the buildings. Everything lit up by it. Electric, intense.

I am sitting on one of the desks, my feet up against the glass, watching it all, when I realise that he's there. Standing behind me, to my right. He might be leaning against something. One of the filing cabinets maybe. I don't know how long he's been there. I hear a match. His breath as he inhales.

I don't breathe.

After a few seconds have passed, I dare to turn my head.

He looks almost the same as before. The same dark suit, but a different shirt this time, plainer, unbuttoned. The same dark, messy hair, as if he's been putting his hands through it. And this time, a tie hangs loose around his neck, as if he's just undone it and not yet got around to pulling it off.

His face is in shadow. I do not dare look at it too hard. I try to breathe. I can feel my heart going. I shut my eyes and then I open them again. He is still there. He can't see me. I don't know what to do. All I know is, I don't want him to go.

When he speaks, I jump so hard I almost fall off the desk.

Rain, he says.

What?

I said, rain.

It's his voice. Is he talking to himself, or can he see me? Blood hammers in my head. The room lights up white for a second or two, shudders, then goes back to darkness. Jags of leftover light floating past my eyes. My voice is a whisper.

What? I say again.

I hear him blow out smoke. I can tell he's smoking the cigarette in a hurried, distracted way. He can't be bothered with it. In the end, he doesn't finish it. He puts it out.

Rain. It's raining out there.

He stands up. What? I think. Is he coming over? I feel myself start to tremble.

Are you talking to me? I say.

Listen, he says as he comes closer. Can you hear it?

I do as he tells me. I listen. Tongues of light lick the sky. A faraway rumble, then such a loud crash that my whole body jumps again.

That's thunder, I say.

He doesn't reply. He is behind me. I know where he is. I can't see him but I can feel him there. He reaches out and puts a hand on my shoulder. The hand is warm. Pleasure falling through me. A feeling so intense you could mistake it for pain.

What are you doing? I ask him.

He doesn't answer.

Matt, I say. Matt – is it really you?

He lifts my hair with his hands then drops it again just as quickly. I shiver. Heat licking the backs of my knees.

Oh, I say. Do it again.

But he doesn't do it again. That's when I realise.

Can you hear me? I ask him. When I speak to you?

His eyes are on me.

Are you real? he says.

I try to look at his face, his eyes. I am sure he is looking at me.

You can't hear me, can you? I say. You can't hear a word I'm saying.

He carries on gazing at me.

I don't care if you're real or not, he says. I don't care what this is. I just don't want it to stop.

I hear it then, the sound he told me to listen for. A million rice grains trickling through fingers on to paper. I see it too. Flecks of wet on the black window. Small at first, then longer, larger ones, some of them joining up, running down. Wet flinging itself out of the sky and hitting the glass.

I try to twist around to look at him, but he won't let me.

You're not really here, though, are you? he says.

Me? I say. I am. Of course I am. Can't you see me? I'm here right now.

He smiles. Touches my cheek.

I mean, I'm sitting here thinking about you and wishing I could talk to you and suddenly you're here. I'm going mad, right?

I take a breath.

You're not mad, I say.

He doesn't hear me.

I don't care, he says. I am mad. Fuck it.

The room lights up. Another crash of thunder.

I think of Sophy lying alone on that drenched and frozen concrete, the grey wool cardigan soaked right through by now and moulded to her face.

He frowns. A tender little frown.

Fucking hell, he says. I'd give anything to see you now. I mean, really see you.

I wonder where he thinks I am. If I'm not here, then ... My blood slows as I work it out.

He pulls his phone out of his pocket, dials.

I lift my head and look up, over his shoulder, and that's when I know. I'm right here with him but it hasn't happened yet. Rain still clings to the window, but beyond it, you can see the neon blur of all those city lights. And yes, the red dot of an aircraft. All that energy still burning away in the old life.

I watch as he props himself on the edge of the desk. Stares at the floor. He has the phone to his ear. He lifts his head and fixes his eyes on the distance, waiting.

At last his whole face changes. His chin lifts. His eyes come to life.

Hey, he says. You OK? Where are you?

Silence while he listens. Bursts into a smile.

All right, but –

He waits.

All right, but you're sure it's OK? You want me to call back later?

He waits again.

OK, he says. Oh no. Oh dear. Poor lad. Christ. How did he manage to do that?

Another wait.

Bloody hell. Oh no.

Another smile. Then a short laugh. The smile leaving his face.

I don't know about that. Well – hmmm.

A pause.

Me too, he says, and again his face loses its smile.

He reaches out and picks up a pencil from the desk. Looks at it without seeing it. Puts it down again. Sighs.

I don't know. Nothing. Sitting here in my office. Thinking about you.

Another pause.

But where's Jimmy now? Is he OK, then? He's not in pain?

Another pause.

That's good, he says. Yes, I suppose – well, until he gets his big teeth . . . Yes, tell him that – tell him I said he's a pirate.

A pause. Laughs.

OK. Yes, you'd better.

Pause.

No, of course – I just wanted –

Pause.

I just wanted to hear your voice, that's all.

Pause and smile.

Yes.

Pause.

Yes.

Pause.

You know I do.

Sigh.

OK.

He turns the phone off, but keeps it in his hand. Sits there looking at it for a moment or two as if it might spring back into life again.

Finally he puts it in his pocket and, after he's done that, he stares into the distance for a long time. He doesn't look happy and he doesn't look sad. He doesn't look anything. He is stuck there in his thoughts, whatever they are. He doesn't move.

He is there for a little while longer and then next time I look, he isn't.

Outside, the storm has stopped, but you can still hear the rain, gentler now, scattering itself on the window. The sky is dark again, dead, frozen, drained of light.

Jimmy was running along the edge of the swimming pool, racing Gloria and another kid, a friend from school, to do a dive. I had told them a million times not to run. Jimmy was a maniac. He always had been. He didn't listen.

We spent the evening in A & E. They were worried he might have concussion, but in the end he didn't. He was lucky that he only chipped a tooth and even luckier that it was still a baby one.

It would grow back. It would have grown back.

Tears are running down my face now. I lick at them and I rub my face on my jumper, but more keep coming. They keep on coming. I don't know what to do. I have no way of stopping them. They keep on coming.

I must sleep all night on that cold office floor. When I wake it is barely light. I know even before I open my eyes that something is different. It is this. There's a baby asleep in my arms.

Black downy hair, black newborn eyes, skinny baby chest, legs that have not yet quite unfolded, feet that haven't yet taken any weight or even touched earth. The soft fat animal place at the back of his neck. The dark silky hairs on the tops of his ears. Fingers you want to kiss and suck, tiny fingernails that peel and shred. The smell of his face. Just born. Sticky and warm and smelling of the insides of things. The inside of me.

It is Arthur.

I yawn and stretch and get ready to shift myself to give him my fullest most bursting breast, but even as I cup his small head so he can fix his mouth on, he takes on the quality of the air, the freezing air all around us and he runs through my fingers like a thought or a wave of the blackest of black salt water, and that's it, that's the end of the feeling, he's gone.

I go and fetch the kid. I know where he'll be. Asleep on the blankets on his stomach, fully clothed, hair flung back from his face, breathing so lightly you'd think he was dead.

I shake him awake.

What? He sits up and stares at me, frowning.

I don't take any chances. I don't even give him time to think. I fling my arms around him, put my lips against his warm and grubby face. I breathe in the asleep-boy smell of his skin. My friend, I think. He's my friend.

I need you to come with me, I say. Right now. You've got to come.

He blinks at me.

Why?

Because I need you to.

But come where?

Don't ask me, Matt. Just do it. Please. Come on.

We go upstairs. The air is cold. Everything's the same as before, the same as it's always been, except for one thing. I know why I'm here.

The first office we come to is empty. A couple of desks, grey computer screens, another dead and dried-up plant, a long glass table with chairs either side. Scattered on the table, though, are some sticks for stirring coffee. Someone has been arranging them into zigzags, making patterns before shoving the rest of them on to the floor.

My heart lifts.

Look at that, I say to Matt. Someone's been playing.

He looks at the sticks and he says something, but I don't hear what it is. I am focused on one thing now. I am excited. I reach behind me and pull him along.

The next room we come to is smaller, another office, the same as the first one – desk and screens and dead air and dust. But the last room, the one at the very end, has its door ever so slightly ajar.

I put my face to the crack. And there, exactly as I expected, fast asleep on that harsh office carpet – with no cushions or anything to lie on and nothing in the way of blankets to cover them – are my children.

My children.

There they are, I say to Matt, as I feel my face grow hot at the pleasure of seeing them, having them, knowing them.

There who are?

My kids.

He peers into the room like a blind person.

What kids? Where?

There.

He looks again. He follows where my hand is pointing. He stares at the spot and then he looks back at me.

Where? he says.

They lie there in a heap on the carpet, all of their heads

at the same end, except of course for the baby, who always manages to turn herself about ninety degrees in her sleep.

Jimmy's foot is pressed into the back of Gloria's thigh, his two hands made into fists, like someone dreaming of the perfect fight. Both of Katie's legs in their woollen tights are resting on Iris's skinny hip, her arms flung up above her head and her mouth wide open.

Iris, meanwhile, is sleeping as she always does – neat as a princess, pale hands folded under her even paler cheek. The dog is curled beside her, head down but eyes open, grave and alert.

Good dog, I think, guarding my children.

As I push the door open a little wider, she lifts her head.

It's OK, I whisper. Stay.

She looks at me – one swift beat of her tail on the carpet at the sound of my voice.

Good girl, I say.

She sighs and, eyes on my face, lets her chin drop back down on her paws. She waits. So do I. At last, somebody sighs and begins to stretch.

Look, I say to Matt. They're waking up.

That's Iris, I tell him as a thin arm unfolds into the air, twisting, fingers opening and closing. She's the eldest. She's kind of nervy, a bit of a worrier, but she's such a good girl.

And that's Katie. She's a real little rascal, but always so happy, loves her food, loves everything actually, slept through the night right from the start.

Katie rolls over on to her back and opens her eyes and, gazing happily at the ceiling, starts to chatter away to herself.

Jimmy sits straight up in one liquid movement, smiling as if woken by a joke. He rubs his eyes. Blinks.

Jimmy, I tell the kid. He'll wear you out. Seriously. I'm warning you. He never stops.

I swallow. There's something about Jimmy. I realise my eyes are full of tears.

As I watch, Gloria turns and snuggles against him and he shoves her off. She opens her eyes and shoves him back, harder. Jimmy clouts her.

Hey, I say. That's too hard. Come on, that's enough now, stop it, both of you.

Four faces turn to look at me. I wipe at my eyes. I don't want them to see the tears. The dog jumps up and comes over to me, tail wagging.

Mummy, says Katie, but she says it in a slow voice as if she's still dreaming.

Mum! shouts Jimmy.

Iris stares at me. I hold out my arms.

By the time I'm down there on the floor with them, the picture that had been hazy at first has warmed up. All the colours are brighter, the sounds louder. The whole thing has come sharp and clean.

The dusty plum of Katie's cardigan, knitted by Simon's mum when Iris was born. The washed and worn-out denim of Gloria's jeans. Jimmy's tawny, springy hair, almost red in certain lights. The warmth of their skin, the glint of a blue eye, a fat finger. Iris's dark lashes. Gloria's creamy tangled hair.

Oh, I tell Matthew. I almost forgot. And this is Gloria –

And I turn back then, ready to tell him all about her, but I'm looking at an empty doorway, sunlight falling through it, nothing there at all. And certainly no kid.

I watch the space for a moment and then I turn back to my children.

Mummy, says Jimmy. Mummy, I love you, I love you! Mummy, why are you crying?

Iris pulls on her jumper and stuffs her feet into her shoes without undoing the laces.

I knew you'd come, she says. I went to sleep just knowing it. I told myself that if I shut my eyes and banged my head on the floor and said, She won't, she won't, about eight or maybe ten times, then the opposite would happen and you'd come.

I laugh. Iris's methods have always been a mystery to me. I cup her pointy chin in my hand.

I've missed you so much, I tell her.

She throws me an anxious look.

You remember now? You know that you're our mum? You're not going to forget it again?

I put my arms around her and hold her tight.

I won't forget it, I say, and I feel her tense for a moment and then relax.

Gloria comes over, silent and smiling at me.

Still not talking? I say.

She shakes her head. I kiss my finger and plant it on her nose.

But we have to go, I tell them as I pull Katie up off the floor and on to my lap. We need to leave as soon as possible.

But leave to go where? says Jimmy.

I'll tell you in a minute.

I start buttoning Katie's cardigan. Her cheeks are red and a string of saliva dribbles down and swings there, wetting my wrist.

Poor old Munchkin, I say. You are teething, aren't you?

She makes a little noise, half a sob, half a laugh.

Never mind, I say. We'll make it better.

Better, she says.

That's right. We'll sort it out.

Mummy, she chants. Mummy-mummy-mummy.

Where are we going? Jimmy asks me again. Are we going on a trip?

Kind of, I say.

I know where we're going, says Iris.

I look at her, standing there watching me with her sad little face, and I think she probably does know.

Well come on then, I tell her. Let's get going. You're all going to have to help me. I don't want any fussing from anyone. Where are your coats? Do we still have Katie's snowsuit thing, the tartan one? It's very, very cold out there.

Colder than Christmas? shouts Jimmy.

Colder than anything you've ever known, I tell him. So get your coat.

Iris is looking at me.

We don't have anything, she says. I mean coats or anything. I told you before. We've got nothing.

She puts a finger in her mouth and tears at the nail.

Then would you mind telling me what those are? I say, indicating a pile of anoraks and duffels on the far side of the room.

Her eyes widen.

Our coats! When did you put them there?

It's probably magic, says Jimmy, and he goes over and gets his coat and puts it on. As he stuffs his arms into the sleeves, I notice how short they are. He must have grown.

And the zip, I tell him. I want it done up properly.

Hey! he shouts. My hat's here too.

He puts on the hat and then he stands, frowning, investigating his pockets.

I had some Haribo in here, he says. And some football cards. Where are they?

Jimmy, I say. It was a long time ago.

He looks at me.

How long?

I don't know how long but a very long time.

He comes and stands close to me then, his eyes full of worry.

This time you're staying, aren't you? he says.

Of course, I say.

I pull him to me and I kiss his small head.

We haven't been out of this place in ever such a long time, he says. Where are we really going?

I take his hand and I take Gloria's and I squeeze them both. I look at their sister.

Iris will tell you where we're going. Where are we going, Iris?

She gives me a careful look.

We've got to go and find Arthur, haven't we? she says. Are we going home?

That's right, I say.

Yay! says Jimmy. I don't know why, but I just knew that's where we were going!

No, you didn't, Iris says.

Yes, I did.

7

The going is hard, slippery and dangerous. Every footstep has to be negotiated.

Though the rain has begun to melt the ice, overnight the temperatures have plunged again and a light snow has fallen. The combination of freeze and thaw is precarious. Holes have opened up in the road, gaping craters which could easily swallow a truck, let alone a child. Other times, the land seems to tilt in an unexpected and frightening way because something or other has collapsed underneath it.

If she starts to slip, you let go of her, do you understand? I tell Iris, who has the dog held tight on a lead.

OK, she says.

I mean it.

I know you do.

Jimmy looks at me with interest.

But, what, even if she, like, starts sliding away and is about to be killed? You mean we're not allowed to rescue her even then?

I look at the dog and the dog looks at me.

I don't want her pulling Iris into danger, I tell him.

He's silent a moment. He has hold of Gloria's hand. We watch the dog's quick breath pumping itself out into the freezing white air.

She's only a dog, Jimmy says slowly. And the life of a human is more important, right?

Right, I tell him.

He thinks for a second then lets out a big breath.

Although I just said that, I don't think I really believe it. You see, I much prefer animals to humans. In fact, I don't really like humans all that much, apart from you, I mean –

Come on, Jims, I tell him, enough of the talking. We have to keep going.

But he stands still, remaining on the exact same spot, a frown on his face.

Because animals don't make wars, right? And they don't –

All right, I tell him. It's a good point, but can we talk about it later?

He's silent for a moment as we walk on.

Mum?

Yes, Jimmy.

But what do I do if Gloria starts to pull me into danger? Can I let go of her?

I look at the pale and silent little girl who is holding on to his hand, and for a second or two I'm not even sure she's there.

It'll be OK, I tell him. Gloria's going to be very, very careful, aren't you, Gloria?

Gloria's eyes are on me. Wordless and yet brimming with words. Exactly like her father's eyes.

It was Christmas Eve. Katie was just coming up to six months old. She sat on her bottom under the tree and pointed to something sparkly and then she laughed. Simon wanted to take a photo. He got down on the floor and looked at her through the lens.

Katie? Hey, Katie – where's my little Munchkin?

She turned and searched for his face but all she saw was the shiny black eye of the camera looking back at her. Immediately the laugh dropped away. Fists clenched, mouth turned down. The cry built to a scream.

Simon took the photo anyway. Katie screaming under the Christmas tree. She had on tartan trousers and a red cardigan that wrapped around her chest and tied at the back. The moment passed and so did the tears, but the photo stayed in our lives.

That night, the night before Christmas, I lay in bed with Simon and I took a breath and said, There's something I have to tell you.

His face didn't change.

I know what it is, he said. It's Matthew, isn't it?

I said nothing. Then I said, Yes.

Simon lay still for a moment, then he turned away.

It's not what you think, I told him after a few silent minutes had passed. Nothing's happened. We haven't done anything.

He turned back and looked at me. I'd never seen his face so empty.

I know, he said. It's worse than that, isn't it?

Matt was my oldest, dearest friend, the one I'd known since we were kids. Simon liked him too. Or at least I thought he did. He certainly didn't think of him as a threat and he was right not to. Whenever I came back from seeing Matthew, I'd make Simon laugh when I related all the stupid things he'd said, the squabbles we'd had, the various interesting ways in which he'd annoyed me.

Telling it like this made Simon feel safe about Matthew. It made me feel safe about him too.

Then, one night, we went out and we drank too much. Matthew had just finished with his latest girlfriend. I'd liked this girlfriend and I told him I thought he'd been mean to her, that I thought he was far too unkind to all his girlfriends. He admitted it was true – adding that the only person he could ever be nice to was me. We talked and we laughed and then we talked more seriously. And then we ordered another bottle.

Come on, he said when the bar staff were waiting for us to leave. I'll take you home.

We got in a taxi. Without thinking, I put my head in his lap. He put his hand on my head. He stroked my cheek, my hair, touched my lips. He kept his finger on my lips.

After less than five minutes, I sat up. But by then something had changed and we didn't know how to change it back. Or, to be more truthful, we didn't want to change it. We liked it too much.

That night, Simon and I stayed awake, crying and talking and crying again. Christmas was ruined. So was our marriage, so was our family, so were our lives.

Tell me how often you've seen him, Simon said.

We've always seen each other –

You know what I mean.

Often, I said.

Have you slept with him?

Of course not.

Have you kissed him?

Silence.

Of course you have, he said. Bloody hell. What a fool I've been. Of course you bloody have.

In the morning, though, he was different. Shaky, white-faced. He pulled me to him, put his hands on my face, touched my nose.

The thing is, he said.

I waited.

The thing is – I just don't want to lose you.

I shut my eyes, bit my lip. I laid my head on his shoulder.

Let's get through Christmas, he said, for the children's sake. We'll talk about it in January.

OK, I said.

But January came, and February too, and even March, and we didn't talk. I hardly saw Matthew. I tried so very hard not to see him. But I missed him, and when I did see him it was miserable, wonderful, terrible. Meanwhile, I hated the lies. I hated that I didn't know myself any more. I hated that when I woke in the morning, the first thing I thought about – before I fed my children or washed or dressed myself – was how not to feel this thing that I felt.

Simon never asked me any more questions. Maybe he was afraid of the answers. I know that I was afraid of the answers.

Then suddenly it was May. Katie's birthday. A blue and sunny day. She had just begun to walk. She pulled herself up on the edge of the trampoline. Gloria, bouncing, light hair flying, saw her and clapped her hands.

Look, Mummy, look! Look at Katie!

Iris came over and took her hand and led her into the middle of the lawn. We all watched as she slowly took her hands away. Katie stood, surprised, swaying slightly, then took two wobbly and important steps before sinking down on to her bottom again in the daisies and clover. We all laughed. So did Katie.

Simon had a beer in his hand. He looked at me.

You're taking all of this away from them, he said. This thing that you're doing. It's ruining our family, everything we've cared about, everything we've made. Think about it. Is he really worth all that to you?

Soon, Iris stops and stares around her. She shivers. Her nose is running. I can see that her school duffel coat is also getting too short. In fact, sometimes I'm not sure she's even wearing a coat at all. The pink of her knitted hat keeps on fading in and out, draining almost to white, and so do her gloves. Sometimes, her face looks almost to be the same colour as the snow, the sky . . .

But where are we? she says. All of this. I don't remember any of it. I don't know where we are. Do you?

I ease the wide cotton straps of Katie's sling to a different place on my shoulders.

You're getting too big for this, aren't you, Munchkin? I say. Way too big to be in a sling.

She laughs and throws her head backwards, almost throwing me off balance.

No, I tell her. You can't do that. Come on, stay still for Mummy now.

I pull her hat down over her ears, hold her small feet in the snowsuit close to my stomach and squeeze them tight. She moans and wriggles her head closer to my chest.

Well? says Iris.

The dog is tugging on the lead. She yanks it back sharply. Wipes her nose on her sleeve.

Well what?

You're not listening to me, are you? Do you even know how to get home?

I hesitate as I think about this.

I'm not sure, I tell her.

You mean you don't.

Well, probably not exactly, no.

Katie tilts her head up at me again and opens her mouth, showing her little row of bottom teeth. I kiss her nose loudly. She laughs. Iris looks annoyed.

You're not taking this very seriously, are you? she says.

I feel Jimmy watching me.

Even though you remember now that you're our mum, he says carefully, I still don't like it when you don't remember things like how to get home. It's like you're not the same person or something.

I take a breath.

Oh, darling, I tell him, I am. I'm the same person.

Well then, OK. But you don't seem worried enough.

You want me to be worried?

He doesn't mean like that, Iris says. I think he just means you're acting a bit too relaxed. For a parent, I mean.

Yeah, says Jimmy. It's like because you don't remember things, yeah, you can say anything at all, even if you don't really mean it.

You never used to be like that, Iris adds.

How did I used to be?

Well, you were always quite a careful person, thinking ahead about everything and always bringing drinks and tissues and everything.

Was I?

Yes. And you don't seem like that now. You just seem like one of us, and it's a bit scary.

The thing is, says Jimmy, you might suddenly forget us again, and then you'll turn around and without even remembering that you're leaving us behind, you'll just go!

I look at Iris.

Yes, she says. I'm worried about that too.

I try to think about this. I notice that Gloria is watching me with her full attention. So is the dog.

I won't do that, I tell them.

Jimmy frowns.

But I'm worried that you will.

I look at him.

Jims, I love you and I won't do it.

Yes, he says. But even though I know that, and I know you mean it and all that, still the thought keeps on coming into my head.

Well, try not to let it.

He gives a little wail.

Even when I don't let it, it keeps on coming!

Iris looks at me.

You say you won't go, but you don't know that for sure, do you?

Dad said he wouldn't go either, Jimmy says.

Shut up, says Iris. Stop it.

But it was a lie. He lied.

Jimmy, says Iris. I mean it.

But it's true.

Shut up.

I feel myself flinch. The jolt of a door slamming. A car starting up. A broken window, or was it a door? Snow falling. Rain and sun and then the whole world freezing.

Hush, I say to Jimmy. Hush, sweetheart. That's enough.

I put my hand out and touch his head, but my fingers have already drifted through his hair into another place that I can barely feel.

*   *   *

In late June I went to Simon. I felt ill, sad, shaky, tired.

All right, I said. You're right. I can't live like this. I agree with you about everything. I won't see him any more.

He looked very surprised. He stared at me. His face was unreadable.

You're serious? You really mean this? I can trust you?

I nodded. Trust. The word sounded lumpy and foreign as I turned it over in my head.

It has to be absolute, he said. I have to be able to be certain.

I told him I understood – well, it was true, I did understand – and that it would be absolute. I told him I loved him, and this was also true. I knew that a part of me really did love him – he was the father of my children. I loved my children. I loved him. I loved our family. I wanted our happiness to come back. I thought it all lay with me, the power to bring it back. I meant every word.

Simon watched my face for a few seconds longer, then he put his head in his hands and he cried.

I rang Matthew. I was dry-eyed, dry-mouthed. My heart was dry, bone dry. I could hear him breathing, waiting. He already knew what I was going to say. Even when we were kids, he'd known what I would say next. It had driven me crazy then. It broke my heart now.

It's the children, I told him.

Yes, he said.

I can't do this to them.

I know.

We didn't speak for a few moments then, we just listened to each other.

Don't go, he said at last. I mean right now. Please. Just stay on the line.

OK.

I waited.

I have to go now, I told him.

Not yet.

I do. In a minute I do.

He asked me to see him one more time, then – to talk it over, to say a proper goodbye.

No, I said.

No one will know about it, he said. We'll just be together for a little while, and then I'll let you go. It'll be something to hold on to. I absolutely promise that's all it will be. I won't make it hard for you.

I hesitated.

No, I told him. You know I can't.

Please.

OK, I said.

We keep on moving. We stumble over that frozen landscape as best we can, but it's hard to tell if we're heading in the right direction. So many of the old landmarks are gone.

Trees have split and fallen and are lying in the road, and so many buildings have collapsed or been burned down. The ones that are left standing make no sense without the others around them – some of them are no more than shells, half demolished so you can see right into them. Blurred and charred remnants of patterned wallpaper. The ghost outline of a fireplace. Skeletal stairs with their fresh carpet of snow.

Look at that! shouts Jimmy, and he points at a hoarding with the words T Mobile still visible on it. I definitely remember that!

He lets go of Gloria's hand for a second, but she reaches over and grabs back hold of him.

Don't be silly, Iris says. That means nothing. It's just an ad. Don't you remember, there were loads of those? Tell him, Mum. They were absolutely everywhere.

I gaze at the hoarding.

She's right, I tell Jimmy. I don't think it means anything.

Iris is pleased. She glances at her brother and then she gives me a fierce, proud look – a look that reminds me of someone, maybe of myself.

I smile back at her, even though it means looking straight through what is left of her to the fallen tree trunk behind.

Gloria is crying. If I think hard about it, I realise she's been crying for a long time. I hold the sleeping Katie against me and I bend down to her.

What is it? I ask her. Sweetheart, tell me what's the matter.

She says nothing. Her face has no colour.

I think her foot's hurting, Jimmy says.

I look at him.

What makes you say that? How do you know?

He sticks out his bottom lip.

I kind of made it up, but all the same, I do think it's true.

I turn back to Gloria.

Is that it? Is it your foot?

She stares at me. She says nothing. Then she gives a little sob. I look at her trainers, sodden with snow.

Are your feet all wet?

Iris comes closer.

I don't think it's her foot, she says. I think she wants to hold your hand.

Is that it? I ask Gloria.

Still she says nothing. But I reach down and take her hand anyway, even though it slips through mine like water.

After ten minutes, or maybe an hour, we pass a low wall with several piles of tiny bones on it. Newly done, because the snow hasn't had a chance to settle on them yet. Each pile contains maybe a hundred bones.

We all stare. Even Katie swivels her head and hangs away from my chest to get a look.

I think someone did it on purpose, says Jimmy in a dark voice.

What do you mean, on purpose? Iris asks him.

Jimmy holds out a hand. His eyes are wide.

I mean that they killed some people and then they got the flesh off the bones somehow and then they put them there, for everyone to see.

Don't be silly, Iris says. How do you know they're the bones of people? And how would they get the flesh off? And who would kill that many people anyway?

Jimmy looks at me.

Some people would. A murderer would, wouldn't he, Mummy?

I look at the bones. Some of them don't even look like whole bones. Just splinters of bones.

I don't know, I tell him.

Anyway, says Iris, they're too small to be the bones of people. Look, they're really tiny. It's probably animals or birds or something.

Or babies, says Jimmy. Maybe a murderer came along and killed a great whole lot of babies and left them there.

It's not babies, says Iris. Nobody kills babies.

Jimmy narrows his eyes.

Why not? How do you know they don't?

Because babies are helpless. They can't hurt you. You wouldn't need to defend yourself against a baby.

Jimmy thinks about this.

But what if you wanted to kill one, say, just for fun?

Now Iris looks at him and shudders.

Jimmy! What a horrible thing to say.

But some things that really happen are horrible. Some things that —

No, says Iris. They're not. And anyway, I've had enough and I don't want to talk about it any more.

But —

I said I'd had enough. Shut up!

Jimmy blinks.

Actually, he says, maybe you're right, because if they're babies, then where are the skulls?

I told you to shut up! says Iris. Mum, could you please tell Jimmy to be quiet?

At the sound of Iris's voice, the dog starts to whimper. And I'm about to speak when I realise something terrible. A weight is gone from my body. It's Katie. She's not there. She's gone.

I look down, cry out.

Mummy! says Iris. Mummy, what's the matter? What is it?

I stumble around in the wind, holding my arms out and calling her name. Katie! Katie!

But, Mummy —

I've lost her. I've lost Katie.

But she's right there! Iris shouts, almost angrily, pointing to my chest, and I look down and see that she's right, there's Katie, still in her sling, her head asleep against me.

I look down at her and now I'm confused. She seems too small. For a moment or two I don't even know if she's Katie or if she's Arthur. I'm shaking all over.

But she wasn't there, I tell Iris.

Who wasn't there?

I thought I'd lost her. I thought I'd lost Katie.

She was there, Iris says. Really, Mummy. All the time, she was there.

But . . . I thought I'd lost her.

Jimmy is staring at me.

But you didn't.

I know. I know.

You really scared me, Iris says.

I know. I'm sorry. I really scared myself.

My body knew straightaway that it was pregnant. It did not change, but the world around it did. Colours ripened, textures grew sinister crests and spikes, tastes and smells turned raw. I waited to bleed but nothing came. I felt him there – Arthur – I felt him clinging on in there.

It wasn't his fault. It wasn't the baby's fault.

I lay on the bed and I sobbed. Simon said nothing. I knew that he knew, and he knew I knew. He sat and stroked my hair. For weeks now, he'd gone out of his way to be careful with me, to be kind. The kinder he was, the more I cried. He knew what I needed. He fetched me a can of soda water.

It's a boy, he said as he snapped the ring and handed me the can, fizzing. Isn't it? You were just like this with Jims. It must be a boy, don't you think?

I said nothing. I could not look at his face. I gulped the soda. It was good; it was clean. I finished it. He opened another one for me. I tried to work out what was different about him. There was something new about the shape of him, sitting there. A different Simon. How did he manage to be so much stronger than me?

When he spoke, his voice was steady.

I want you to know that I love you. That I think we can do this. I am up for it. We'll do it together. You don't have to say anything right now. Just think about it, OK?

I looked at him. I wasn't crying any more but I could feel the sobs waiting there, deep down inside me.

Why are you doing this? I said.

Doing what?

Why are you being so nice to me?

He sat still for a moment, his head to one side.

I don't know, he said.

But why?

His face hardened just the tiniest touch. He didn't say anything else.

The following Christmas – Katie was walking properly now, she had her first pair of proper shoes – I told him the truth.

It's nothing to do with what happened, I told him. It's nothing to do with Matt. But I just can't do it. It doesn't feel right.

I saw him flinch at the mention of the name.

What exactly are you saying? What can't you do?

I looked at the ground.

It's not fair on you, Simon.

What's not fair on me? What are you talking about? Who are you to say what's fair on me?

I took a breath. Don't make me say it, I thought. But he was waiting.

I can't love you. I've tried and tried and I just can't. I just don't think I love you any more.

He kept his face steady. He did not shout or cry or even act very surprised. Back in the spring, when I'd been trying so hard not to see Matthew, we'd had a few counselling sessions and we'd both agreed that it had been a waste of time. Now, though, he asked me to go and have one more session with him.

Why? I said.

Whatever you think you've decided, I just want us to talk it through with a third party.

He told me, then, that after we'd stopped the sessions, he'd continued seeing the counsellor without me.

I stared at him.

You've been going all this time? But why?

When he replied, his voice was cold.

How else do you think I've been getting through this? How else do you think a man lives with a woman who's expecting another man's baby?

I said nothing. Then I said, OK. I'll come.

Thank you, he said, as if I was a total stranger. Thank you. I'd really appreciate that.

This time he didn't say he loved me.

It has begun to snow again. At first very light and then more heavily. Snowflakes blow into our eyes and mouths. The wind stings our cheeks. Sometimes it's so raw and strong that we have to turn the other way to get some relief.

I think we've been walking round in circles, says Iris. I mean it. I keep seeing things that I'm sure I've seen before.

I think so too, says Jimmy.

Copycat.

I'm not copying. I'm just saying what I think, that's all.

Then try and think something of your own, instead of always thinking other people's thoughts.

Hey! says Jimmy.

You two, I tell them, always fighting.

Iris sniffs.

So what do you think? she asks me. About the circles?

What circles?

Are we walking in them?

I look around me. The landscape ahead of us is both familiar and not familiar. A sign says All Bar One and another says HSBC and another says Lloyds. None of the words means anything to me.

I don't know, I tell her. I'm doing my best, OK?

Iris lets out a breath.

My arm's hurting, she says. It's really aching. Can someone else have a go with the dog?

I glance at the dog. For a second or two, she's not there at all. Then I see the outline of her nose, a whisker.

Try and keep going a bit longer, I tell Iris. Then I'll take her.

I'll take her! says Jimmy.

Iris hands him the lead, but I can no longer see an animal on the end of it. Jimmy seems unbothered. He pulls the lead along.

What would you have done, if you really had lost her? he asks me after we've walked on a bit.

You mean Katie?

Yes.

I don't know, I tell him.

What would you do if you lost us all? Not just Arthur, I mean.

I let myself think about Arthur. His dark wet weight as he came slipping out of me.

Jimmy – I begin.

Would you cry? I mean really, really cry. Would you scream?

I look at him.

Do you think that Arthur will be there? he says. When we get home?

I don't know.

What will you do if he isn't?

Jimmy . . .

What?

Oh, Jimmy. Just come here.

When he comes, I wrap my arms around him, hold him very tight. I shut my eyes.

Don't go, I say. Please don't go.

But I'm not going.

You are. You are.

I hold on, trying to feel the warmth of his body.

Hey, he groans. You're annoying the dog. And you're making all the air come out of me.

I open my eyes. As I expected, the dog's not there.

I'm sorry, I say. I just want to hold you properly.

Why?

So I can feel how warm you are.

But you know how warm I am!

No. I want to feel it.

Why?

Because I love you. Because it feels so good to hold you and know that you're there.

OK, he says, and he shoves himself hard against me, almost throttling me with his hug. Can you feel it now?

Yes, I lie. Yes, I can. Thank you. I can.

It was February when we sat them down to tell them. Iris — tense and wary, her bitten fingers resting in her lap, sharp enough to guess what was coming. Jimmy and Gloria laughing and fighting and kicking each other on the sofa, oblivious. Katie sucking her cloth on my lap. The baby's knees and elbows moving visibly under my T-shirt.

He said I should do the talking. Because this was all my doing. Because I was the one who wanted this. So I did. I began to speak the words we'd agreed on with the counsellor. The careful, difficult words. I unloaded them, in all their unkindness, in front of our little family. My voice shook, but I tried hard to keep it calm and loving. I told them how much we loved them, how we would always love them, but . . .

My voice was soft. The words were hard and terrible.

I could not look at Iris.

Their reactions were precise and entirely typical. Jimmy cried. Katie saw his face and cried. Gloria stayed silent, gazing up at her father, searching for clues. Iris stood up and ran from the room.

Sometimes the children are with me, sometimes they aren't. I have no way of knowing whether or not, when I look down, I'll see Katie's head, feel her feet hanging there. Sometimes I do manage to grip Gloria's little hand in mine, but other times my fingers hang loose and empty at my side. Mostly they hang loose.

Iris's anxious frown is still there now and then, waiting for me to say something, to do something. But more often there's nothing, an Iris-shaped space where she ought to be. Jimmy comes and goes. I never know when he'll next disappear. Halfway through one of his mad conversations. In the middle of a laugh . . .

Hold my hand, I tell him.

Oh, he says. Do I have to? I'm not a baby, you know.

I just think it's better, that's all.

But Mummy I just gave you a hug –

Yes, but this is different. I just want to know that you're still there.

But I am here! I'm right here, look!

I'd rather you held my hand. I don't know you're there if I can't feel you.

OK, he says. Can you feel that?

I look down.

I don't know, I say.

He laughs.

I just gave you a great big smack. Didn't you feel it?

No.

OK, then. Can you feel this?

What? Feel what?

I look around me.

Where are you? I say.

As we – or maybe it's just me now – make our way towards Elephant, I see people crowding round braziers, shouting things out, pushing and banging against each other. Men and boys mostly. Maybe they're fighting for something I can't see. I have no idea what they are shouting. Sometimes I catch snatches of obscenities, mostly yelling and laughter.

172

A small person, probably a child, in jeans and a grey hoodie, is slumped against a wall by the side of the road, legs drawn up, wrists dangling over his knees, head dipped as if in sleep. Something about the shape of him is familiar and I call out to see if he's OK, but he doesn't reply. I call again. He doesn't move. In the end, I go and ask if he's all right.

When he still doesn't respond, I lean over and touch the grey hooded head.

I won't hurt you, I tell him. I've got kids of my own. I just want to know if you're OK.

He stays so still under my gloved hand that I reach out and gently pull back the hood. Under it the bone is white and a few longish clumps of ginger hair still cling to the skull, lifting, now that I've exposed them to the wind.

The children are mostly gone, their shapes and colours, the touch of them, all dissolved, but their voices remain. Their questions.

Do you remember everything now? Iris asks me, her voice almost drowned out by the wind.

I remember some things, I tell her. I remember more than I did.

But not everything?

Not everything, no.

Maybe you don't want to remember everything?

I give her a swift look. She's always been a clever girl.

OK, but do you remember about our dad? says Jimmy.

What about him?

Everything. What he was like and all that.

I think so, I tell him.

Why did he have to go away?

It's a long story.

Do you think we'll ever see him again?

I don't know, Jims. I hope so.

And if he saw us now, say we just saw him over there walking along or something, do you think he'd remember that he was our dad?

Oh darling, I say. I'm sure he would.

A troubled look crosses his face.

And you do still remember that you're our mum, right?

Iris's voice is sharp.

What is it, Mummy? Why are you crying?

I don't know, I tell her. I don't know.

I hear her lower her voice.

Is it because of what you did to us?

I hold my breath.

What?

You know what.

She swallows. I think that her eyes are on me.

I know I ought to be afraid of you, but somehow, I don't know why, I'm just not.

What did she do? says Jimmy.

Iris says nothing. Grief sweeps over me.

I couldn't help it, she says. I was just so amazed and happy to see you again.

What did she do! Jimmy almost shouts.

Before I can think about what to do next, I feel something heavy in my arms – a fierce, dragging weight between my shoulder blades.

I look down. It's Katie. She's in my arms. She's wearing her old snowsuit, not the tartan one that she had on just now, but the other one, the red one, the one I put her in before when . . .

And there's no sling. The sling has gone. And her head is heavy and she's just about asleep, and I'm aching all over and she's a raw tired weight in my arms, this child, and I can't remember how we got here and all I know is I'm struggling to carry her just as I did when I left the house . . .

The house. We left it an hour or is it a day ago? Katie. She is mine. She is my child. I carry her in my arms. My face is on fire. I do not have a plan.

The world is still burning but the air is frozen, and once we are past Camberwell Green and on to Newington Causeway – snowflakes coming down in silence – the air grows quieter. No one is screaming. No one is making a sound. There are fewer people now and those that you do see slip and stagger along in terrified silence, heads down, anxious to avoid trouble.

How many days has it been? Was it yesterday? Today?

Some carry suitcases or armfuls of blankets, but others must have left their homes as quickly as I did, and seem to have nothing. Some people sit in cars, but the cars aren't moving and they'll have to get out of them sooner or later. An oldish man with bloodied hands calls out to me for help, but I keep on walking. When his shouts grow more urgent, I move faster.

At Elephant, someone has set light to the top of the shopping centre and it's still smouldering, and all of the upper windows are thoroughly smashed. The eating places have been looted. A sign says Tai Tip Mein and then Noodle. The Eat As Much As You Like sign is hanging right off and flapping in the wind. Same for the Chinese – smashed up and burned. Bright nylon sacks of rice have been tipped in the snow. Down by the old kiosk – Chocolate-Chewing-gum-Patties-Jerk Chicken –

someone has built a snowman and forced a bright-blue plastic bag over its head.

Katie's asleep now. My arms are really hurting. I try shifting her up so she's half on my shoulder, but have to change sides so often it doesn't really work. There's some dried blood on her hands, and for a second or two I can't work out why it's there. Then, a moment later, I can, and my stomach twists. I hear a strange sound and I realise it's my own voice, gulping and wailing. I shut it off quickly. Katie doesn't budge. She stays asleep.

The freeze has already turned the trees in the middle of the roundabout black, and you can see the cars there too, stopped for ever in their rush-hour queues. You can't any longer see the people inside those cars, but there are no signs of any footprints across the snow.

A pretty, long-haired girl in a purple snowsuit and a fur hat is sitting cross-legged on a piece of corrugated metal on the charred back of a lorry. So still she looks like she's meditating. Her eyes are wide and the wind whips the strands of her hair around her face, and at first I think that she's mad to sit there, looking like such an easy target. But as I pass her, I see that nothing moves, not even her eyes. I'm tempted to try to get the hat, but even if I didn't have Katie, I'm not sure I'd be able to get up there without hurting myself.

By the tube is some rubble with thick snow on it and beside it a tarpaulin beneath which you can see the shapes of at least two people huddled together. The tarpaulin flaps around them. They aren't moving either. I don't stop to see if they're alive or dead.

A small red-haired person, wearing jeans and a grey hoodie is sitting against a wall by the side of the road, legs drawn up, wrists dangling on his knees, head dipped as if in sleep. I gasp and stare for a second. It looks so much like Jimmy.

Even though I know it can't be Jimmy, still I call out to him, but he doesn't move or speak and I stand there for a moment, thinking and worrying and wondering what to do. I call again. He doesn't move. In the end, I go over and ask if he's all right.

Holding Katie propped on my hip, I lean over and touch the grey hooded head.

I won't hurt you, I tell him. I've got kids of my own. I just want to know if you're OK.

He looks up at me. His eyes are empty. He isn't a child, but a man, red-haired, white-faced, a few days' growth of hair on his face. The skin on his neck is mottled with black.

Piss off, he says. Some spit comes out of his mouth as he says it.

I do as he says. I walk away, my heart thumping. When I dare to look back, he's still sitting there.

Man, says Katie.

Yes, I tell her. Man.

I stop to rest a moment, squatting and leaning against a wall with Katie propped on my knees. My face is still burning. I feel sick. The air seems to wobble. In the distance, I see another thing that confuses me. London Bridge.

I blink. It's still there. It's not possible. Surely we can't be back there already.

I look at Katie. I swallow. My throat is raw and tight.

Maybe Iris was right, I tell her. About us going round in circles.

She smiles. Dribble is running down her chin, which is getting sore.

Isey, she says and she rocks back against me. Her hair is damp and cold but it still smells like honey.

I hold my wrists up to the light and watch them moving all on their own.

I'm really shaky, aren't I? I say.

She looks at me. I can almost see the circles of her small brain going round and round. She puts a finger in her mouth and pulls it out again.

Dod, she says.

I shake my head.

The dog's not here, I tell her.

She listens. Her mouth is open. Her two new little teeth. Her fat wet bottom lip.

Isey?

Iris isn't here either.

She blinks at me.

And neither is Gloria or Jimmy and neither is Arthur, I add quickly, before she can sit there breaking my heart by running through all the names of all the other little people we'll never see again.

My mouth is dry. I scoop a handful of clean snow off the top of the wall and push it in my mouth. It tastes of cold metal and it hurts my teeth and the brief moment of pain is enough to put me back on track. I straighten up slowly and I hear his voice again. Jimmy.

Why did you do that? he asks me.

Do what?

Why did you make a face when you put that snow in your mouth?

Because it hurt when I bit on it.

Oh. Did you know it was going to hurt?

Yes.

So you're brave, then.

I'm not brave.

You are, says Iris. You are brave. You had babies.

Having babies is OK. You don't have to be that brave to have babies.

Well, I don't ever want to have a baby. I can't think it's worth it, if it hurts that much.

It doesn't hurt that much. It's hard to explain, but it's an OK kind of pain.

Even though when you had Katie, you were screaming and screaming?

You remember that?

Jimmy got really scared. Dad had to send us next door to watch cartoons.

I shut my eyes and open them again, hoping to send the voices away. It doesn't work. I think about whether we should in fact head towards the bridge. If we cross it, at least I'll know where we are. I can get us back to the building. I think about the building then and I feel happier.

And what about when you had Arthur?

What about it?

That was awful.

I don't want to talk about Arthur.

Why not?

Don't, Iris. That's enough. I mean it. Don't ask me any more questions.

Why not? Why can't I ask you?

Iris.

What?

Iris. Iris.

What?

I walk on, with Katie held tight against me. The snow has stopped falling and the wind has dropped. Soon we are moving towards London Bridge.

A church has a sign outside with the words Good News! Jesus has the Answers! in big slanty letters. In front of it, a man is slumped on what is left of a wall, quite a young man, smoking a roll-up and drinking from a bottle.

He sees me and, very slowly, as if he's holding his breath, he puts the bottle down. I try not to look. The blood jumps into my throat. I walk faster, but I know he's watching me. My heart sinks when he throws the cigarette in the snow and slides down off the wall. In three seconds he is beside me.

I've got nothing, I tell him, as I feel myself start to tremble.

He looks at me and he doesn't smile. Then he looks at Katie. Katie returns his gaze.

Boy or girl? he asks me.

I say nothing. I can tell from his voice that he's drunk. He moves in closer. His breath is rank. I see that his hands are shaking.

Is it a boy, or is it a girl? he says again, louder this time.

I shake my head and he stares at me.

You what?

He keeps his eyes on me. Katie's still studying him.

Man! she says and, without any warning, her small hand flies out towards him – one of her grand toddler gestures.

Straightaway, he raises a fist and shoves it close to her nose. His eyes are hot and hard. I gasp and my heart bangs in my chest. Katie thinks it's a game. She laughs loudly.

He lets his hand fall. His eyes are on my face. Very slowly, I take a step backwards.

You got somewhere to go?

What?

I'm saying d'you want to come in?

He indicates a house whose broken windows are angrily barricaded with planks.

I shake my head but he grabs my arm, squeezes till it hurts. I see his grey wool mittens. The black hairs on his knuckles, the sliver of dirt under each long yellow nail.

What's your name? he says.

I say nothing.

Tell me your fucking name.

I bite my lip.

What? he says. You don't have a name?

I turn to face him. I'm shaking all over now.

Please, I say.

Amazingly, he releases me.

You've got lovely eyes, though, he says, as I lift Katie higher on my hip and begin very carefully to walk away.

The snow and ice are slippery here but I speed up, moving as fast as I can. I think he'll call out or come after me, but he doesn't. He doesn't do anything. I try to breathe, but it's harder than I thought. I do not breathe. I do not allow myself to look back.

The place where we are now doesn't look like London Bridge. It doesn't look like anywhere. To the left, there's a superstore, its windows smashed, already thoroughly looted. Heaps of rubbish smouldering in the car park. Beyond it, a clock tower, the hands pointing to 9.22, the moment when everything stopped.

A railway line sprawls away into the distance and I stand for a moment, confused. In front of us, a library which no one has bothered to break into. And next to that a coffee shop, also intact. I peer through the window and –

The blow comes from behind. A blow and then someone grabbing me around the waist. Almost before I can cry out, someone takes Katie from me and a big hard hand closes over my mouth. Another on my breast.

Katie begins to scream. I try to reach out for her and then I smell his whisky breath again. Right on my face.

Really sorry, he says. Second thoughts. I hope you don't mind, I brought my friend along. He's good with babies.

It's not just the friend. There are more of them. I don't know how many. Several more. At the very worst moments it feels like there might be quite a crowd.

They take us down into a basement room, blankets pinned at the windows. Flames everywhere – the yellow wobble of candlelight. The smell is of unwashed clothes, smoke, piss.

Katie is screaming.

Give her to me, I keep on begging them. I'll do anything you want. Just let my daughter stay with me.

Can you make her shut up? someone says.

I can, I cry. I can do it. I can shut her up.

No, another one says. Not her. We meant you.

Someone hits me in the mouth. My tongue swims with the bright taste of blood.

Please, I say, just give me my child.

The second blow is much harder than the first. I feel all my breath leave my body. Something cracks, but it sounds much too far away to be something of mine.

I like your hair, someone says.

More blood spills from my mouth.

The mattress is on the floor. They push me down and pull off my boots and my jeans. I don't know where Katie is. Two of them holding me while another tugs off the rest of my clothes. It feels important to try to hold on to my shirt, but they prise my fingers off easily and pull it over my head. The more I struggle, the more they laugh.

Katie, I say. Katie.

Nothing stops them. They carry on. They get the job done.

The mattress is filthy. It has a pattern of roses. Dirty satin. The word Sleepeezee. I'm reading the word over and over when I hear a match being struck and a door opening and closing. Freezing air on my bare legs.

No, I say.

A rough hand reaches out for my breast and someone else says something but I don't hear what it is.

Where is she? I whisper because I can't see or hear her any more. What have you done with my baby?

She's OK, someone says. She's having a nice time.

Yeah. She's watching TV.

A burst of laughter. I try to listen for her voice in the laughter but it's not there.

Desperate now, I list the reasons they should leave me alone.

You've got the wrong person, I tell them. I'm a mother. I've got young children. I'm bad luck. I'm already dead.

But they aren't listening. They tip something down my throat. It comes back up my nose. Whisky. I feel for my coat and try to pull it back over me. It doesn't work. Right by my face, a candle has been burning, but now someone leans to blow it out. I taste smoke and wax as the darkness unwinds itself.

That's when I begin to scream.

8

I wake. It is night. My head is in someone's lap. The person is humming. I know the tune. What is it? Is it a programme that used to be on TV?

Sophy? I say. Ted? Iris?

Oh, he says. You're awake.

I don't think so.

You are.

I can't be.

Fingers come down on my face. His fingers. I know them. I know his hands.

I do a daring thing then. I turn my head a little so my lips touch his thumb. Just the smallest touch, pulling at my lower lip slightly. I'd like to kiss the thumb, but I don't. I wouldn't dare. I hear him sigh. Lights bending and blurring, moving through the cab before they disappear again. The swish of tyres in the rain.

We shouldn't do this.

What? he says. What shouldn't we do?

I don't know. Whatever.

Say it.

I don't know.

I listen and I hear it again. The sound of those tyres.

Is it raining?

But he doesn't answer and instead it starts all over again.

You're awake, he says.

I don't think so.

I open my eyes and I look around for some sign of the building. Carpet. Desks. Windows. Corridors. Lifts. Graham handing me an orange. Sophy, hunched there, complaining on her bed of coats.

But I don't see any of this. All I see is snow. Right by my face, more snow. Above me, a black night sky sprinkled with stars.

Are we outside? I say.

Again, no one answers. Oh well, I think, and I shut my eyes. He touches my face again.

Hey, try and answer me. Are you awake?

I yawn.

No. I'm not awake. Go away. I'm busy.

I hear him laugh.

What are you busy with?

I say nothing. I just get on with it.

Squatting down to do up the laces on Gloria's trainers, my knees pushed wide apart by the hot, hard curve that will soon be Arthur. Cutting an apple into quarters, putting one on each plate. Pulling out Jimmy's wobbly tooth for him, feeling the membrane crunch as the blood comes.

Hey, let me see it! – he takes the tooth from my fingers. But oh, it's tiny. Can I get the money now?

But just as I'm settled on the sofa with a cup of tea and Katie's backing into my lap with the same old favourite picture book, he interrupts again.

I need to wake you up. I'm sorry, but I need to see if you're OK.

I'm OK, I tell him. I'm fine.

I go back to my children.

Mum? says Jimmy.

Yes, sweetie?

I can't eat this apple. My other tooth's too wobbly.

Try eating it on the other side, then.

But that side's still sore from where you pulled it out.

OK, well then you'll just have to risk biting it on the wobbly side.

But I don't like it. I can feel the skin hanging down.

That's OK.

Yes, but I don't like the feel of it flapping and it tastes all bloody . . .

Blood. My eyes are open now. Cold air is on my hands. A dragging feeling in my stomach. I try to move my feet, but they're stuck to something. Or stuck together. I feel his fingers, picking at the knots.

I've been trying to untie you, he says. Do you know what happened? Do you remember anything? What did they do to you? Did they hurt you?

Snow is falling. It falls on every part of my face. I put out my tongue, interested to see if it will fall there too. It doesn't. Then it does. I lick my lips. I taste blood. I put up a hand and feel my teeth. They all seem to be there, a tight little row of them.

Is it mine? I ask him.

What? Is what yours?

The blood. Is it mine?

He doesn't answer. Maybe he didn't hear me. Or maybe I didn't say it.

I hear a match being struck and I smell his cigarette. I put out my tongue and let another snowflake melt there. He asks me what I'm doing, and I tell him – eating snow.

And I begin to laugh. I start and I keep on laughing. I can't stop. I feel like I've never heard myself laugh before. Or not in a long time, anyway. Isn't it funny, I'm thinking, how one laugh always leads to another . . .

I feel his hand on me again.

Oh, he says. Oh don't. It's all right. I'm here. Oh, please don't cry.

Something is crackling now – smoke coming off damp wood.

Clever, I say.

What's clever?

You built a fire.

He doesn't say anything. I have this feeling that he doesn't hear a thing I say.

Has this happened before? I ask him.

Now he answers.

What? Has what happened before?

All of it.

He hesitates.

I don't know what you mean, he says.

I put my hand up to touch my face and see that my fingers still have the brown streaks of someone's blood on them.

Whose is that? I ask him again.

What?

The blood. Whose is it?

I think it's yours, he says.

Here, he says. You're freezing. Put your gloves on.

He takes hold of my wrists as if I was a child.

I don't know why you keep taking them off, he says.

I watch with interest as my two cold hands are worked inside the gloves, each finger eased in, the thumb too, a sharp tug as they are pulled over my wrists.

Who are you? I ask him.

He doesn't hear me.

Now try and keep them on, OK?

OK, I say. But I don't know who you are.

You'll be much warmer if you keep your gloves on.

OK, I say.

After we'd sat the children down and we'd told them, Simon went to stay with his golf partner, Jock. It was what we'd agreed. Till we sorted out something more permanent. He was only a few tube stops away. He could see the children as much as he wanted.

That afternoon, the kids and I watched videos. We watched all the old ones, stuff they'd had all their lives – the more babyish the better. We watched *Thomas the Tank Engine* and we watched *Postman Pat*.

I haven't seen *Postman Pat* since I was about five years old, Jimmy said happily, as he kicked his legs in time to the theme tune.

We watched *Fireman Sam* and we watched *Teletubbies*. Even Iris watched *Teletubbies*. In fact the children were very specific about what they would and wouldn't watch.

Not Beatrix Potter, said Gloria. I don't like the fox. And not *Stingray*. I don't like the fish with the teeth.

And not *Rupert*, said Jimmy, when he saw me getting the box. *Rupert* gives me a horrible faraway lonely feeling in my tummy.

Yes, said Iris with a shudder. It's the woods. They're too dark and I don't like Algy Pug.

Why don't you like Algy Pug? Jimmy asked her.

There's something wrong with him.

What's wrong with him?

I don't know. There just is, OK?

So we skipped those and began all over again with *Thomas the Tank Engine*. We watched all curled up together on the sofa. We watched as if our lives depended on it. After a while I got up and made honey sandwiches and they all drank milk. When dusk came, I got up and drew the curtains. The outside world had never looked so dark.

Then, after a few days, Simon phoned and told me he was coming back. He'd decided he would not leave after all. It was his house just as much as it was mine. He refused to go. I would have to be the one to find somewhere else.

Why should it be me, he said, when it's you who did this?

His voice was quiet and strained. I could tell he was listening hard to this new version of himself. I listened too. My thoughts were tumbling.

But what about the children? I said.

What about them?

Where will they go?

They'll stay at home with me. The less disruption for them, the better. Remember this was all your idea, he added, when I stayed silent for too long.

But this isn't what you said before, I reminded him, when we first talked about it. You agreed it was important for me to be with the kids.

I heard him take a sip of something. He swallowed.

Well, he said, that was then. But I've talked to people now. They say I've been too reasonable. And I have to say I think they're right.

I caught my breath. Inside me the baby's feet touched my ribs.

What people? I said. I had a quick vision of the golf partner's wife, a pale, nervy redhead who had never liked me, her arms folded, a bottle of wine open on the table in front of her.

He was silent a moment.

Let's just say I've had a lot of support from a lot of people. And I've changed my mind.

That night I packed a suitcase. Several suitcases. A small one for me and huge ones for them. Everything they could possibly want. Jumpers and fleeces and jeans and socks. Gloria's favourite Thumbelina trainers. And toys. Jimmy's superhero sticker books and his dirty old cuddly giraffe. Iris's bead kit and her new guitar. Gloria's Sylvanians. Katie's raggies – the one she loved best and the other that she would only have if her best one was in the wash. All of the stuff I might need when the baby came.

I staggered out and put the cases in the boot of the car. There was only just room. I tried to get the Moses basket in but it wouldn't fit. But then I thought that the baby could probably sleep anywhere when it came. I remembered a bowl for the dog. A lead, some biscuits, a bag of food. The stained old towel she liked to lie on.

I thought for a second and then I went back to the car and pulled Jimmy's giraffe out of the case. He'd miss it if it wasn't in his bed tonight. We'd have to make sure we remembered it in the morning.

I didn't hear Gloria creep downstairs. She stood in the kitchen doorway in her socks and T-shirt, watching me. Her face was the face of an old woman.

Where are we going? she said.

Shh, I told her. You're not meant to see. It's a surprise. We're not going anywhere.

Next time I wake, I feel a man's hand touching the inside of my elbow. A dark snag of memory kicks in and I fight to sit up.

No! Leave me alone! Get away from me!

I try again to move my feet but I can't.

It's OK, he's saying. It's OK. It's only me. You're OK.

I feel my heart turning over and over, thumping and thumping. It makes my whole body shiver.

Please – don't hurt me.

Why would I hurt you? I'm not going to hurt you.

The hand is on my head again. I reach out and try to see whose hand it is, but all I can see is my own bare wrist, the one that belongs to me, with the snowflakes melting on it.

I'm here, the voice says.

You won't hurt me?

Of course I won't.

I yawn. The hand pats my head.

That's right, go back to sleep.

What are you doing?

I'm not doing anything. I just think you need to sleep for a bit longer.

Is it safe?

Of course it's safe. It's perfectly safe. I'm here.

Who are you?

You really don't know who I am?

No, I don't. Why would I?

I hear him hesitate.

I'm just a friend, OK?

OK.

I think about this.

But I don't have any friends.

Yes you do. Now you do.

OK.

I say nothing. I keep my eyes closed. After a moment or two the humming starts up again.

That tune. Now it really is beginning to get to me. Jimmy would know it. I can't think of the name of the show but I know exactly when it comes on – at 6.35, just after the news.

That night it rained and rained. It rained harder than I'd ever known it rain. Thunder and lightning, a wild storm ripping through the sky. Gloria and Katie both crying. Me getting the Calpol. Jimmy running to the loo with one of his bad tummies. The baby kicking and turning inside me. My heart in my mouth as the gutters poured.

Next morning, though, it was the brightest, bluest day. Sunshine. Uncommonly warm for the time of year. A heat-wave in February, said the radio. Already, at eight in the morning, the temperature climbing. The planet heating up. Not possible, the weatherman said. Well, let's enjoy it while it lasts, the presenter said.

I don't enjoy anything any more, I thought.

I got out of bed and water came rushing out of me. So much

193

water – more than I'd ever had with any of the others. Three weeks early. And it had black in it.

Gloria was standing watching me as I gazed at the wet carpet and tried to move my feet.

It's OK, I told her. It's not anything to worry about.

Straightaway she began to cry.

My head is still in his lap. It feels good. When I reach up and try to touch a part of him – his arm, his chest – a gloved hand comes and gently puts mine back down.

I think I might be a bit drunk, I tell him.

You're not drunk. You've been hurt and you probably don't feel too good, but don't worry, you'll be OK.

Who hurt me?

I don't know. Poor girl. I don't know.

It reminds me of being drunk in a taxi, I tell him. With my head in someone's lap –

I stop for a second and listen to myself.

Who's saying all of this? I ask him.

I feel his lap move as he laughs.

You're saying it, he says. And I'm surprised you remember that.

Remember what?

About the taxi.

What about the taxi?

Nothing. Don't think about it now.

Don't think about what?

It's not important. Never mind.

I can tell from the way his lap feels under my head that he's still smiling.

* * *

I thought I would feed them first, then call an ambulance. I wondered if I could send them all next door to Mrs Gregson, then see if I could get hold of Simon to collect them later.

I stuffed a bathroom towel between my legs and I made them all breakfast. Sugar Puffs bouncing all over the table, scattering and crunching under our feet.

It doesn't matter today, I told them, as the dog went around snaffling the spilt cereal. We're having a holiday from being tidy today.

Yay! said Jimmy, bashing the table with his fist and watching the milk slop over his plate.

Iris looked anxious.

But why? she said. Why don't we have to clear up?

Lots of complicated reasons, I told her. Just trust me, sweetheart. We don't.

But what about her teeth?

What about whose teeth?

The dog. She's not meant to have sugar. Remember what the vet said?

I was about to tell her that the dog would be all right just this once, when a pain went through me – a hard, hot cramp that stopped my breath. I bent over, held on to the kitchen table. I tried to remember how to breathe. I saw my fingers turn white as I gripped. I wondered who I should call first – Mrs Gregson, the ambulance, or Simon.

In her highchair, Katie looked at me and banged her spoon and laughed.

Again!

But Iris was staring at me.

What is it, Mum? Are you OK?

I'm fine, I told her as I took a few deep, panicky breaths.
It's just a cramp.

Outside, the garden, drenched by the storm, was bone dry
already. The heat of the sun had made the hellebores wilt, crisp
and brown as if someone was cooking them. Petals were dropping. Leaves lay strewn and curling on the lawn, like autumn.

Far away, you could already hear sirens.

Things change. They change all the time. Now the snow has
stopped and the night sky stretches high above us.

Look at the stars, I say. So many of them. You'd think they
were so close.

How close are they really? Jimmy asks me. Could an astro-
naut touch them?

Of course no one can touch them, Iris says.

But just say they did, what would happen?

They'd burn up and die.

They're millions of miles away, I tell him. So don't worry.
There's no possibility –

No possibility of what?

Of you touching one.

What are you talking about? he says.

The stars. I was telling Jimmy about the stars.

I hear him hesitate.

I think you've slept enough now. I think we're going to have
to wake you up, he says.

Under my head, something shifts. My cheek sticking to something cold.

What is it? I ask him because I don't like the feel of it.

It's a bin bag, he says. Remember those?

Why've you got it?

To sit on. To keep us dry.

I don't want to be dry.

He doesn't hear me.

Do you mind if I have another go at untying your feet? he says.

What?

I blink. It's still so dark. I can barely see him. I can barely make out his shape.

Your feet. Can I untie them? I gave up on it before because I didn't want to wake you.

My feet. Something in me goes cold. I try to sit up, but I can't.

What happened to me?

I already told you. I don't know. I just found you here, lying in the snow like this with your feet tied.

But – what was I doing?

I hear him take a breath.

Well, you looked like you'd been hurt, he says finally.

And?

And – nothing. You looked like you'd been attacked. Do you remember anything? Have you any idea who did this to you?

Did what? What did they do?

I touch my face. The pain makes me shake all over. Even my hand shakes. I remember a mouthful of blood.

I think someone punched me in the face, I say.

Yes, he says softly. I think that too.

I feel some sick come up in my mouth. I swallow it back down.

Was there a baby with me? I say.

* * *

Jimmy went out in the garden. But seconds later, he ran straight back inside.

The fish! he was yelling. The fish! They're all floating on the top of the pond!

Iris looked at me.

That means they're dead.

I looked at her. I didn't want to upset Jimmy.

Not necessarily, I said, as I panted through another wave of pain.

She rolled her eyes.

But Mum, if they're lying on top –

Come on – I straightened up and took Jimmy's hot hand in mine. Let's go and have a look.

Out in the garden everything had changed. The light was metallic, eerie. The sun was hotter than I'd ever felt it. It burned our heads.

Ouch! said Jimmy, who always suffered in the sun.

I touched the back of his neck. It was pink, raw. I felt another wave coming.

We should go back inside, I said.

Why? said Iris.

I cupped my hand beneath my belly and felt it tighten. February. This was February. I crouched on the ground for a moment.

I don't like this weather, I said.

On the pond's steaming surface, the fish bobbed, some of them swollen, others split right open, the edges curling back as if on a hot grill. There was a strong smell.

Like fish and chips, Jimmy said. Only without the chips.

I looked at the fish and, as I looked, another pain zigzagged through me and I had to bend right over. Again, I struggled to breathe. Heat poured over me.

What's wrong with you? said Iris, and I saw that her face was wet, her T-shirt dark with sweat.

Go inside and put Katie in her cot. Then dial 999, I told her. Tell them your mum's having a baby and needs an ambulance. Tell them our address and our phone number and then open the front door and prop the hall chair against it so it stays open.

Iris ran inside, her sandals flapping on the melting path. We watched her go.

I could feel that Jimmy was about to ask me a whole lot of questions but he didn't get the chance, because, as he ran, there was a sound like a blade tearing through the sky. We watched as the house next door and the one behind it burst into flames.

Jimmy screamed. The sun disappeared. The air turned icy. Thick fat snowflakes started to fall.

He gets to work on untying me. I keep trying to see him through the darkness. Every part of me is hurting.

Did I have clothes on? I ask him.

He hesitates.

Yes, he says.

And the baby. Was she with me?

Yes – I can hear the rapid thinking in his voice. Yes. Don't worry, they were all with you.

All?

All of them. The kids.

I stop very still for a moment. I don't breathe. I don't move. This is it. The bad moment I've been waiting for.

That's a lie, isn't it?

He stops what he's doing for a moment. His hands resting on my feet.

Why do you say that?

Because it's not possible.

Isn't it?

No. You know it's not. And anyway, if they were with me when you found me, then where are they now?

He turns to look at me. I can just about see his face now, in shadow. Longish hair, down to his shoulders.

Look, he says. They're safe. I've taken them to a safe place.

Where?

It's just a place I know. A building.

I don't believe you.

I'm not lying to you.

You took them there?

Yes.

And then you just left them?

I left Iris in charge. She was fine about it. I had to come and find you. She knew I was going to find you.

I think about this. I try to imagine how the kids would be if they were left alone in a building somewhere. Would they worry and panic? I decide that Jimmy would do his best to be cheerful and that Iris would probably be pretty quick to organise them. She knows most things about dealing with Katie, I think. Sometimes she's better with her than I am. I hope that Gloria won't just mope and disappear into herself. I worry about Gloria.

Can we go there? I say. Will you take me? I want to go there right now.

We will. We'll go in a minute. I just need to get you walking first.

I can walk. I'm fine. I can walk any distance. I just want to be with my children.

He's looking at me.

Really? You think you're OK to walk now?

Yes, I say.

You're feeling OK?

Yes.

Well, good, he says. That's good.

What's the matter? Why are you looking at me like that? Don't you believe me?

No, he says.

Haven't you done it yet? I say when I see that he's still fiddling with the knots.

He says nothing. I continue to watch him – the back of his head. Hair touching the back of his coat. Something about the way he bends himself to my feet makes me feel soft.

Who are you? I ask him. Do I know you?

You keep on asking me that.

Yes, I say. I wonder why.

He laughs to himself.

Seriously? You really don't know who I am?

I remember some things very well, I tell him. But not others.

And you don't remember me?

I don't know. I haven't really seen your face, have I?

I feel the rope around my ankles give. A hand pats my leg.

There you go, he says, and he sits back on his heels and turns around. I see that he is nice-looking. Dark-eyed, a few days' growth of beard.

Someone hurt you, I tell him. On your face. That's a bad cut.

He smiles. Touches the place.

It's not too bad, he says. It's getting better.

I try to get up on my feet but I can't. He comes to help, but I don't want to let him.

It's OK, I say.

Let me help.

No.

But I want to. Why can't I?

I don't look at him.

Look, how am I going to get myself back to my kids if I can't even stand up on my own?

Don't be so hard on yourself, he says, pulling me up anyway.

I thought I was OK but, as I straighten, I feel something trickle down between my legs. All my clothes feel like they've been put on wrong. There are tightnesses in places there usually aren't. I begin to shake.

It's hopeless, I say.

What's hopeless?

I say nothing. I start to cry.

I'm so sorry, I tell him.

Sorry? What have you got to be sorry for?

For being so . . . stupid.

What? Why do you think you're stupid?

For letting myself get hurt and . . . I don't know. I feel stupid and I feel sad. I just want to get back to my kids, I say.

He looks at me.

You know something?

What?

I just want to put my arms around you.

I flush.

No, I say. Please don't.

I sway on my feet. I think I hear a dog howling somewhere. It's still dark and grey shadows are moving over the snow.

I wish it was light, I say. When will it be light?

Soon.

But will it definitely get light?

So far it always has.

I look at him.

But we can't be certain?

About what?

That it will get light.

He seems to think about this.

No, he says. I suppose we can't.

I think about this and then I hear myself laugh.

What's funny? he says.

I sound just like Jimmy, don't I?

He smiles.

You do, he says. Him and his questions.

I look at him.

You know Jimmy? You remember him?

He glances away.

I know all your kids. You think I'd know you and not know your kids?

I think about this. I look at his face and my heart lifts. I don't say anything. He smoothes out the sheet of black plastic I was lying on before. The bin bag. He doesn't look at me.

Sit down, he says.

No. Please. I want to go.

Not yet. We'll wait for it to get light. You'll feel better then.

Really? You think so.

Yes. I really do. So sit down.

I look at the black plastic.

Come on, he says. Just do it.

I look at it but I stay where I am, standing. My legs and stomach hurt. My thighs ache.

Come on, he says again, more softly now. You can at least sit down. What terrible thing is going to happen if you let yourself do that?

I look at his face again. I sit.

Upstairs in her cot, Katie had woken and was standing up rattling the bars and gasping out tears.

Maybe she'd seen the flames across the road. Maybe she'd heard the sound of next door's windows shattering, one after another. I listened to her scream for a moment and felt a prickle of panic, then I shut the sound from my mind while I got my thoughts straight. Downstairs, Iris was banging my mobile hard against the kitchen table.

Stop it! I yelled at her, as I bent forwards over the table to deal with another wave of pain. What are you doing?

The pepper mill got knocked over. It rolled very slowly to the edge of the table, then dropped to the floor. Peppercorns spilling and bouncing everywhere. We both looked but did nothing. The dog edged over and started sniffing at them. Iris banged the phone again.

For goodness' sake, I said. We need that phone and you're going to break it.

She looked at me. Her eyes were hard and scared.

But it's already broken, she said. Don't you ever listen?

That's what I've been trying to tell you. I can't even make it work to dial 999.

I grabbed the phone from her and I pressed dial and listened. Nothing. I tried punching buttons but nothing happened.

Jimmy was at my elbow.

We need to get the fire engines as well, he said.

Why? said Iris.

He was gazing at me. His face was white. He could hardly get the words out.

All the houses in the road! All the houses!

What about them? Iris said.

They're – they're catching on fire!

Iris stared at him.

They can't be, she said.

Well they are! Jimmy cried. Go and look out of the window if you think I'm fibbing.

I looked at Jimmy's small white face as another wave of pain went over me.

Go and get the cordless phone from my bedroom, I told him. Bring it here, fast.

I dropped to the floor on my hands and knees and the dog, surprised and already tiring of the peppercorns, skittered out of my way.

The air outside the kitchen window was turning thicker and greyer, like dusk but not like dusk. As if someone had stuck a lid on the world and screwed it shut. It was getting colder.

Put on some lights, I told Gloria, but I already knew what would happen when she flicked the switch – absolutely nothing.

* * *

Dawn comes. I had thought we were nowhere but it turns out we are on a road with shops and houses. Some are burned, but most aren't. There's a pound shop and a sign that says Iceland and another that says Fitness First. Also a nail shop and a betting shop and a chemist with its front smashed in, a couple of people lying dead on the ground in front of it.

Above us, the sky is an odd shade of red – almost brown in places. Everywhere, you can see smoke from all the fires that are burning. I think about the building where my children are. What if that has caught fire?

It's light now, I tell him. Can we go back?

Back?

To the place where you took the children.

He looks thoughtful.

You think you've already been there?

What?

You said back.

I tense for a second, thinking about this. Pictures turning over in my mind.

I don't know, I tell him at last. Is it in the City? Is it an office?

For a few quick seconds, I can almost see it. Empty corridors, windows that go down to the floor. A wide concrete terrace, a white dome. My heart speeds up. He looks embarrassed. As if he can see it too. He glances away from me.

Yes, he says. That's the place.

And have I been there?

He looks at me. He says nothing.

What? I say. Well, tell me. Have I or haven't I?

I look at his face. The slight chubbiness around his jaw. His dark eyes, dark lashes. The gash on his cheek.

He shrugs. His eyes are full of pain.

I don't know, he says. Maybe once.

Jimmy brought the upstairs phone, but of course it didn't work. There was pain on his face as he handed it to me. I stared at it for a moment. I couldn't think why I'd asked for it. Then I remembered.

Are you sure it's plugged in at the socket? I said, even though I already knew the answer. Iris went and checked and came back. She shivered and hugged herself as she spoke.

It's in.

What?

I said it's in.

Gloria was still flicking light switches on and off. Every light, flick, flick, on, off.

Stop it, I told her a little too harshly. Can't you see it's making no difference?

She gazed at me.

But I only want to make it be a bit light, she said in a whisper.

Me too, Jimmy started to moan. Can't you just get another light that works or something, Mum?

Can you both just shut up? Iris said as I gasped and leaned down over the kitchen table. Mummy's really hurting and she can't do anything except breathe right now.

She was right. It was all I could do. I wasn't even doing that very well. I tried to breathe, but my chest kept on wanting to empty itself and not take any air back in.

I tried to remember how it had been with the other births. I remembered the panic and the pain of Iris arriving. People shouting and running. I couldn't remember Gloria or Jimmy or Katie. I remembered the metal frame of a hospital bed,

Simon's hands, a chair with a green PVC cover, ripped so that the foam showed through – but hadn't Katie been born at home? I couldn't remember how it was, having a baby at home.

I tried to concentrate on the shape my own hands made as they gripped the edge of the wood. Sweat pricked my under-arms, my back. It poured off my face.

Iris was standing and rubbing my back like I'd told her to.

Aren't you worried about our house catching on fire? she whispered.

I shook my head.

You aren't? But why not?

Trust me. I just know it won't.

I felt her take this in. I knew from the way the pressure of her hand on my back lessened for a second or two, that she didn't believe me and she didn't trust me.

I'm worried that next door is just going to burn down completely, Jimmy said.

Then what will happen to Mrs Gregson? said Gloria. Will she just scream and run out into the street, do you think?

No, said Iris. If she did we'd hear her. And anyway, she would come round here.

Well, maybe she was out shopping or something? Jimmy said.

Iris stared at him. I could feel her hand trembling on my back.

She never goes out shopping. People do her shopping for her, because of her leg. And, I think all the shops will be on fire.

He looked at her carefully. You could see he was thinking about whether or not to ask her the next question. He decided not.

Well, I hope the cats escaped, he said.

*　*　*

208

The dog was drinking water – lapping and lapping it in a frantic way as if she knew it was her last. Upstairs, Katie was finally quiet. Maybe she'd given up and gone back to sleep.

My waves of pain had lessened slightly. Was it all slowing down? I didn't know if that was a good thing or a bad thing. I tried sitting on a chair. The towel between my legs was sodden. When I sat down, I felt more water seep out.

I looked around me. The room was so dark. The children's faces were a mass of shadows. I asked Iris to fetch me another bath towel and I told her where to find candles. Gloria came and stood in front of me with a roll of kitchen paper and I almost laughed. Jimmy whispered to me that he had matches in his bedroom. Two boxes of them.

I don't want to know why you had those, I told him. And you're not in trouble this time. But never again, OK? They're not for kids.

Never again. Never again. Another, worse wave of pain came then and I got up and bent over the table again. I gasped and waited for it to finish, but another followed straight after. Three or four more coming after that.

I tried to put my hand down to feel what was happening, but I couldn't get far before another wave swept me off. Again and again, I tried to remember the breathing but the pain kept getting in the way, gripping on to me and giving my lungs no space. Upstairs, Katie started crying again.

Oh God, I said. Oh God. Oh please, oh help me.

Jimmy made a sound, halfway between a scream and a sob.

I don't want you to die, Mummy, Jimmy said. His words flew around my face and I batted them away.

Oh God, I said again.

Iris went and got Katie and brought her downstairs. Katie

209

held out her arms and started crying, Mummy, Mummy, Mummy!

Get her away from me, I told Iris.

Where shall I put her?

I don't know. Anywhere. Put her anywhere.

Iris stared at me for a moment, then she thrust the towel at me. I pushed it away.

There are about six houses on fire across the road, I heard Iris say. Six houses. And I don't think anyone has called a fire engine, but I suppose their phones aren't working either.

She strapped Katie in her highchair and gave her some keys to play with and also the plastic beaker of milk, which she poured straight down her front in her hurry to drink it. She cried again.

Don't die, Mummy, Jimmy was saying, and I saw that he was holding his cuddly giraffe tight against his chest and really crying now. I don't want you to die.

I won't die, I told him. But I might need to scream soon, OK?

OK, he said. His face wobbled. I could see him thinking about how to control himself. Can me and Gloria go and watch TV?

How are you going to do that? Iris said. Don't you realise, there's no electricity?

What about the computer?

That won't work either.

Gloria put her head near mine. She lifted my hair so she could whisper in my ear. The tickle of her breath was like an extra pain.

Mummy, why did you put our toys in the car? Is it OK to go and get them now?

No, I said. Of course you can't!

When I thought about the car, I wondered what on earth my plan had been. What had I been doing? Where had I imagined I was going to take them all?

No, no, no! shouted Katie from her highchair.

The room bobbed in the candlelight. Outside, the snow was falling fast. The pain had its own rhythm now and I didn't care if I died or not, I was going to follow it. Beneath me I saw a dark, wide pool on the floor. Its edges were moving, creeping outwards. I didn't give it a second thought, but Iris gasped.

Is it blood? she said, but I was in my own world now and couldn't answer her.

We make our slow way back towards London Bridge. We stick to the smaller streets, icier, more deserted. The snow squeaks beneath our feet. Sometimes I almost slip and he has to help me, but on the whole I manage it alone. I make him walk a step or two ahead of me. He thinks it's so I can grab on to him if I need to, but it isn't that. It's so I can watch the back of his big dark coat, his hair.

We walk mostly in silence, but now and then he tries to tell me things.

Do you remember where you lived? he says.

I shake my head.

Your house was pretty. Roses all around the front door and you and Simon had knocked the two downstairs rooms into one.

Simon?

Your husband.

I think about this for a very long time. I feel that he's waiting for me to say something, but I say nothing.

Roses? I say at last.

Well, I think they were. You like roses?

I don't know. Not much, I don't think.

Well, you did. You grew vegetables too. Potatoes, beans and stuff. You even had a pond, with fish in it.

To eat?

He laughs.

No, of course not. Just, you know, goldfish.

Goldfish. I feel myself tense.

I wouldn't know how to grow vegetables, I tell him quickly.

Well you did, he says. You do.

In the middle of the road, a large dog lies on its side. Its black lips are pulled up around its teeth and its eyes are wide open.

Flies dance around it and I think it's a long time since I saw any flies. And then I realise. The air's been getting warmer.

We walk around the dog.

And did you go there? I ask him a moment later.

What? Go where?

To the – to our house.

He looks at the ground.

Yes, he says. Well, of course I did, yes.

You were our friend, then?

He looks at me.

I was your friend, yes. We go back quite a long way, you and me, Izzy.

Izzy? I say. My heart drops. I'm staring at him. He looks straight back at me.

That's your name. Short for Isobel. But no one ever calls you Isobel. You really don't remember your own name?

I think about the name and I think about the person called Isobel who was never called that, and I shake my head.

I remember my children, I tell him. I remember everything about them. But I don't remember myself.

Do you want to know what my name is? he asks me a bit later.

OK, I tell him, though the truth is I don't really care about it all that much.

I'm Matthew.

Matthew? – the name twists itself in and out of shape and then settles in my head like an ache. It's a nice name, I tell him.

He smiles.

You don't really think that.

I look at him.

Well, it's OK, I say.

Suddenly he leans forward. He stares at me. He touches my shoulder.

Oh, he says. Oh, Izzy, what is it? What's the matter?

I put my fingers to the corners of my eyes, try to take away the tears. I squeeze my eyes shut, but it doesn't help. More of them come falling out. I push his hand away.

Are you OK? he says.

I shake my head.

Izzy?

I don't know, I tell him. That's enough now. Leave me alone. I don't know.

On the floor, on my hands and knees, on the towels which Iris had spread out for me, I put my hand down to feel between my legs. My fingers touched something hard and hot and wet.

It wasn't a part of me – what was it? Was it the head? I waited for a moment. I blew out more air.

In another world, very far away now, I heard the children saying things, their voices coming and going like voices on the radio. I heard Jimmy whining that he wanted to go out to play in the snow.

Me too, I heard Gloria say.

I heard Iris objecting.

But we've already got our coats and hats on, I heard them say.

All the houses are burning down, said Iris, and then she added something else which I could not catch.

We promise we'll keep away, said Jimmy.

I heard Iris say something else then, in a ruder and crosser voice.

But what are we meant to do, I heard him reply, if we can't even watch TV?

Stop moaning, Iris told him then. Stop being such a stupid little baby. Don't you see that something really terrible has happened out there? No one's to even open the back door, do you hear? Mum would go crazy. You're staying right here, both of you.

I tried to raise my head, to check they were obeying Iris. Sweat trickled down the back of my neck. I saw that their coats were off, so maybe they were. I tried to speak, but my voice was swallowed up in a bubble of pain. My breaths were coming much too fast. But too fast for what?

I cried out. Iris rushed over to me.

What's happened? Gloria was asking her. What's the terrible thing?

Maybe she thought the terrible thing was what was happening

to me, but at that moment, the world decided to answer her. Outside there was a crash like thunder, only louder and closer than any thunder should be. You would think the sky had been ripped in two.

Gloria screamed and so did Katie, and the dog ran to the furthest corner of the room and sat there panting. From where I was I could see her sitting and staring at the wall. Saliva falling from her mouth.

I saw that Iris was struggling not to cry.

I wish Dad was here, she said in a shaky voice. And then I felt her glance at me, wondering if it was OK to say that.

I said nothing. More sweat fell out of my hair and ran down the back of my neck. I tried to hold on to myself. I held myself in one place, which was all I could do. I panted hard.

When this baby comes out, I told her, you're going to have to help me catch it and wrap it in the towel, OK?

Now Jimmy looked interested.

And what happens if she doesn't catch it?

I didn't answer him. I began to push.

We walk on through those streets towards the river. It seems to take a long time. Once or twice he tries to take my arm to stop me slipping, but I don't let him and I don't slip.

I went there, you know, he tells me. A few days after it happened.

I look up.

Went where?

To your house. Well – to where your house had been.

I stare at him.

It wasn't there?

The whole street burned down, Izzy.

But – then why did you go there?

He looks at the ground.

Why do you think I went there? I went everywhere.

I'm silent a moment, trying to work this out. I try to think about everything he's told me. The roses. The goldfish. The two rooms knocked into one. The woman called Isobel who is never called that.

Matthew? I say.

What? His face softens.

Do you mind if we don't talk about it any more right now?

OK, he touches my shoulder. That's nice, by the way.

What's nice?

Hearing you say my name like that.

We reach the river. The weather has definitely changed, there's no question about it now. It's warmer. It's lighter. A fog or a mist has come rolling in. It hangs just above everything, a cloud of wetness that you can feel on your hands, your face, your hair.

We walk on to the river until we're standing right in the middle of it. In the strange afternoon light, the ice is smooth and white as a cup of milk. I lick my lips.

In front of us, some dogs are fighting – a snarling, sliding ball of teeth and fur. We both turn our heads as a man speeds past us on a bicycle, grizzle-haired and wearing black clothes, ringing the bell and spraying us with water before the fog swallows him up again.

We both stare after him.

Was that real? I say.

He laughs. He thinks I'm joking. He gives me a careful look.

Do you know what was interesting, though? Did you notice the water?

What water?

As he went past. The spray. It means the ice is melting.

I look down at my feet. It's true – there are slick, shallow puddles all over the surface of the ice.

We walk on a moment, but then he stops and feels around in his pockets and I watch as he lights a cigarette and smokes it fast, holding it down by his thigh between puffs, looking around him as if someone might at any moment come and try to take it off him. He reminds me so much of someone and I can't think who it is. And then I can. It's the kid.

He breaks off then, head on one side. Looking at me. He smiles.

What? Haven't you ever seen anyone smoke before?

No, I tell him, it's not that.

What, then?

I don't know, I say. But can I ask you something?

He looks happy. He flicks the cigarette, ash lands on the ice. You know you can ask me anything you like.

The man who you say was my husband –

Simon.

Yes. Simon – I test the name aloud for a moment and decided it doesn't feel any more likely. Well, was he – I mean, were we happy together?

He looks at me, blows out smoke. He looks down at the cigarette, then back at my face.

Oh Izzy, he says.

What?

You're putting me in a very difficult position, asking me a question like that.

9

Arthur's bright, raw cries filled the kitchen. The dog shuffled herself under the table, terrified.

I tied the cord as tight as I could with Jimmy's shoelace and tried to get Iris to cut it with the kitchen scissors, but they weren't sharp enough and she was shaking so hard she was afraid she would hurt me or the baby, so in the end I did it myself.

Gloria screamed when the placenta slid out.

It's OK, I told her. That's just what comes out when you have a baby. There was one just like that when you were born too.

But not when I was born? Jimmy said.

You too, I said.

Oh yuck.

I told Iris to get a baking dish from the cupboard to put it in.

I don't want the dog trying to eat it, I told her. Though in fact the dog didn't look like she was capable of eating anything ever again. I'd never seen her so limp and ratty and scared.

I lifted the placenta into the dish because Iris didn't want to touch it, and she put it up on the counter. Then she pulled Katie out of the highchair, where she had got herself all slumped and grizzling, and we all went over and sat on the sofa, where I fed Arthur by candlelight.

For a while everyone was quiet. Just the sound of Arthur

218

sucking. Occasionally, still, the sound of glass breaking somewhere further down the road.

You have a new brother, I told them.

I hate him, Gloria said very quietly.

That's a horrible thing to say, said Iris.

You can't hate a thing that doesn't speak and is as small as
a monkey, Jimmy pointed out.

I looked at Arthur. Jimmy was right. He did look like a
monkey. A beautiful, perfect, adorable little monkey, with his
dusky black hair and flattened nose and folded-up limbs. A flush
of love made my heart speed up. I felt it in my cheeks, my
scalp, just behind my ears. The sweet excitement of a new baby.
I sighed with pleasure and I put my hand out and touched
Gloria's cheek, but she shivered and pulled away from me.

You're just tired, I told her.

Everyone was silent again. Jimmy was holding his giraffe
by its two front legs and twirling it round and round.

Can you stop doing that? Iris said to him.

Why?

Because it's really annoying me.

Jimmy carried on twirling.

He needs to do it. He needs to do his loop-the-loop, he said,
and then he thought about what he'd just said and he laughed.

Iris looked at me.

Mum?

What?

He's being annoying. Do something.

Try to be still for a bit, darling, I told Jimmy.

He stopped twirling.

I thought Arthur was asleep, but when I looked down he
was gazing into the distance with his big glinty monkey eyes.

He's just a few minutes old, Jimmy said. He'll never be this young again.

That's right, I said.

He thought for a moment.

If it wasn't pitch dark in daytime, and if there wasn't blood everywhere, and if next door hadn't burned down and maybe even killed Mrs Gregson, and if the TV was working, and if you hadn't just had a baby all on your own without Dad, this would be a perfectly normal kind of day, wouldn't it?

He finishes the cigarette and chucks it down on the ice. We are almost across the river now. Cannon Street is ahead of us, a creamy, blue-white line against the even whiter sky.

With every step we take, I feel a little stronger. I think of the building, with its long grey corridors, its huge wide windows, its snowy terraces.

I think I have been there, I tell him as we climb up some icy steps to what would once have been a road.

Been where?

To the building. The place where you took them. I think I know it. If you left me here right now, I think I could almost find it.

He gives me a long look.

I'm not going to leave you here, he says.

Do you know a girl called Sophy? I ask him moments later.

Sophy? Sophy who?

I don't know her other name. She has blonde hair. Very pretty. She's about fifteen.

He thinks about it.

There was a Sophy who used to babysit for you, he says.

I brighten as I realise that might be who I'm talking about.

Yes, I say. I think that's her.

Why? What about her? Have you seen her?

I try to think about Sophy. Her pale hands, coming out of Graham's jacket. A grey cardigan over her face. The rain coming down.

Yes, I say. I've seen her.

She seemed like a nice kid. Is she OK?

I hesitate.

I think so, I tell him. I'm not sure. I hope she is.

A few moments pass. He says nothing. I don't know what he's thinking. I'm thinking about all those names. Sophy and Simon and Matthew, and the woman who they never call Isobel.

Is she just the same? I ask him.

What? – he looks puzzled. Sophy?

No, I mean me. Am I the same as I was when you knew me?

He looks at me. His eyes are dark.

I recognise you, if that's what you mean.

No, that's not what I mean.

He sighs.

Well, all right, your mouth looks a bit swollen and there's a fucking awful bruise on your cheek. But if anything you look even more beautiful, especially with your hair all long and wild like that.

I feel myself flush. My hand flies to my cheek.

I wasn't talking about looks, I tell him.

He glances away.

I know you weren't, he says, and he sighs again. A long sigh. For a second he looks as if all the air has gone out of him.

You said it was OK to ask you questions, I remind him.

It is. It is OK.

Then what is it? What's the matter?

He says nothing. Finally he takes a breath.

What are you asking me to do, Izzy? Are you asking me to tell you what you used to be like? Or are you asking me to tell you how I used to feel about you?

The day, Arthur's birthday, rolled on. One o'clock came and so did two o'clock, three o'clock, and it did not get any lighter. We stayed in the house. We sat around. There was nothing else we could do.

Mummy? Gloria said.

Yes?

What are we waiting for?

Nothing, I told her. We're not waiting for anything.

So what's happening?

I don't know what's happening.

But — are we going to be OK?

I saw Jimmy watching my face.

That's enough questions for now, I told her.

We couldn't hear the fires burning any more, but the blackness outside remained as suffocating as ever and when Iris opened the back door to try to let the dog out, smoke and something else that wasn't smoke came in. The dog braced herself in the doorway and would not go. In the end, she peed on the mat.

Iris had a look of distress on her face.

It's awful, she said. There's nothing but snow everywhere and burned stuff. And the trees in the garden are all black.

What about Mrs Gregson's house? I said.

She gulped.

I tried to look. It just isn't really there any more.

I stared at her.

But what do you mean? What's there?

She bit her lip.

Just, I don't know, half a wall. Black stuff.

But could you see anything? Jimmy asked her. Did you see Mrs Gregson's dead body? Did you even see the cats?

Iris ignored him.

There's no sound of anyone anywhere in the road either. It's so weird and quiet. It feels like everyone has just gone away or died.

I looked down at Arthur. His face was so still that for a second or two I felt worried. Then his eyelid flickered. His mouth moved. I breathed again. I looked at Iris.

There must be someone out there, I told her. It isn't possible. Other people must be staying in their houses the way we are. We can't be the only ones.

Why didn't our house burn down as well? said Gloria, who'd been staring at Iris and listening with round, shocked eyes.

I don't know, I said.

She waited for me to say something else but I didn't have anything else to say, so I said nothing. We were all silent for a moment then. We watched Katie, who was sitting on the floor and leafing through a picture book which she was holding upside down. She realised we were all watching her and she looked up and grinned.

Butch! she said, lifting it up with such force that she almost tore a page.

Yes, I told her. Book.

Mum, Iris said to me at last, what do you think this is?

I looked at her. My mind was going round and round. Ever since Arthur had come out of me, I'd been feeling more and more unsteady.

This?

Yes. What is it? What's happening?

I held Arthur's warm damp weight against me. I put my lips on him. His head smelled of cheese.

I don't know, I said.

But do you think something bad's happened? Could it be the end of the world?

If it was really going to be the end of the world, Jimmy said, it would have been on the news.

Iris turned on him.

Shut up, Jimmy. This is serious, OK? I'm trying to ask Mum a really important question.

I reached out and took Jimmy's hand. I squeezed it. Then I looked at Iris, my anxious and speedy and clever Iris, who always worked everything out.

No, I said. Don't be silly. Of course it isn't.

But how do you know?

I don't know, I told her. I don't know anything for sure. But I just don't think it is.

You're not scared?

No, I said. I'm not scared.

She lifted her chin and she looked at me then, and I knew what the look meant. It meant she already knew the truth. That I was no use and I couldn't help her.

I'm scared, said Gloria.

I don't know if I am or not, said Jimmy.

Iris said nothing. She looked at them both for a moment and she looked like she was going to say something else, but she didn't. She went over to the window and she folded her arms and stood looking out at all that darkness.

*   *   *

We were cold. We were all so cold. Everyone shivering, everyone's teeth chattering. Katie's lips had turned quite blue. I told Iris to put another jumper on her. A jumper and a hat.

She'll never wear a hat, Iris told me, and sure enough she tore the hat off, wailing, and threw it on the floor.

I shouted at her from where I was stuck with Arthur on the sofa.

One more trick like that, I said, and you get a big hard smack.

She watched my face for a second or two and then she burst into loud upset tears.

Jimmy stared at me.

Mummy, he said. You don't smack babies.

I said nothing. I thought it was time Arthur had another feed, but he wouldn't do it. His mouth slipped off the nipple as if he didn't even know it was there. I cupped his small brittle head in my hand, touched his cheek. It felt cold. I drew him up to my breast again, tried to warm him against my own hot skin.

I was burning. My head was burning. My stomach and my legs hurt and my mouth tasted rough and sad, like old newspapers. I touched my face. My fingers slid around in the sweat.

Jimmy was sitting next to me and bouncing up and down. It was giving me a bad headache. I told him to stop it and be still. He gave one more bounce, then he looked at Arthur.

Are all new babies that funny colour? he said.

I looked at my baby.

What do you mean? What colour?

He shrugged so his shoulders touched his ears.

I don't know. He kind of looks like someone's coloured in his face with a felt-tip.

I tried to smile.

A felt-tip?

Yes, a grey one. A grey felt-tip.

I saw Iris watching me. Our eyes met for a second. She held my gaze and then she looked away.

I was hot but I knew the children needed to get warm.

You can't do anything about it, Jimmy said when I put my arms around him and tried to warm him up. There's absolutely nothing you can do.

Of course there is, I told him. Of course I can.

He gave me a sad look.

But what?

Don't worry, I told him. We'll get the room warm.

You're just saying that because you're really sick.

I stared at him.

I'm not sick, I said, but he just looked at me and said nothing.

I told Iris to look for firelighters in the cupboard behind the washing machine. She found them, but I couldn't remember if we had any wood, any coal. I didn't know where Simon would have put it. Jimmy found half a bag of kindling under the stairs, but there was nothing else.

Fetch some newspaper, I told him as I tried to keep Arthur tight and warm against me. I'm going to show you how to make a fire.

I know how to make a fire, he said, shivering all over with cold but now also with excitement.

No you don't, I told him. Not in real life you don't.

Gloria was staring at me. She was trembling. She looked empty and frightened.

What? I said. What is it, darling?

She said nothing. Her eyes were wide. I put out my hand

to her, patted the sofa. It was so cold you could think it was wet.

Come on, I said. Come and sit here with me.

She shook her head as if that was a terrible idea, and then she backed away from me as if I might grab her at any moment. She went to sit on the stairs with her chin on her knees.

I instructed Jimmy. I told him to pile up the kindling on top of the scrunched newspaper and crumble a firelighter on top of that and light it.

He looked astonished.

What? he said. With a match? You mean I'm allowed to do it all by myself?

I heard his concentrating breath as he stood back and watched the little flames dart into life. At the sound of the fire, the dog ran away to the kitchen. Jimmy sniffed at his fingers.

Smell that, he said to Iris. It's the loveliest smell, like petrol.

But what are we going to use for coal? Iris said, ignoring him.

Katie had fallen asleep on the floor by the sofa, her hat still off. I put Arthur down on the rug next to her. He startled for a second, splaying all ten of his fingers out like he'd had the most brilliant idea, then he drifted back down into sleep.

I tried to get up then. I tried to make my brain stand me up, but it didn't want to do it. The signal wasn't getting through. My legs felt like someone else's legs.

Finally, I gripped on to the arm of the sofa and I pushed. That was it. I was up. The other person's legs were hot and wet. Or maybe it was her heart, my heart. I could feel it pumping the liquid round my body and I wasn't at all sure it was going in the right direction.

The coffee table was made of some kind of lacquered pine. Simon's mother had given it to us. It was tiny, useless, ugly.

I picked it up and put it on the fire. For a second it seemed to stop the flames, but then they leaped up and embraced it, spat out some bright violet sparks.

Jimmy gasped.

We're burning the furniture!

It's all we've got, I said.

Oh my goodness, said Iris in a horrified voice. Oh, oh, Mummy, look!

She didn't mean the fire. She was staring at the sofa which was soaked dark with my blood.

Back on the other side of the river, towards Southwark, there's the sound of music. Laughter. Guitars and maybe a drum. Some singing. Flames bouncing on the ice. There's a smell of fat, of burning meat.

I remember Ted then. The night he came back drunk and we all walked to the river, looking for the party. And we never found it. But there was something else about that night – something that happened, or maybe didn't happen. Maybe it still will. It was to do with the kid. It was . . . I'm silent for a moment, trying to remember it.

He puts his head on one side.

What? he says. What are you thinking?

I was thinking about something that happened. And then I thought that maybe I got it wrong and it hasn't happened yet.

Maybe it's not the answer he wanted, because he looks disappointed. He rubs at his hair, takes a breath, looks away across the ice.

It probably did happen, he says.

You think so?

He turns back to me.

Well, what? You're saying you can look into the future?

I look at him. I don't have an answer to that.

I know what you're thinking, he says at last. You're thinking you just want to get back to the building, get back to your kids. And I'm just thinking that I would like to keep you here.

I don't say anything. Then I say, Why?

Why? – he looks at me and he doesn't smile. Why? Because I like being with you. I always did. Haven't you got it yet? Do you mind me saying that? Is it OK with you, if I tell you something that's true for once?

I listen to his words. I feel my face get hot.

I like you too, I tell him.

He shakes his head but he still looks unhappy. He swallows. Well, thank you, he says.

I keep my eyes on him. I look at his face, the crinkles at the corners of his eyes, the dark of his lashes, the way his hair sticks up slightly on one side. I look at the hollow parts of his cheeks, the little curve at the top of his lip, the line where his beard starts.

Actually, I say, can I ask you something?

He doesn't say anything. He waits.

Did we used to . . . did we once . . . I mean, were you my . . .?

He doesn't look at me.

Was I your what?

I don't know. You say I had a husband and so –

Have. You still have a husband. As far as I know.

But what was it, then? You and me, were we somehow . . .?

He looks like he might be about to say something, then he changes his mind. His face is tight.

There's no point in talking about it, Izzy.

Why? Why is there no point?

Because it's over, isn't it? So what is there to say?

I stare at him.

Why would you want to talk about it? he says. If you don't feel it now, if I have to tell you what happened and what you're supposed to feel, well really, what's the point?

I think about this.

But, I tell him, I don't have my husband any more.

You don't know that for sure. And anyway, whether Simon's still around or not, that makes no difference. It won't come back.

It?

His face is hard.

The feeling.

But, I say, struggling to find the right question to ask, did we feel things then?

I felt things, as you put it.

And me?

There's pain on his face.

Look at you, Izzy. Look at yourself. You don't remember a thing, do you? You don't even remember what you did a moment ago.

I do, I tell him quickly. I do remember.

What did you do?

I thought about you.

And before that?

I think I thought about you then as well.

He looks back across the ice towards the party.

Everything's melting, I say.

I know.

I go over to where he's standing. I go right up close. I put my hands on him – his chest, his stomach, his thighs. I push my hands under his coat.

He doesn't move. I look up at his black eyes and I touch his face. The line of blood – I touch the edge of it. I put the inside of my wrist against his hair. When he doesn't do anything to stop me, I put my lips against his. Very gently, I put my tongue on his top lip. Then the bottom one. I lick them both. They taste of ice. I press my lips against his. He groans.

Izzy. What are you doing?

I say nothing. I pull his mouth back to mine. He doesn't speak and he lets me do it, then he draws back and says it again, less gently.

What are you doing?

I don't know, I tell him.

He shuts his eyes. I take his hand.

Do you want to go and lie down somewhere? I say.

What?

Do you want to?

He steps away from me quickly. The sound he makes is terrible. He puts his head in his hands.

I stare at him. I think he's crying.

I thought you'd like it, I tell him. I thought . . .

He doesn't look at me. He doesn't look up. His head stays in his hands. I watch him and at first I feel helpless, stupid. But after a few moments, I work out what it is I need to do. I go over to him and very gently I put my hand on his head. No kissing. Nothing. Was this how it felt, loving him?

I'm not afraid of you, Matt, I tell him. I don't care what you think. I like you best when you're like this.

Still he doesn't look up. I don't need him to.

I lied to them. I told them it was normal. I explained that mothers always bleed for a bit after they have babies.

231

But that much blood? said Iris, still staring at the dark slick of wetness that had begun to drip on to the floor. I mean, going everywhere like that?

Yes, I told her. That much blood.

I told them we'd get a new sofa.

But when? said Jimmy, gazing at me, hands on hips, trying to catch me out.

When the shops are open, Iris told him in a steely voice.

But when will that be? What if they never open again? What if all the shops have burned down?

No one knows whether they've burned down or not, Iris said. And anyway, even if they have, someone will build more shops and we'll go shopping again.

That's my girl, I thought.

Gloria said nothing.

I got Iris to go upstairs and fetch me every towel she could find, as well as aspirin. She brought down temazepam by mistake. I'd forgotten we had temazepam. Good, I thought, I might treat myself to one of those later.

Iris, I said, you're a great nurse. I don't know what I'd do without you.

She gave me a look that was full of doubt, but even so, she looked pleased and she insisted on carrying Arthur around for a bit, to give me a break. He looked as small as the smallest black mouse, resting there on her shoulder. Every time I looked at him, he seemed smaller and more fragile and unlikely and further away.

That night we did not move. We all slept exactly where we were.

Excellent! said Jimmy, when I told him he didn't have to put on his pyjamas or clean his teeth or go up to bed. So we're just actually going to camp in front of the fire?

If you like, I said.

To keep the fire going, I'd added the wooden bread bin and a couple of chopping boards as well as some of Simon's golfing magazines. I was tempted to put his expensive bag and the fringed leather shoes on there too, but I didn't think Jimmy – who occasionally went to watch him play golf – would like that, and anyway, I worried it might make noxious fumes.

Are we just going to burn every single thing we possess? Jimmy asked me, eyeing the flames.

I smiled.

Why not? I said. But then, when I saw his devastated face – Of course not, Jims. That was just a joke. Of course not. Not really.

I looked around the room and felt suddenly brighter. With the little children and babies and firelight, and minus the blood, it could have been a scene from an old-fashioned Christmas card. My heart sailed upwards.

Well, isn't this nice? I said.

No one spoke. There was something a bit frightening about so many silent children, so I tried to encourage a bit of comment.

Is everyone warm? I asked them.

Iris glanced at Jimmy and I saw him look at her.

Kind of.

Are you having a good time?

Gloria gulped.

Not really, Jimmy said.

I touched my face. It felt damp and cold now. Even though I was burning. I'd put another bath towel between my legs and

I could tell that it was already soaking. It made a comical squelching sound when I moved. I thought how we would all probably laugh about this later. The thought made me wild and cheerful. And I looked down at Arthur, so still and sweet and peaceful in my lap and I thought how at least on that count I'd struck lucky. I didn't think I'd ever had such a well-behaved and easy newborn baby.

If it gets too hot, we'll open a window, I said.

Iris gave me a worried look.

What? I said. What's up with you now?

She shook her head and looked at the others, then she chewed on a nail.

The kids hadn't eaten for hours. Iris got some stuff from the larder and they ate hoops and beans spooned straight from the tin and they drank some milk. Then she took a torch and she and Gloria fetched pillows and duvets and blankets from upstairs.

I noticed that Gloria climbed the stairs after her and did everything she was told to do, but she did not speak. She moved in silence and in slow motion. She said nothing at all. Now I thought about it, she hadn't spoken a word for at least an hour or so.

What's the matter with Gloria? I asked Iris.

She glanced at me, trying to decide something.

She doesn't like the black outside, she said at last.

But none of us do, said Jimmy. It's horrible. And I'm not at all keen on the way everything keeps on bursting into flames.

Iris looked at him and then she looked at me. Her eyes were grave. She looked at us as if we were both fully signed-up members of the same mad team.

Yes, well Gloria really, really doesn't like it, she said.

The blood had stopped coming out of me, but I couldn't stop shaking and my teeth clattered together like the teeth of a cartoon character. I took a temazepam to deal with that. Then I showed Iris how to swaddle Arthur tightly in a towel and got her to lay him on the floor between two sofa cushions. He did not sleep, but lay awake, staring around him with his glinty monkey stare.

I picked up Katie and gave her a cuddle. She arched her back and struggled in my arms. Her fist hit my lip.

Naughty girl, I said, and I grabbed her fat wrist to pull her hand back down away from my face.

No! she said, still struggling.

Yes!

I held her all the tighter then and I shook her a little bit harder than I meant to, but I needed to show her who was in charge. She grizzled away, gazing at me with angry, worried eyes, then she stuck her fingers in her mouth and used them to comfort herself.

Just for the hell of it, I had a go at turning on my phone again. Then the lamp by the sofa. Then the television. Then the radio. Nothing. It was a fact. The world out there had fallen away.

I'm not at all well, I thought – then, quickly as it had come, I pushed the idea away. What did it matter, really? We were all here together, weren't we? That was the main thing. It was the only thing. I had all my children around me – even my brand-new little baby, my Arthur.

I felt suddenly sorry for Simon, wherever he was. Because he wasn't with his children and also because now he would never get back to the house and have the satisfaction of asserting his moral rights and reclaiming it as he'd intended. I wondered what Jock and his wife would think of that.

I realised I had no idea what time Arthur had been born. Was it lunchtime? Was it even today?

In the morning, I told the children as we fell into a strained and shivery kind of sleep, everything will be OK. In the morning, I'm sure it will be light.

On the street that looks out over the river, we come to a wall with a bench in front of it. The snow on the bench has all melted away and the wood's damp and bare. Then I notice the thing that's different from last time. On the piece of ground beneath the bench, some blades of grass are showing, coming up through the snow. The green is intense. We both stare at it as if it's a miracle.

I know what will happen next and it does. He sits down on the bench and he looks at me and, after one quick moment of thinking about it, I go and sit beside him. I am ready for this. I feel the slats move under us. And I feel it, too, as he puts his arm around me, and this time he's a man, fully grown, so his arm reaches properly around, his hand resting on my shoulder. I feel the rough of his coat sleeve, like last time. But this time, I can lean back for a moment against him.

We did this before, I tell him as my body caves into his shape.

He looks at me.

Your memory's better than mine, he says, and then he realises what he just said and he laughs.

I try to laugh too, but the sound that comes out of me is not quite like laughter.

He pushes some hair out of my face, but it falls straight back. In the end, I push it away myself. I want to say other things to him, but I don't. I don't speak at all. I sit there. I tell myself that I can even feel his heart thumping, and for a few seconds I almost think I can.

We sit there together for a long time. I don't know how long. Mist is still rolling off the river, so thick that you can no longer see over to the other side. After a while I yawn. He asks me if I'm sleepy.

No, I say.

I'm sorry, he says at last.

You've got nothing to apologise for.

Come here – he puts his hand on my face and turns it gently towards him, but I shake my head and I pull back.

I'm feeling too wound up, I tell him.

He gives me a long look.

Don't be wound up.

Or too sad. I don't know which.

He gives up and settles me back against his shoulder. He says nothing. After a moment, he puts his hand on my knee, squeezes it gently. I put my hand on his. I like the feeling of his fingers under mine.

Don't be sad, he says.

I don't know where I want to be, I tell him. Right now, I mean. I just can't stop thinking about them. Even though I know there's no point.

I know, he says. That's all right. I know you can't.

In a minute we'll go back there, won't we?

He nods.

Don't worry. We'll go and find your children.

I hope they're all OK.

They're OK.

You don't know that. You don't have to say it just to make me feel better.

None of it was your fault, you know, he says at last.

None of what?

What happened between us. I just want you to know that. What I mean is, it was all me. It was entirely me. I knew exactly what I was doing.

I twist my head to look at him. I try to think about what he might have done. I can think of nothing. When I try to remember him, my heart always lifts. To me he is blameless.

That night in the taxi, he says. Remember? I wanted it. I started it.

I say nothing. I snatch another glance at his face. Arthur's face. His dark head. The dark, dark eyes.

But it was me too, I tell him. I knew what I was doing as well. I knew what would happen and I still did it. I put my head in your lap. I shouldn't have done that.

He smiles. He touches my head again, ruffles my hair.

You don't remember do you? You were just obeying orders. I told you to put it there.

I think about this. I'm trying to remember if it's true. All I remember about the end of that evening is that I did not want to leave his side. I didn't care what happened next, just as long as it kept on happening.

I was drunk, I say.

We both were. But not too drunk. We were just about drunk enough.

Drunk enough for what?

To know what we wanted.

* * *

238

All the same, he says, when you did it, when you ended it, I honestly didn't know what to do. I didn't know how I would go on.

I say nothing. I wait. From somewhere above or behind us there's a drip-dripping sound. Ice melting.

I just wanted you to know that, Izzy, he says. How I felt about it. Not to make you even more sad, but so that you know – because I never got a chance to tell you.

I feel myself twist against him.

Even though, he continues, I'm sure you were right to do it. I'm sure you did the right thing.

You are?

I wipe my face on my coat sleeve. Then I have to wipe it again. When he answers, his arm is still around me, it's even tighter, and his voice is hoarse.

No, he says. All right. All right, I'm not.

At last, he takes his arm away. I can see that he's upset. His eyes are shaky and sad. I tell him to go ahead and have one.

What?

A cigarette. It's OK. I don't mind.

Without smiling, without thinking, he pulls them out of his pocket. He's not looking at me as he lights it. He frowns, his eyes on the flame.

I went after you, you know – that night.

What, the night of the taxi?

No, not that one – he looks at me for a second. No, I mean that last night. The last time I ever saw you. I know I shouldn't have, but I did. And I think I would probably have caught up with you, except – he breaks off to inhale – there was this bloody bomb scare. Somewhere on Bishopsgate. Police, loads of vans. They cordoned off the whole street. They wouldn't let me through.

I shut my eyes for a second, but he doesn't notice. He laughs to himself. He shakes his head.

So instead I went back up to the office. I couldn't think what else to do. I just went up there and sat alone in the dark and I cried. Maybe because you'd just been there, I could almost make myself think that you still were. All I wanted was to carry on feeling close to you. But I cried like a fucking baby, Izzy. I don't think I've ever cried so much in my whole life.

I hold my breath. I think of him sitting there on the edge of the desk in the dark. The tearing sobs.

When I speak, my voice is a whisper. Even I can hardly hear it.

And then? I say.

And then?

What happened after that?

He shakes his head.

Oh Izzy. Don't make me tell you the rest.

I shut my eyes. I see his hand, picking up his phone and keys. The brief rattle before they go in his pocket. The sensation of him passing very close to me, suddenly almost hopeful, hurrying.

What happened? I say. When you left the office? Where were you going?

He is silent for a long moment. He sucks at his cigarette. He looks at the ground. I glance at the side of his face. His hollowed-out cheeks. The terrible grey colour of his skin.

Matt? I say, suddenly afraid.

He turns and looks at me. He chucks his cigarette down. His eyes are dark.

I thought I'd go and find you anyway. Fuck the consequences. I thought I might even confront Simon, have it out with him – you know, in a calm and adult way. I wasn't going to be unreasonable. Christ, I must have been deranged that evening, because I even told myself I might be able to make him understand.

I stare at him.

Understand?

That I loved his woman. That I'd always loved her. That I needed her more than he did. That I was more likely to make her happy. Yes, it was stupid and selfish of me, and it would have been a very bad idea, wouldn't it? It's not what you wanted, I know that. I'm very glad it didn't happen. I'm very glad, Izzy, that I didn't get a chance to do it.

I say nothing. He wipes his hands across his mouth, looks at the ground.

Do you hate me now? he says.

I look at his beautiful face, full of sorrow and shadow.

I could never hate you, I tell him.

He draws me to him then. He draws me close. He puts his lips against my hair, my cheek. And I know how they're going to feel before they even touch me, and I'm right, they do – icy cold.

As he speaks, his lips are in my hair. My tears are falling on his coat. A tear rolls off the rough weave of his sleeve.

Matt –

I was trying to call you, as I went across the street. But your phone was off and I didn't want to leave a message. So I started to send you a text, not saying anything really, only to tell you that nothing had changed, that I still loved you.

He looks at me and he shakes his head.

It was all my fault, I wasn't even drunk, for God's sake, but

I was in some kind of a crazy fucking dream . . . I felt nothing, no pain. I knew I was entirely to blame. And you know the worst thing? I could imagine what your face would be like, when you heard. That was the part I really couldn't bear. All I remember thinking, over and over, was that. How the hell am I going to stop Izzy finding out about this?

I stand up. The snow beneath my feet has turned to slush. I can smell soil, earth, air, ripeness. My boots are quite wet. The earth is coming back to life. When I finally speak, I can't look at him. I look instead at the smallest, greenest blade of grass. It looks so hopeful. It gives me courage.

I had a baby, Matt.

What?

I had a baby. A little boy. I had a little boy.

10

I was right. In the morning it was perfectly light. The dark-ness had dissolved, or at least it had receded, and though the sky was still a strange, harsh colour, a sharp acid light pene-trated the glass of the windows, illuminating the room. You could see it all now, the things you needed to see and even the things you'd rather not.

I saw all the chaos and mess that had crept in and taken over the room. The sputtered-out candles. The blackened things in the fireplace. The bloody towels all over the floor. The half-eaten tins of spaghetti hoops. The dark sodden place that was the sofa. The pale, untroubled faces of my children as they lay sleeping, waiting for whatever this day would bring.

But Arthur. He didn't look at all happy. Maybe I'd never seen him in this savage light of day before, but his skin was yellower than it should have been and his eyes had lost their glint and his breathing didn't seem right.

I wondered if he was hungry. I tried to remember when he'd last let me feed him. Last night? Yesterday? I wondered if he was cold. The room was freezing. We're going to have to find some more things to burn, I thought, and I remembered Simon's study upstairs full of big fat expensive art books that he never looked at, and I smiled.

Arthur gave a little moan – it wasn't a cry. I almost wished it had been a cry. It seemed all wrong that he wasn't crying. I realised I hadn't heard him cry in a lot of hours.

I tried putting him on my breast but he gasped for breath and spat the nipple out. His face was naughty but I knew it wasn't naughtiness.

He's ill, I thought. He's definitely ill. And I'm not too good myself either.

I picked up my phone, stared at the buttons. I realised I was shaking. I tried to get a grip on myself. I tried to tell myself the facts: that the phone was dead, but I should not panic. What good would panicking do? It certainly would not fix anything. I tried to bring myself back – to think about normal people, normal reactions, normal things.

I thought about what Simon would do, what Simon would say, the different ways in which he would stride in and take charge. Even without the phone, I knew he would have done something – gone out to find someone, demanded someone do something, explained very calmly and clearly what he thought might be going on.

But I reminded myself that he wasn't here. That he wasn't going to be here. So I took some big breaths and tried to think calmly about my situation, ran through the kinds of things I would have said if the phone worked. I'm all alone with my four children and their new brother. And there's something wrong. The birth wasn't good. I think I might be haemorrhaging. I'm feeling very sick. I'm afraid of what will happen if I can't look after them. My eldest is only nine years old. I think I might need some help . . .

I began to cry. My crying woke Iris.

Luckily my eldest daughter was the only one who woke. The others were all still sleeping soundly, a row of little white mice under their duvets and blankets. This suited me. I told her what to do.

You're going to put on your boots and coat and go out into the street and try to find someone, I said.

She looked at Arthur, who was making a bad face and moving his tiny arms and hands in a kind of grey slow motion. Then she looked back at me. She bit on a nail.

But find who? she said. And anyway, how will I walk? The snow looks so thick. I think it'll come right up over my boots.

I tried to think. Iris was no fool. It was important to tell her something convincing.

You'll have to take a shovel with you, I told her. There's one near the back door, just behind the bins. Use it to clear a path in front of you as you go.

She stared at me. I knew what she was thinking — that I'd forgotten that she was only nine years old. Going out into the snow with a shovel was a grown man's job — the kind of thing her dad would have done. I tried to ignore the look in her eyes.

Walk along the street, I said. See which houses are still standing — there must be some that haven't burned down. And bang on the doors as hard as you can. If there's anyone in there, they must be able to hear you.

Iris blinked.

What if they're all dead? she said.

Then try going round the corner to Sophy's house. See if she or her mum are there.

Her eyes widened.

I'm really worried that they won't be there.

What makes you think that they won't?

I don't know. I just have this bad feeling.

Well then, I said – I'd had enough of her negative attitude now. Just stand in the middle of the street and shout for help as loudly as you can.

Iris scrunched up her face. She was studying me carefully, listening hard to these instructions, but I could tell she was also looking for something. She was looking for the thing that I'd left out, or not thought of, or even wilfully ignored. She was looking for the one thing in all of this that wasn't quite right.

I waited. My face was slick with sweat. I could smell my own skin, my own blood. I felt impatient but I had to admit her next question was a very sensible one.

But what exactly am I asking for? If I find someone, then what am I asking them to do? To take you and Arthur to the hospital?

I looked out of the window. The sun was still bright but the sky was the colour of tarnished metal – dead and pointless.

That's right, I said. I need a lift to the hospital. Arthur needs help. All of us, we all need some help.

She kept on staring at me. I knew that she didn't want to go. She was trying to think of a reason. She knew there was still something wrong.

But the snow – what if there aren't any cars driving?

I blinked.

Someone will think of something, I told her.

But what if I can't find anyone?

I touched her skinny shoulder. I thought that really she ought to try to humour me now.

See what you can do, I said. Just do the best you can, OK? And I turned away, back to Arthur.

*   *   *

We are almost at the building now, Matt and I. The streets are light, dusty, bathed in early-evening sunshine. Even the shadows are alive with the stored-up heat of the day.

Shops are closing and bars and restaurants are filling up. Men stand on the pavements with their suit jackets off, smoking and talking and drinking beer. Women in tight dark skirts and high heels, hair swinging, briefcases under their arms, laughing loudly and talking on their phones. By the Ship Tavern someone has put a piece of chipboard on the pavement and a kid who can't be more than twelve years old is tap-dancing on it, alone and vigorously happy, without any music, hoping that coins will be thrown down into a plastic cup, which they are.

We walk along next to each other. We're not touching, not out here, but we might as well be. I'm so completely alert to the fact of his presence. His tall shape. The way the jacket of his suit swings open. The way he's pulled off his tie and stuffed it in his pocket. The hair, just long enough to touch his shoulders. The fact that I don't think he has shaved for a couple of days.

He feels me looking at him and he turns.

You OK?

I don't know.

That means no.

I bite my lip. I say nothing.

Izzy –

I suppose I'm scared.

Don't be.

Not of you. Of me. Of us.

You're scared of us?

That's about it. Yes.

He's silent a moment. A man is squeezing oranges outside

Liverpool Street Station. People rushing down the steps and escalator to get to the trains.

Izzy, he says, you've nothing to be scared of.

I say nothing.

Honestly. Do you believe me? I love you.

Don't say that.

Why can't I say it?

Another silence.

OK, I won't say it. But that doesn't stop it being true. In fact, I don't think it's ever been more true than right here, right now at this particular moment.

He stops to pick up an evening paper. By the kiosk, something awkward happens. We run into Sophy.

Oh, I say, Sophy! Where are you off to?

She looks at me quickly, breathless. Notices that I'm blushing. Also that I'm not with Simon but with Matthew, whom I think she's met maybe once before, at our house. She keeps her eyes on me, pulls a face.

Dance class, she says. Don't laugh. I haven't done it before, but you get the first three for free.

I'm not laughing, I tell her. You remember Matthew?

She nods and smiles at him and for a brief moment none of us says anything. I feel myself take a little step away from him. For all she knows, we are just friends. I ask her where the class is.

Oh, just around the corner from here. I'm just so sick of being such a blob, she adds. I want to get fit.

You're not a blob, I tell her. You're curvy in all the right places.

All the same, she says, wrinkling her nose.

Well, good for you, I tell her.

I take a breath – I really can't think of anything else to say. Matthew comes to the rescue.

I'm taking Izzy to see where I work, he says.

He laughs and so does Sophy.

OK, she says, holding her head on one side and waiting, as if there might be more to it. Which there is.

None of us says anything for about five seconds. Then she asks me if Jimmy's better.

Just about, I tell her. But he might have to have his tonsils out now.

Oh, poor thing, she says, with real feeling.

Yes, I say. It's one thing after another with him. He just seems to attract accidents and operations – which of course, deep down, he loves.

We all laugh.

I ask her then if by any chance she's free to babysit tomorrow night. I see him looking quickly and carefully away into the distance when I ask her this, as if it's not his business, not his life. She says she can't see any reason why not, but can she text me later on tonight or tomorrow morning? I say that's fine.

Well, bye then, she says, as she slings a nylon rucksack over her shoulder. Have fun.

We watch her go, bright trainers moving fast over the sunlit pavement. Matthew looks at me and feels around in his pocket for a cigarette. He frowns.

Was that difficult? he says.

I shrug.

Why should it be difficult?

I just wondered.

It was fine, I tell him. Sophy's a good girl.

OK, he says.

He threads his fingers through mine for a quick and daring second and then he lets them go again. Then he lights the cigarette and smokes it fast, but throws it down half finished, impatient to get in the building.

We go in through the main entrance and are hit by the cool of the air conditioning. A marble floor. A jazzy little fountain. Tall shiny pots with plants in them. A bank of white-leather and steel sofas for people to wait on. Newspapers and magazines spread out. I stand for a moment, looking around me.

What? he says.

I shake my head.

Nothing, I say.

The doorman is missing a front tooth. He makes a joke with Matthew that I don't understand. Maybe it's about working too hard. Most people are leaving the place, after all, not arriving. Suit after suit pouring out through the turnstile and into sunny Bishopsgate.

We have to wait for a lift because they're all so full of people coming out. One of the men who steps out is about to walk right past us, but then he turns and grabs Matthew's arm, punches it in a lively, jokey way.

He has on a suit and trainers but no tie, and his eyes are glittery and a little wired, his hair dark and springy. Under his arm, a copy of *The Times*. In his hand, an orange. I don't catch what he says. He looks at me and so does Matthew.

Izzy, this is Graham, Matthew says. Works on my floor. He's a total waster. Don't be taken in by him. Don't listen to a word he says.

The man called Graham laughs and looks at me, then his eyes change and he looks away.

Don't listen, or don't believe? he says.

Ha! Both, says Matthew. Neither.

Graham claps Matthew on the shoulder and then he looks at me again, more carefully this time, and he smiles. Then he stops smiling. His whole face alters.

What did you say your name was?

Izzy.

He hesitates, staring at me.

Have we met before?

I feel my cheeks get hot.

I don't think so, I say.

Your name doesn't ring any bells, he says. But your face — you're not a friend of Caroline's are you?

Caroline?

My wife. Well, soon-to-be ex.

I shake my head. I'd been worried he was going to say that he knew Simon. I try to smile.

I don't think I know any Carolines, I tell him.

But he seems unconvinced. He continues to stare at me.

You know where I think I've seen you? he says, chucking the orange from hand to hand as if he's about to juggle with it. I think I've seen you here.

Here?

Yes. In this building.

I laugh.

I don't think so, I tell him.

Not possible, Matthew says. Seriously, she's a very old friend of mine and she's never been here before. I'm about to give her a tour.

But Graham looks serious. He bites his lip and looks straight into my eyes.

I'm not making it up, he says. Honestly. Your face – oh God, I'll get it in a moment.

Matthew glances away across the foyer.

You're doing a pretty pathetic job of chatting her up, he says. And we're missing all the fucking lifts now.

Graham steps away. His eyes still on me.

OK, he says. OK, mate. Sorry. Go on, off you go.

He throws the orange up in the air and catches it one more time. But as we step into the lift he turns back suddenly and puts his hand on the door to stop it closing. His eyes are intent, serious.

Right here in this building, he says. I don't believe you've never been here because I've seen you. I'm not in any doubt at all. I know I have.

I take a breath. Matthew touches me somewhere.

Christ, he says, and his voice is only half warm. Come off it, Graham. What are you saying? That she's lying?

Graham keeps his eyes on me, and I feel my blood start to jump.

I don't know what I'm saying.

Matthew shakes his head.

Well, whatever it is, just leave it, OK?

I push a strand of hair behind my ears, fiddle with my earring. I look straight at Graham. I keep my eyes steady.

I've never been here, I tell him. I think I'd know if I'd been here, wouldn't I?

He says nothing. He carries on looking at me. But someone else gets in the lift then and we have to let the doors close. We go shooting up through the shaft, seventeen floors up, to the floor where Matthew works.

*　*　*

The room felt even colder once Iris had gone. I tried doing normal mother things. I tried walking around with Arthur drooped over my shoulder, the way you're supposed to do with small babies, but he wouldn't do it. He kept on shuddering and falling backwards, his head at an awkward angle, not behaving how newborns ought to behave. And my own head was hurting too now, a dull, throbbing ache. The more I walked, the more it throbbed.

So in the end I sat back down on the sticky sofa and laid him on his back across my knees, and I tried to take a proper, responsible look at him.

Arthur, I whispered, keeping my voice low because I didn't want to wake the others. Arthur.

His breath was coming fast and his eyes were wide open, but they weren't really looking at me. The change was subtle. Only a mother would have seen it. But it was as if he'd decided not to be there in quite the same definite way as he'd been there before.

I squeezed my eyes shut and felt a tear slide out.

Arthur, I whispered, where are you? Come back to me.

I thought I heard him whimper, but I wasn't sure. I knew that I could have imagined it. Nothing else changed.

I saw that there was a little bit of sick at the corner of his mouth. Had he been sick when I last fed him? Would I have noticed? I struggled to remember but my mind was dark.

That was the problem, I thought, as I wiped at his mouth with the cloth – he was starving. He was going to starve. The same went for all my children. I had failed them, all of them. I knew very well that the mission I'd sent Iris on was hopeless. What was I thinking? A nine-year-old girl, out on those streets. I was a bad mother, a reckless and irresponsible person. Because the world had gone, hadn't it, and it wasn't coming back in a hurry. The world was freezing, it was on fire, it was nothing, it had gone.

I sat and watched my baby. I didn't think he could see me now. Sometimes his breath seemed to be there and sometimes it didn't.

Arthur, I said again, louder. Arthur!

Katie stirred for a moment, smacking her lips together and beginning one quick little half-cry, before going back to nuzzling her raggy in her nest among the cushions on the floor.

Iris had been gone a long time. I didn't know how long, I just knew it was long. I sat there and did the only thing I could do. Kept watching my baby.

I tried to tell him things. I told him how much I loved him, how much we all did, what a special baby he was, how very much he was wanted – how sorry I was that he'd been born into such a difficult and frightening and upside-down world.

You came on the very worst day, I told him, as the tears began to fall down my face again. Honestly, it's not always like this – you should see us normally. Your brother and sisters, they're just the best, they're so funny and lively, they're such good kids. And we have a garden with a fish pond and a climbing frame – when you're older, you'll appreciate those things . . .

Arthur?

His face had relaxed, or maybe it had hardened. I was shaking all over, but I tried to keep my legs together so he would not slide off my knees. I held him there. I touched his soft cheek.

You're safe, I said. Don't worry about anything. I'll take care of you. Nothing can happen to you. I'm your mum. You're safe with me.

And maybe he'd listened to me, because he seemed to have settled. He was very still. I felt still too – still and calm. I gazed at him in silence for a while.

I thought I should really tell him about his father – about how much I'd loved him, how we'd loved each other all our lives and could never really tear ourselves away from each other, how proud and happy he would have been to see and know and hold his baby son. I wanted to tell him all of this – and for a quick second or two, I thought I could actually see it. Matt's beautiful face – his hands, his arms and fingers, the laughing way he would have scooped this child up, and then the trembly, disbelieving way he would have gazed and gazed at him.

I wanted to tell him all of this but I didn't manage it, because when I tried, when I thought about that hungry-happy look of Matt's, no words would come, only more tears.

So instead I touched the top of his small monkey head, where the black hair swirled in all directions as though it didn't know where it should go next. And I touched my lips on his tiny nose. And I put a finger in the clenched nub of his hand.

And I thought about how so much of him was new and undecided. How none of it was his fault. It never had been. So much of him was just waiting to see what would happen next.

That morning, the next morning, when Simon took a phone call from someone who knew us both, and then sat me down and told me he had some very bad news indeed about Matthew, I sat there, with my hands folded in my lap, as calm and still as anything. I know that I kept my eyes on Simon's face as he took me through it, and I know that I listened very carefully to the words, as if they were a set of instructions, which in a way I suppose they were.

Accident. Very late last night. Near his office. Instant. No one's fault. Would not have known. Nothing they could do.

Then I thanked Simon for telling me in such a kind and careful way and, even though he said he wanted to get me a brandy, a temazepam, put me to bed, hold me in his arms, I got up, and without taking anything with me – keys, bag, phone – I walked right out of the house.

I walked away in no particular direction, down the road, past the place where the builders were singing along to the radio and throwing scaffolding into a lorry, round the corner, past the newsagent's and the launderette and through the little gate that always squeaked, and across the playing field where they did the football on Saturdays.

I walked fast. The sun was on my face. It was a bright, warm morning. I went past people and dogs. The grass was dry. I saw a hedge with pink roses in it, a yellow frill at the centre of each. I saw a dead animal, on its back with some worms moving in it. I saw a little boy, crying loudly because his mum wouldn't let him go in the pushchair.

When I thought I'd walked far enough, I picked a bench, just any bench, a random bench where no one else happened to be, and I sat down on it. I felt its slats give slightly under my weight. The wood was rough and warm. It was kind. And, keeping my hands on that warm, kind wood, so that I wouldn't fly off or slip or come to some other kind of unimagined harm, I sat there and I repeated Simon's words over and over several times, until I was certain I had them properly and securely in my head.

Accident. Very late last night. Near his office. Instant. No one's fault. Would not have known. Nothing they could do.

They weren't true, of course, the words. I didn't believe them, not for one single moment. But they were all I had left of Matt now and so I clung to them. Or not quite all, because there was also that little spark of something that, even at that very moment, as I sat on the bench, was doing everything in its power to put down blood roots inside me, beyond me, around me, clinging on.

Arthur.

When Iris came back, when she stumbled in the door all pink and ragged from the freezing outside air, I think she was crying quietly to herself.

I didn't get anywhere, she said. I didn't manage to do anything. There just wasn't anything I could do. There's no one there. There are no people.

She stopped and she stared at me. She stared at Arthur. Her eyes were dark.

What's the matter? she said.

I tried not to look at her. I shook my head. She rushed to get closer.

What's happened? What's wrong with him?

I lifted my head. Felt my chin wobble.

I don't know, I said. Nothing. I'm sure he's OK. I don't know.

Iris stared at me. There was terror on her face. She said nothing. I waited for her to say something but she didn't. She just carried on standing there and staring at us both and saying nothing.

Another tear slid down my cheek. It landed on Arthur's little arm. It was uncovered. Who had uncovered it? I pulled the blanket up to keep him warm.

Iris took another step towards me. I didn't think I'd ever seen her look so afraid and unhappy.

What are you going to do? she whispered.

I shook my head.

I don't know, I told her.

I waited. And then I said something else. At first I couldn't hear what it was, the other thing I said. And then I could. I heard it. It was: Help me.

His office is huge – empty and bright, quiet apart from the faint hum of the air conditioner. The glass of the windows going right down to the floor. A corner room, so you can see everything – the cluttered city skyline, the dome of St Paul's, bathed in evening sunshine.

I sit in the big chair. I want to find out for the first and last time what it's like to sit where he sits, to see what he sees, to feel the things that he might feel.

I know that he's watching me. Even if I didn't know it, I'd still know.

I look at his dark screen, the power off, but alive and somehow alarming because it belongs to him. I place a finger on the keyboard. Lay my hands on his cool desk. Pick up a pencil, turn it around and hold it in the palm of my hand, where it sticks for a second. I put it up to my face, smell it. I slide open a drawer – noiseless, clean, not much in it really – slide it shut again.

He sees me doing all these things. He says nothing. I say nothing. He stays on the other side of the room. He folds his arms and leans against the wall. He never takes his eyes off me. He keeps on looking. I feel it everywhere in my body, his look. Shoulders, wrists, elbows, thighs.

On the desk are some papers, a magnet with paperclips stuck to it and, in a thick glass frame, a photo of some blond children.

A girl and a boy, bright T-shirts, sweet, eager faces. I pick it up.

My sister's kids, he says. Holly's the eldest, she's a nurse. The little one on the left, Ted, is coming here to do work experience in a few weeks. He's a bit bigger than that now, of course.

I put the photo back exactly where it was. He comes over then and stands very close to me. Very close but not touching any part of me. I breathe in the air between us, around us.

What are we doing? I whisper. He places two fingers on my bare neck and I shiver.

Well, he says, his voice staying low to match mine, we can either go out and find a bar, get a drink . . .

I look at his eyes.

Or?

Or, if we go two floors up from here, there's a place where we can be entirely alone and see the whole city spread out before us.

I smile.

I know, I say.

You know?

I mean that one. Let's do that one.

All the children were awake now and they all knew what had happened to Arthur. Iris had told them. She told them he'd died.

Jimmy looked amazed, impressed even.

Completely dead? You mean that's the end of him now?

Iris shuddered.

The end of him. What a horrible thing to say.

But you mean he won't ever come back to being alive, not even if he has an operation or if the doctor comes?

Iris hugged herself. I noticed that she couldn't stop shaking. Even her eyes were shaking.

He's dead, she said. Don't you know what dead means? Dead isn't a thing that suddenly changes.

Jimmy looked at me. I could see he was thinking hard. His face was white.

We're not going to die, are we?

I tried to say no, but I found I could not speak. I kept my eyes on him. I shook my head.

Don't talk to Mum, Iris told him. Just don't say anything. You've got to leave her alone for a bit. She can't talk to you right now.

Jimmy scowled.

Why?

What do you mean, why?

Why can't she talk?

Why do you think?

Jimmy ignored Iris's last question. He looked hard at Arthur's small body.

I wish he was alive, he said. Because I thought at least he would be fun when he got bigger. But I'm quite glad as well that he's dead.

Iris gasped.

What? Why are you glad?

Jimmy blinked. He looked at me. Like Iris, he was shivering.

Because at least we know what happened to him. And we don't know what's going to happen to us, do we?

At the sound of his words, something swam up in my throat and I gripped the sofa for a moment. When I recovered my balance, I laid Arthur on a cushion on the floor and tucked a blanket round him. Now that I saw him properly – his whole body too thin and his face the colour of pee – I almost laughed. How could I ever have thought he was a well baby?

From the very first moment I gave birth to him, as I'd squeezed him out, the odds had been stacked right against him, hadn't they? And Jimmy was right. We didn't know what was going to happen to us. We had no idea. But Arthur knew. It had already happened – the worst had happened and he was safe now. At least he was out of it. He wasn't waiting for the next thing.

Light blazed in through the window but the room was colder than ever. I asked Iris what the light was and she said that several cars parked in the road were blazing. She hadn't even managed to get to the end of the street. So many of the houses in the street were on fire. She said that at one point she'd glanced back down the road at our house and panicked because she thought she saw long flames coming out of the upstairs window.

But you didn't, did you? said Jimmy.

No, she said. I didn't.

Baby! Baby! – laughed Katie, and she hurled her beaker at the TV. Milk dribbled down the blank grey screen. She gazed at it and then she chuckled again. No one picked the beaker up.

Jimmy took hold of my hand and patted it.

Don't worry, he said. She's not laughing about Arthur. But she's maybe just a tiny little bit glad to be the youngest again.

Iris looked at him, a kind of disgust on her face. She was crying. She was the only one.

That's a terrible thing to say, Jimmy. And you're just making it up. You've no idea whether she feels that or not.

He gave her an uncertain look.

Stop bossing me, he said.

Iris sucked on one of her fingers. She'd bitten it so viciously it was bleeding. Every time she took it out of her mouth a bright new jewel of blood appeared.

I just can't believe it, she said through her sobs. I can't believe our brother has actually died and no one's doing anything.

I put my arm around her, tried to gather her close. I looked at Gloria, who hadn't said a word for hours now. I didn't know what I was going to do about Gloria, but I knew I would have to do something. I would have to do something about all of them in the end. They were relying on me. I was their mum.

Don't worry, I told Iris. I'm right here with you and I will do something.

As I spoke the words, they sounded like the words of a song, brave and believable in their way. Maybe Iris thought they sounded good too, because she leaned against me. She didn't look at me. She gave a last little sob.

But what, Mummy? What will you do?

I have a plan, I told her. That, too, could have been the title of a song.

I have a plan. I touched my hand to my forehead. It was icy, damp still. Outside, the sky was the colour of ash and the snow kept on falling.

We don't take the lift. Instead we walk up two flights of concrete stairs, our two pairs of feet echoing, then out into a quiet, wide, carpeted corridor, past a couple of locked office doors. I don't look at the doors. No one else is around. Just the faraway sound of someone hoovering. A snatch of music from a radio.

In the corridor, he puts a hand out behind him to take mine, and as soon as I'm joined to him like that, I feel a little less sad and shaky. Something snaps and lifts inside me. I let it.

Trust me, he says. I know what you're thinking, but it's going to be worth it.

He doesn't know what I'm thinking.

He pushes a heavy metal fire door and suddenly there we are, out on that big, empty corner terrace. That smooth grey concrete, a wall and a metal railing all around.

I stare at the city spread out beneath and around us, lazy and soft in the evening sunshine. You can see as far as St Paul's on one side and what I imagine is Whitechapel on the other. Barbican, Spitalfields, Holborn.

Above us, the gulls. Screaming and lifting and dropping on the warm evening air. The chalk line of half a dozen aeroplanes tracing their way through the sky.

He looks at me. I feel him looking at me and for a moment I can't speak. I can't do anything. I don't know what he wants me to say.

What? he says.

Nothing. Just – it's strange, I suppose.

What's strange?

This – being here.

Being here or being alone together?

Yes.

Which?

The second one. I've never been alone with you –

You have.

I think of the loud, dark bars we've been in. The taxis. The one time that we took a risk and kissed each other in the park.

I haven't. Not really. Not completely alone like this. Not without anyone else around at all. Or at least, not since we were kids.

Oh well, he says. Kids. That doesn't count.

I don't look at him. I shut my eyes. I let the building hold me.

It did count, I tell him. When we were kids, I mean. I promise you – for me it did count.

He waits. I feel him watching me. I feel the space. The silence. The possibility. I wish I didn't keep avoiding his eyes. I wish I didn't love him. I'm dizzy with all the things I wish.

I don't know what else to say, I tell him at last.

He smiles. Then he walks over to me and he touches my cheek. His hands go to my neck.

That's it, he says. That's enough. You don't have to say anything else.

It was true. I hadn't lied. I did have a plan. I told them we were going to make some biscuits.

Iris frowned at me.

But we can't cook. There's no electricity, remember? How are you going to make the oven work?

I saw Gloria watching me carefully to see what I would have to say about this. I took a breath and it came back out white. The air in the room was freezing. Now and then I thought I smelled burning, but it had to be in my own mixed-up head. My ribs and stomach hurt. My heart was clammy. I knew I was still bleeding. I didn't know how much longer I could be like this – upright, bright, alive.

Not cooked biscuits, I said, in the tight and magical voice I used when I told them stories. These are special biscuits.

Straightaway, they all adjusted their faces to match my tone. They put on their bedtime-story faces. They couldn't help it. Even Katie. Even, slightly, Iris. Wide-eyed and waiting.

Are they the sort that don't even need cooking? Jimmy said. He rubbed his nose with a grubby hand.

That's right, I told him. Well done. That's the sort.

OK, he said, rubbing his nose again.

Shouldn't we wash our hands? said Iris, glancing at Jimmy's, which were now somewhere down in his trousers. I tried to think. I knew I didn't have the strength to go through the whole thing of soap and hands and towels at the sink.

Not today, I said.

But why not?

I had a brief moment of dizziness. I stepped backwards, then forwards again.

Iris, I said, just go with me on this, OK?

She said nothing. She scowled and bit a nail, then, remembering she shouldn't be doing it, she wiped it on her jeans.

Very slowly, because I was so weak, I opened every kitchen cupboard and I got out what we had, put it on the counter. I could only lift one thing at a time, but I knew the children thought I was doing it on purpose – spinning it out, making a drama of it.

The dog saw that food was going to be involved and got up, yawned, stretched, came over. Half a pack of chocolate digestives, the one on top slightly soft and stale. An unopened box of Jaffa Cakes. Two fig rolls. Some mini-packs of Jammie Dodgers.

Aren't those supposed to be for packed lunches? Iris pointed out in a shaky voice.

I looked at her and she looked at me and I watched her face change as she worked it out. Rules didn't count any more. They were over and done with, probably for ever. I felt suddenly sorry for her then, and I did my best to make it easier.

Today is special, I told her. Today we're making works of art.

Works of art? And then we're going to eat the art? Jimmy said, getting the hang of it with his usual energy.

That's right, I told him. We're going to gobble up the works of art!

Katie laughed loudly. Not because she understood but because she knew I was doing my funny voice. I pinched her tummy and she laughed again. Her night-time nappy hadn't been changed and I noticed there was a pale pool of liquid under her highchair, but she didn't seem to mind. Good old Katie.

I found some years-old glacé cherries and also a pack of malted milk biscuits, the sort with the cows on.

Oh, not those. They're boring, Jimmy objected.

Ah, I said. But we need some boring biscuits as building blocks, you see.

Jimmy nodded as if he'd already thought of that.

On the counter was some butter. I told Iris to get icing sugar and vanilla essence if there was any.

For butter cream? she said, her voice lighting up a little, because she couldn't help it – in her heart she really loved cooking.

Yup, I told her, as I steadied myself on the counter and sweat pricked my hair. That's the glue. Butter cream is going to be the glue.

The glue for the art? said Jimmy.

You've got the right idea, my love.

Ten out of ten for knowing it? he said, an unhappy little smile on his face.

Ten out of ten, I said.

* * *

I lie on top of him, every part of me pressed against every part of him.

The air's still warm, but the sun is creeping away over the concrete, fast disappearing, leaving nothing but shadow behind it. His face now in sun, now in darkness. The light going. The day going.

I never thought we'd do this, he says.

I know. I didn't think we would either.

You think we shouldn't have done it?

No, I say. No.

No, we shouldn't have done it? Or no, you think it's OK?

I think it's OK — I take a breath and I lift my head to look at him. I'm very happy to have done it.

Me too, he says quietly.

I put my head back down on him.

Right now, I'm just very happy, I say.

You are?

Yes. I'm not thinking any further ahead than this moment. And at this moment, I feel happy.

I feel him stroking my cheek. My ear.

I just don't know how it happened, he says then.

What, you mean just now? This?

I feel him swallow.

No, I mean all of it. These last months. And before, actually. Everything. Our whole lives. Us.

I'm silent. I can feel my own heart beating. Or maybe it's his.

I didn't mean to fall in love with you, I tell him at last.

He laughs and I feel it, the laugh, vibrating in my chest.

I know you didn't. Ha! Never has a truer thing been said. You didn't even used to like me.

What are you saying? Of course I liked you. I've always liked you.

I feel him laugh again.

Oh come on, Izzy, not when we were kids, you didn't. In fact I think you really hated me. Remember the time you pushed me down the stairs?

For a moment I'm silent, remembering this.

I didn't mean to do that.

Yes, you did. You absolutely did. Don't you dare deny it.

I got into big trouble for it.

Rightly so, he says, kissing me.

Well, you were the strangest child. You never smiled. Or at least you never smiled at me.

I was shy of you, Izzy. I just couldn't handle it. Try and remember that in the future, will you? If a boy doesn't smile, if he ignores you, if he can't look you in the eye, it almost certainly means he likes you too much.

I think about this. I remember him then – Matthew as a kid. Lifting his eyes to mine, then looking away again.

And you had a beetle called Arthur, I tell him. Who on earth names an insect Arthur?

Arthur! I remember Arthur. Well, I like that name. It's a noble name. It suited the beetle anyway.

So, if you ever have kids, that's what you'll name them?

What? Arthur, Arthur and Arthur?

No, I say more quietly. Just Arthur.

He's silent a moment. We both are. I slide my hands under his head, feel the weight of him, his skull, the warmth of his bones. I kiss him once on the mouth, then once more. He lets me do it. Then he pulls my face back down and makes me do it again. Lifting us back out of the unhappy place.

All the same, I tell him, you were a strange kid. I never understood how you could spend so much time grubbing around with insects and animals.

He sighs.

Like I said, you hated me.

Not hate. Of course not hate. But –

But what?

Well, you were ever so slightly unappealing.

This time his laugh is bitter.

I still am, he says.

No you're not, I tell him. Not to me anyway – not even slightly. No way. Every single thing about you – I can't begin to tell you how many things – you are completely appealing to me.

He's silent for a moment.

You know that I mean it, I tell him.

I know, he says.

He touches my nose. Runs his finger from the top of it along to the tip.

You're my oldest friend, he says then. My dearest friend. And my only love. How can we just turn our backs on this? Why can't we just go on knowing each other?

I swallow. I say nothing.

Seriously, Izzy. It's a serious question. Answer me.

But I don't answer him. Instead I see my kids' tired little faces. Jimmy going on about something or other. Iris frowning and biting her fingers. I see Gloria and Katie sitting together and sticking bright foam animals on the side of the bath, content and serious-faced, without any idea that life can change shape in an instant. I say nothing.

He knows what I'm thinking.

269

I could make a really serious promise not to love you.

No, you couldn't.

You're right. I couldn't.

And I can't either. I can't do it. Not any more. I can't not love you, Matt.

He's silent a moment.

Maybe we could meet up just occasionally to talk about it?

Talk about what?

About how we're going to manage to stay away from each other. Though now I think of it, occasionally wouldn't be enough. Maybe we could do it weekly, or perhaps every other day would be better, or maybe even –

I start to laugh and feel my eyes fill up. I put my head down on him. I wipe my eyes on his shirt. I put my hand on his mouth.

Stop talking, I tell him.

He obeys. Silence.

You know what the deal is, I tell him and he says nothing, because he does.

We lie together and do nothing. I feel his hand moving up and down my back. After a while it stops.

Oh, I whisper. Don't stop.

He continues. I close my eyes.

You're going to break my heart, Izzy, he says at last.

I don't look at him. I turn my head to the side, still resting on his chest.

You are, you know.

I don't want to. I don't want to break your heart.

Well, you're going to.

I don't want to.

You will. You know you will.

I shut my eyes.

Don't tell me I know things. I don't know anything, I say.

A gull alights on the railing and looks at us, yellow-eyed and interested, head twisted to one side.

Fuck off, he says. Go on. Shoo. Go away.

The gull stays.

I feel my phone vibrate and reach for it. Lift it, look at it. Simon. I put it back.

You need to get it? he says.

I shake my head.

Really? You can if you need to. Talk to him, if it makes you feel –

I put my head down on him again, shut my eyes.

When each child had made their own work of art – Jaffas and Dodgers and shards of crumbling digestive held together with slabs of butter cream – I said that I was going to judge the competition.

The competition? But that's not fair! Jimmy said. You never said it was a competition.

I only just decided, didn't I?

He stuck his bottom lip out and kicked the kitchen counter hard.

It's not fair, he said again.

But, I said, as I felt another clot of blood slip out of me, would it really have changed the way you made your biscuit, Jims?

He didn't say anything. He gave the kitchen counter another hefty kick.

Any bad behaviour and you'll be disqualified, I said.

Katie was singing to herself and hanging sideways out of her highchair, oblivious, but Iris and Gloria were staring at me. Gloria had only half finished making her biscuit before giving up and trying to cram part of it into her mouth. I'd had to put my hand on her small cold one.

Not yet, I'd told her, even though she'd already had the cherry. The eating part comes later.

Why can't she eat it? Jimmy said.

Just because.

Gloria made a little circle with her fingers and looked at me through it.

Why are you doing that? I asked her.

She said nothing. She continued to look at me.

She's spying on you, Jimmy said.

Yes, said Iris. She's suspicious. She's wondering what you're up to.

I looked at her and I flushed. Then I went over to the dark, bloodstained sofa and felt around under the cushions. Where had I hidden them? I knew I'd put them somewhere.

Arthur was still lying there on his cushion on the floor and even though I knew he was in a happy place and well out of it, still the sight of his perfectly lifeless body gave me a quick snag of pain.

I love you, I whispered to him, making sure to be quiet enough that no one else would hear. I love you and it's all going to be OK. I have a plan.

The pills were part of the plan. I found them at last.

See these little white sweeties? I told the children, continuing in my special magical storytelling voice. These are the prizes – and everyone gets one. Two if your biscuit is particularly good.

272

Jimmy automatically reached out a hand – I knew he would take anything I gave him – but Iris was staring at me.

Those? But those are just aspirin, she said.

I held the temazepam up out of Jimmy's reach.

They're not, actually, I told her. They're something much nicer than aspirin. They're good for you and we're going to stick a couple of them in every biscuit. Really good people can have three.

Her face darkened with worry.

And then we have to eat them? But are they OK for children? I mean should Katie have them?

Katie will be fine with them, I said.

I put my two arms on the concrete and I look down at his face, trying to take it in. The precise beauty of him. The ideal spacing of his eyes, his nose. The sheer, exact brilliance of his mouth. He looks back at me.

Izzy, he says.

What?

What are you doing?

I pause. I search around for it.

I'm making a study of you. A serious, scientific study.

He keeps his eyes on me. They don't move.

Why?

So I can remember you.

He carries on looking at me. His eyes. My eyes. It feels like touching. A little flicker of something starts to move inside me.

Oh, I say, suddenly in pain. It won't stay.

What won't stay?

The picture of you. I can't keep it. I can't put you enough into my head.

He keeps staring at me, says nothing.

I was trying to take something from you, I tell him. I wanted to steal something of you and put it into me.

His eyes remain on mine for a second, then he turns away.

Don't say that, he says.

OK.

I mean it.

OK. I know you do.

Anyway, you already have me, he says. Look. What's here? Nothing. It's all gone. There's nothing here at all. You took it long ago, Izzy. It's all right there, inside of you.

I rest my head on him again, on his body, on the place where I think his heart might be. And maybe I sleep, because when I next open my eyes, the air is a whole different shade of velvet. Oh, I think, we're still here.

What are we going to do? he says at last.

Do?

The word jolts me out of where I was. It jolts me out of here and into there.

Yes. Oh Izzy, what am I going to do with you?

I stay where I am. I try to think.

I'm here, I tell him.

I know you are, he says. Right now you're here. But I don't think I can do this.

Do what?

I love you, Izzy. I just do – I love you. I don't think I can do what we talked about. I think I need you. After all these years. I don't see how I can let you go.

* * *

I stuck two temazepam in each biscuit. I wanted to be on the safe side. I thought about having one myself, but then it struck me that I was going to need to stay alert for quite a bit longer than the children, so I didn't.

Jimmy ate his straightaway.

Yum, he said, as he wiped the crumbs from his mouth. I think I definitely won the competition. Mine was the best.

He slipped down off his stool and went to the fridge and poured himself some milk. Drank it. Wiped his mouth again on a tea towel, just like I always told him not to. Outside, the sun was trying to come out, even though the sky was darker than ever. You could clearly see several feet of snow outside and at the far end of the garden, beyond the pond, tiny flames licked the bottom of the shed.

Gloria held on to the kitchen counter and rocked backwards and forwards on her stool, her legs hanging down like the tentacles of some silent sea creature. She picked her biscuit apart, holding it in her fingers and examining it while eating it a mouthful at a time.

I saw that one of the pills had dropped off the biscuit and on to the counter, a blob of butter cream sticking to it. I picked it up and blew on it and popped it in her mouth, and she gazed at me and I thought for a moment that she would spit it out again, but she didn't. She swallowed.

Good girl, I said, and I felt like pulling her on to my knee and hugging her so hard that she'd giggle and gasp for breath, but she didn't look like she wanted me to, so I didn't.

Katie was making a big old mess with her biscuit. She'd thrown the cherry on the floor and was bashing her fist into the rest. It was going to be hard to make sure she ate both of her pills. I stared at her for a quick and horrible moment, confused, and briefly all my strength and resolution fell away. Then I collected myself.

I'll come back to her later, I thought.

I realised I should try to get a couple of pills into the dog as well. Easy, I thought. I slipped her a piece of digestive with a pill butter-creamed on to it, but she ate the biscuit in a very slow and careful way, licking the cream off first and then holding the biscuit in her mouth as though she was chomping on something very hot.

Then, just when she'd finally swallowed the last bit down and I thought I'd got away with it, out popped the pill, clean and whole and white.

Fucking animal, I thought. I got a piece of cheese instead. It worked. She was so greedy for cheese, that dog, she forgot about all of her suspicions and swallowed it whole.

Iris licked at her biscuit and looked at me.

What? I said.

I don't like this.

You don't like the biscuit?

No. The whole thing. I don't like it. I don't like the cooking without an oven or the stupid competition or the way you keep talking in a strange voice and seem kind of happy and excited about everything even though Arthur's dead before he even had a chance to live. And I don't want to eat any of your aspirins, either, she added.

I tried to stay very calm. I knew I needed to be strong for her. I looked at my hands on the crumb-sprinkled table. Was it my imagination or were they the wrong colour? I looked at Iris.

I told you, darling. It's not aspirin.

She bit her lip.

All the same, it's medicine and I don't want to eat it.

I sighed.

Iris, sweetheart, I said. I'm only trying to make things better for everyone. It's really hard if you won't trust me. Please trust me. Please help me.

She stared at me. Her eyes were not helpful.

I love you so much, I said.

It was true. Even now I felt a raw little pain in the pit of my belly, which I knew was the dread I'd had right from the very first moment I ever held her against me – dark and keen and warm as Arthur, as all of them – that I could never keep her safe enough.

She said nothing.

I didn't want this to happen either, I told her.

She lifted her head. Her eyes were purple and splotchy from all the crying.

But Mum, she said, where's Dad?

I tried to think. None of the answers I could think of sounded right.

Does he even know you've had the baby?

Of course he doesn't. You know I have no way of getting hold of him. How could he possibly know?

She looked at me carefully.

But if he did, he'd come, right?

I thought of Simon then. The genuine kindness with which he'd tried to get me through the shock of Matthew's death. The electrically bad moment when I admitted that I was expecting Arthur. The long, hard silences in our bedroom at night.

Iris was still watching my face.

I'm sure he would, I said.

*   *   *

After the second time, it's like I can't stop feeling him. Rings and rings of excitement going right through me, each one smaller and tighter and brighter than the last. Maybe they'll go on for ever, I think. Maybe that's what I'll always have of him, just this delicious, rolling brightness, echoing on and on through me.

It's like a bell, I say.

What's like a bell?

Nothing. Me. I'm rocking and singing inside like a bell.

Iso-bel?

That's a really terrible joke.

But then I can't help it – I laugh. I take his wrist in my hand and he tries to grip on to me, but I don't let him. I turn it around so I can see his watch.

How much time is left?

His eyes are closed.

As much as you want, he says.

I mean what time do we have to go from here?

Any time. No time. We can stay all night if we want to.

I can't stay all night.

I know you can't. I'm just saying.

But – we won't get locked out up here or anything?

I'd like to get locked out here. It would please me very much. I could spend all night doing things to you – days and nights, I could spend months. Summer would turn to autumn and winter would come – we'd be out here in the ice and snow and the gales, just stuck here lying on top of each other . . .

I shiver. Suck in a quick, terrified breath.

To stop him talking, I kiss his face. I kiss his mouth, his nose,

his eyelids, then back to his mouth again. A long kiss. He takes
over the kiss. He pulls me in.

Don't go, he says.

The terrace is cool now, entirely in shadow. The sky is the
colour of ink. The air smells of the river – dirt, wet, salt, bones.
I shiver again.

I've been here before, I tell him.

I wait for him to say something, but he doesn't. He says
nothing. I wonder if he knows. Maybe he does know, because
he shivers too and he reaches out and pulls me closer.

Don't go, he says again. Please, Izzy. I feel like all we've
ever done, all our lives, is say goodbye. But this time I just need
a little bit longer. Don't start saying goodbye before we've even
begun.

Iris ate the biscuit in the end. She didn't do it because she wanted
to. She did it to please me, because she found it hard, in the
end, to disobey me, her mum – because she felt that she should
be a good girl and do as she was told. That was the worst part.
That she did it because, deep in her heart, she was a good girl.
A good and responsible girl. I knew when it came to it, that
would be the worst part, the worst thing, and I was right, it
was.

As she finally swallowed the last mouthfuls down, it took
all my strength not to cry out and shake her and make her sick.
She saw me watching her. She must have seen my face.

What? she mouthed.

Nothing, I told her as my heart turned right over. I love you.

She stared at me for a second. Her watchful little face.

Me too, she said.

What?

I love you too.

I touched her head, then turned away from her quickly.

It was impossible to get Katie to eat her biscuit. Nothing I tried seemed to work. She just wasn't having it. Her cheeks were bright red now, glazed with tears and snot, and she seemed very unhappy indeed. There was no way I was getting anything down that child.

Does it really matter if she doesn't eat it? Iris mumbled over and over again.

The pill was working now and her eyes were huge and trippy, her voice wobbling. She trudged around in tight circles, unable to decide where to put herself. It was painful to see her. It made me want to cry. Jimmy and Gloria had already lain themselves down like good children. Why on earth couldn't Iris do the same?

I looked at her and I didn't answer the question. She glanced at Katie.

I think it's her nappy, she muttered.

Iris was usually right about Katie. So I tried changing her, even though it took all my strength, getting her over to the table and laying her on it and getting the heavy, pee-soaked nappy off her, dropping it on the floor and wrapping a clean one round her.

She kicked and she cried.

As I fastened the tapes, I saw that she was red and chafed in lots of places from sitting too long in her own wet. I felt a quick flash of guilt, but there was no way I was going to get myself up those stairs to fetch her nappy cream.

By the time I'd finished changing her, everyone was properly out for the count. Jimmy in Simon's saggy old chair by the TV, sideways on, his small foot in their grey socks slung over the arm, his giraffe dropped on the floor. Gloria in a heap on the floor quite close to Arthur.

And Iris, who had finally drifted to a standstill at the foot of the stairs, one hand still on the banister, where she'd been on her way up to the bathroom to fetch her baby sister some of that cream.

We stand together on Camomile Street. The sun has gone now, but the air's still warm. The bars are noisy. I can smell beer, trees, bus fumes. Far away, the sound of sirens.

If I turned and looked back, behind me, I could still see the building, looming up at the end of the street, dark glass towering over everything. I don't turn.

He looks at me. I know that, despite the fact that his heart is ready to burst, he wants a cigarette.

Have one, I say.

What?

You can smoke. Go on. It's OK.

He looks upset, confused.

I can't, he says. But at the same time that he shakes his head, he's already feeling in his pockets. He lights it swiftly and looks at me, dragging the smoke in like it's oxygen. His face is dark.

It's very hard not to touch you, he says.

My phone buzzes. A text. I look at it.

Who is it?

Sophy, I tell him. It's only Sophy.

Can she do it?

I look up at him in surprise. I know he's not even slightly interested.

Tomorrow, you mean? Yes.

What is it? What are you going to?

Simon has a thing. A work thing.

His face falls.

Oh.

He takes two more vicious puffs of the cigarette, then he puts it out.

Come here, he says.

He pulls me into the shadows. I think he's going to kiss me then, start up the kissing all over again, and that will be the end of us, of all our resolutions, the end of everything, because I don't think I could go away from him then – but he doesn't. He doesn't kiss me. Instead he holds me very close against him. Our faces don't touch. We don't speak. We stay very still.

What are you doing? he says after a few seconds have passed.

Nothing, I tell him, as my tears fall into his shirt. I'm just trying to remember the feeling.

What feeling?

This – what it feels like – being loved.

He holds me away from him for a moment, so he can look in my face.

You're allowed to change your mind about this, he says.

I gaze at him. I can't speak. I shake my head.

Not just now. I don't mean tonight. I mean any time. Nothing will change, not for me it won't.

Don't say that, I tell him.

It's the truth.

It's not true, I tell him. You're just saying it. Things change. People change. It's right that they do. They should change. They always do change.

I might change, but my feelings about you won't.

You can't know that. How can you know it? You can't possibly know it.

I can. I can know it. Ever since I was a kid –

I don't believe you.

Try me.

Seriously, Matt . . .

I stop for a moment, confused. All our lives we have argued like this. I take a step away from him. He looks at me.

You're going? he says.

Yes.

There's a silence. It wants me to fill it by turning and walking away. I'm about to do it. I will do it. I'm about to. My legs might do it, but my eyes won't let me. I keep on looking at him standing there.

What are you going to do? I ask him.

Do?

Yes. Now. What will you do?

He shrugs. His mouth is trembling.

Fuck knows. I don't care. What does it matter? I might go back to the office for a bit.

And do what?

Nothing. Sit there. Feel sorry for myself. Cry. Think about you.

I look at him.

This is unbearable, he says.

Yes.

Finally, he is the one – he does it. He puts a hand on my cheek. I turn my head to kiss his finger, but it's already been pulled away – it's gone. He takes a single step backwards, away from me. He's trying to smile, but his eyes are doing something else. I can't look at his eyes.

OK, he says. OK. Take care, Izzy.

And I do the next bit. I do it myself. I turn and I walk away. It's easy, I think. Far easier than I imagined. It's just a question of taking some steps. One step at a time, one foot in front of another. And then another and another, until it's so many of those footsteps that the distance between us is beyond repair and I'm completely gone from him and that's it, I'm gone, I'm no longer there, I'm lost.

I don't look back. I walk away through those warm and dusty streets, still filled with people shouting and laughing and having their drinks, with the buses and the taxis and the sirens that are screaming even louder now.

On Bishopsgate, police vans are blocking the street, tape, uniforms everywhere. A suspected bomb, someone says. People are being asked to cross the street. I walk fast. I don't care where I go.

Not here, lady, a man shouts at me. You need to cross over. We're clearing the area.

Sirens. More vans arriving. A fire engine too.

I turn and go in another direction, any direction. People are shouting. I don't feel safe. and I don't want to feel safe, I don't know where I am or where I'm going – I don't think I ever will again. I don't care what happens next. My life is nothing. I don't have a plan.

Maybe I should have a plan.

Maybe I shouldn't be surprised, when, many minutes or maybe it is hours or even a whole lifetime later, I find myself back in that same blue darkness, my last surviving child in my arms, fires still burning, thick snow all around me, and even more of it coming down now, faster and harder, falling, falling, on Camomile Street.

I did the dog first. The dog was easy. She was lying on her side. You could barely see her breathing to start with. I just put the cushion on her head and I sat on it for a moment. It was quicker than I thought it would be. Easy. She didn't even whimper.

But when I got up and took the cushion off, I jumped hard – because her front leg started fidgeting, as if she was chasing rabbits in a dream. But it must have been a muscle spasm, because her breath had stopped and her tongue was out and it was clear from the emptied way she lay there that she was dead.

The dog was dead. It was a fact. I thought about how furious Jimmy would have been. With me. How the tears would have fallen down his face. The lecture he would have given me.

Dogs trust you, he'd have said. They trust you completely. Just because they don't go attacking you with guns and knives doesn't mean you should creep up and kill them.

I shut his voice out of my head and I went over to Gloria.

She was on her side on the floor and her head was back, her chin up, her small, pale face pointing across the rug to where Arthur still lay. She still had butter cream on her fingers, a trace of biscuit crumbs around her mouth. Her eyelids were a violet colour, shadowy.

Gloria. She didn't look like the rest of them. She never had. She didn't look like me and she didn't look like Simon. She was a fairy child. If you believed in changelings, then you'd say she was one. One of them. Not one of us – and certainly not mine to play this game with. She never had been.

I thought about how she'd gone silent, all the words emptied out of her, and I shivered. Had she seen what was coming?

I took her fingers and I kissed them, breathed in the warm smell. I couldn't go near her face. I couldn't put my face near hers. I had to look away at the blank TV screen as I took a breath and put the cushion over her face and held it there.

I hadn't thought I was crying, but I must have been, because, as I turned my head back, so many tears came falling on to the cushion, plopping on to the velvet and then rolling off, salt falling into my fingers, my wrists wet with them.

Gloria didn't struggle, she didn't do anything, but I thought I felt a little gasp of surprise come out from under the cushion. I also thought I saw two or three of the small fingers I had kissed clench themselves, but so very briefly and gently that I couldn't be sure.

When she'd been still for a while, I took the cushion away – only to see that her face continued to move, her mouth working away, soundless, her eyes still open and alive, gazing at me. I put the cushion back and held it there. I held it for a long time. I didn't take any chances. When I finally took it away, her face was the same colour as her eyelids, her lips were blue. There was no question.

I was shaking. Every part of me moving all on its own. I got up and walked into the kitchen and I bent over the sink, my arms on the draining board. Nothing came out. I waited. My body would not be still. My shaking arms made a cup and a bowl fall over. The bowl rolled around and around on the floor but it did not break. It still had butter cream in it. I looked away quickly.

I told myself I could stop right there, that I did not have to finish the job, but I knew it was a lie. I saw blood on the kitchen floor under me.

I'm dying, I told myself.

I didn't know if that was a lie or not.

I thought Jimmy would be the hardest, but no. Darling Jims. He always was a good sleeper, but the pills had knocked him right out. As I pressed down on his small face, I felt nothing, heard nothing, maybe the smallest sigh, but that was all.

I couldn't believe it was so quick. I waited and waited even though I sensed he was gone.

I was his mum and he trusted me. Though in some ways he was a boy who questioned absolutely everything, still you would have to admit that he accepted everything too. It was a happy balance. He would probably have grown up to be a good person, lively and content and satisfied. He liked this life, this world. It excited him. I had given it to him and I felt terrible to be the one to take it away from him.

When I'd done Jimmy, I dragged another chair over and I sat with him for a while. I did not know what I had done. I stared at him. I looked at his face, as he sagged there with his legs slopping over the arm of the chair. I laid my head back against the chair. The room went round. I lifted my head again and opened my eyes hard and steadied myself. I got up slowly, my blood was everywhere. I bent and picked up the giraffe and put it in his arms. The giraffe eyed me happily. I looked away.

I could hear some raw sharp cries coming from somewhere – the sound of a person in real distress. It took about three minutes for me to realise that the person was me.

By the time I went over to Iris I was sobbing and sobbing. I could not get my breath. I hadn't known how much strength this would take. My stomach and my arms and my legs and my face were hurting. Every part of me, inside and out, was hurting. I'll die next, I thought. It won't be very long. Give me a few more minutes and we'll all be together again.

I'd put Katie in her highchair in the kitchen, turning her to face the back door and giving her some things from the kitchen drawer – slightly irresponsible things if I was honest – to play with. A metal nutmeg grater with a not especially blunt edge. A can opener. A corkscrew with a blade on it for cutting foil. A risk, perhaps, but I was no longer a good mother in any proper sense of the word, and, more than anything, I needed to keep her entertained.

Iris's hand had slipped down off the banister and she was sleeping now with her head on her hands, the way she always did. Even in her bed she would sleep like that, with her mouth closed and her hands neatly folded, as if she'd taken sleeping lessons and passed with distinction.

I looked at her and I seemed to lose all energy. It dropped away. I put the cushion on my knees and I sat down next to her at the foot of the stairs and I put my hand on those parts of her I knew so well. The strands of dark hair that fell across her face. The small blue veins in the crook of her wrist, the inside of her little finger with its anxious, bitten-down stump of nail.

I thought about how she was my first baby, how her coming along had changed everything, made me into a different person. How there was never a moment after that when I could properly relax and not care. There wasn't a single moment when I could exist without this huge and beautiful and extraordinary thing at stake – this thing to live for, this thing to die for.

Iris.

I thought about leaving her then, letting her stay alive. But I looked outside and I saw that already the trees at the bottom of the garden were drowning in flames. And then I imagined the look on her face when she saw what had happened to Gloria and Jimmy and the dog . . .

I put the cushion on her face.

I don't know what I expected. I suppose I thought it would be like Gloria and Jimmy, but it wasn't. She gagged. She started. She struggled. She struggled hard. She fought me. The pills hadn't worked – she could not have been properly asleep. It turned into exactly what I had not wanted – a fight.

I heard her say, No! I heard her say, Mummy!

For the first time in my life, I did not answer her. I did not speak. I shut my ears, my face, my heart. I kept the cushion held right down. I could not bear it. I did not want to see her face. I did not want her to have to see mine.

Her fingers clawed at me. She had no nails, but still she managed to draw blood on my hands, my wrists. I held the cushion firm. Her cries grew weaker. Her fingers stopped moving. Her hands dropped away. She became slower, gentler. Then stiller. I heard a little moan. Then finally she was still.

Her head was at a bad angle on the stairs. She looked so uncomfortable. More than anything I wanted to make her better, prop her up, sort her out.

Iris? I whispered.

I waited.

I was so afraid to take the cushion off. I stayed there for as long as I could, holding it on her face and sobbing. I don't know how much time went by. I didn't want to leave her. I didn't want it to be the end. I wanted to tell her I was sorry. I wanted to find out that it hadn't worked after all – to have her wake up, get up, look at me in that accusing way and take care of me in the way she probably would have if I'd let her grow up to be a young girl and then a woman and then . . .

Iris. My Iris.

I could hear Katie in the kitchen, happily making music with the can opener and the nutmeg grater, banging them hard against the table of her highchair.

I went in there and undid the harness and pulled her out of the chair. Blood on her hands, on her face. I tried to wipe it with a tea towel but she wouldn't let me. She drummed her feet and yelled at me when I tried to prise the grater from her fingers.

I got it away from her, then kissed her head and shook her hard to shut her up. She made a funny noise when I shook her. My tears in her hair. Our faces knocking together as I tried to pull her against me. I bundled her into her old red snowsuit – my hands shaking so hard I could hardly do up the poppers so in the end I didn't bother. I left it open.

There was thick black smoke in the hall and a crackling sound coming from upstairs, as I carried her, still screaming out of the back door. The last thing I saw as I got us away from the house was the car, flames sneaking around the edges of the boot, smoke pouring out – the smell of burning plastic. I thought of all the children's things in there and, for a few stupid seconds, I wondered if I should try to get Gloria's beloved Sylvanians. Then the memory of why I shouldn't swung back over me and my thoughts went dark and my legs carried me away.

I walk through the snow on Camomile Street with my child in my arms. She is getting to be quite a big girl now, a real dead weight. I think that her second birthday must be coming up soon, but most of the facts have already slid away and I have no idea for sure of when she was born or even if she is definitely mine.

I don't know how we got here.

I don't know how much longer I can go on carrying her through this snow. I don't know what's been happening or how much time has gone by. I don't know what kind of person could do that to their child, their children. I don't know what kind of person I am. I don't know who I am. I thought I would be dead by now. I don't know if I am dead or not. So many things I don't know.

And across the road from us, a man is slumped on what is left of a wall, quite a young man really, smoking a roll-up and drinking from a bottle. Drunk. And he sees me staring at him. Slow motion now. He puts the bottle down.

And I wait. And even though I know exactly what is going to happen, because there are no longer any surprises – just this endless, heartbreaking loop of consequences – still my heart sinks a little when he throws the cigarette in the snow and slides down off the wall.

It won't be long now, I think, and it isn't.

In three quick seconds, he is beside me.

The one thing he got wrong, the kid: he didn't start it. It was me. It wasn't the night in the taxi – that was already right in the middle of it. We were certainly both too deep in it by then.

It was all my fault. We were children. On the carpet, playing with the beetles. And I wanted to have an effect on him. I wanted him to see me. He was not looking. He never looked. I wanted him to look. And I could not resist the shape of his mouth.

Whoa, he said. I can't believe you just said that.

What? What do you think I said?

He shook his head, rubbed at his face.

I can't say it. I just can't. It's just so raw.

He looked at the carpet for the longest time. Finally, he scratched his head. Still he did not look at me. His face was red.

I will if you want me to, he said at last. I can, you know. I could. I quite like you actually. What I mean is, I don't really care. I wouldn't mind doing it. If you want me to.

The first time we went to see the counsellor, during that first summer when I was trying so hard not to see Matthew, Simon told her it was the lies he found hardest.

Me turning my phone off, pretending I'd left it at home. Telling him I was in one place when I was in another. Telling him I had put it all behind me when, clearly, I had not. How was he supposed to trust me after that?

The counsellor looked at us both and she waited. I waited too. Was that the question? I didn't know if I was supposed to answer it. I didn't have any answers. Anyway, Simon was right. I had lied. I was not trustworthy. I didn't trust myself. That was the worst thing, if I stopped to think about it. Trust. I never had.

So I said nothing. I looked at my hands. I touched my fingers on the cool back of my neck. Put my lips to the flat inside of my wrist, breathed it in. The smell was of nothing. I looked at my knees, but they were the same ones I'd always had. They gave me no clues. I said nothing.

This, he explained to her, was why he'd told me it had to be all or nothing. It had to be over. He had to be certain there

would be no contact. If I wanted our family to stand a chance.
It had to be a clean break.

This had surely been reasonable, hadn't it?

Had it?

Hadn't it?

The counsellor looked at us both and waited. I waited too.
I wanted to find out the answer. I didn't know the answer. I
thought I would make them wait.

He throws the cigarette in the snow and slides down off the
wall. In three seconds he is beside me.

I've got nothing, I tell him, but he looks at my bleeding hands
and wrists and then he looks straight at the child. She returns
his gaze.

Boy or girl?

Just like last time, I say nothing. I pull her against me. He
moves in closer. His breath is rank. I see that his hands are
moving too fast.

I said what is it, a boy or a girl?

I shake my head.

You what? he says.

There are two of them now. His friend has joined him. They
stand there in the snow, the two of them. They ask me again
if it's a boy or a girl. Then they ask me what it's called.

And I look down at this child who I am holding now in my
arms, her eyes round with fatigue, her breath hot against my
neck, and I tell them the truth – that I don't know.

The look that they exchange is quick and complicated.

You don't know your own kid's name?

I look at her again. Is she my own? I look at her hands, my
hands. The blood from both of us has rubbed off on my coat.

I can't think why anyone would do that – why would anyone want to cut the hands of a child?

The first man looks at me and he doesn't smile. The child is studying him with glassy, tired eyes. Suddenly, though, she looks amused, delighted. Without any warning, her small hand flies out towards him.

Man! she says.

Taken by surprise, he doesn't wait. He raises his fist and shoves it hard in her face. As my arms open and I let her fall, he reaches out for me – for any part of me.

I smile. I knew this was coming.

The last thing I see is the water closing over her astonished face. A million crystals waiting to meld together. Ice forming.

I thought the world was frozen. I didn't know there was a puddle there. That's the very last thing I think before the world goes dark. Surprise, puddle, ice . . .

The last time we saw the counsellor – all those months later, after Matt was gone and I had decided that the only truthful thing was to leave Simon – she already knew everything, because he'd been seeing her all this time.

But still, he sat there, explaining – for my benefit, I supposed – and he asked her more or less the same question. Did she think he had acted reasonably? Had his thoughts and actions at least been understandable? Hadn't he tried his best to be loving and kind?

And I looked at him, sitting there on that sagging brown sofa with the William Morris pattern, the picture of a surprised-looking cat propped, just like last time, among the dead grasses in the fireplace. And I looked at her, with her frizzy hair and her calming ethnic jewellery and her box of Kleenex and the three untouched glasses of water lined up.

And I thought about how it was true. Simon really had been very kind, very understanding. And he was right, it was a disappointment that I had been unable to respond to his continued kindness and reasonableness with the energy and love that he felt was his due.

And then I thought about how dark and cold the world was. I thought about the way that everything that was good and kind and hopeful always had to be taken from you. I thought about how everything always ended in a cold place, bones and ashes, life sucked out, in darkness.

I shivered. And I thought about crying. But then I thought about how I'd had enough of crying, so I started to laugh.

Simon turned to the counsellor. He said nothing. He kept a very straight and level face, but his eyes said it all.

Now do you see what I'm up against?

She didn't speak. She kept her eyes on me and said nothing.

Me too – I did the same. I stopped laughing, finally, and I said nothing. I waited and waited. I pushed my fingers into the corners of my eyes, to try to keep back the tears, but it didn't work, they rolled down over my hands, my wrists, and still no suitable words came.

And I thought that I wasn't going to get away with it. I thought she would soon tell me that it was time to speak, to account for myself, but she didn't. She never did. I felt very grateful to her.

I felt Arthur hiccup inside me then. Hanging there. Keeping me in this world.

And I took a breath. I decided to speak.

* * *

I wake. It is night. Cold. Snow. My head in someone's lap. The person is humming. I know the tune.

Sophy? I say. Ted? Iris?

Oh, he says. You're awake.

I don't think so.

Fingers come down on my face. Grubby boy's fingers. I try to move my legs but my feet are stuck together.

It's all right, he says. I'll undo it in a moment.

What?

Shh.

His thumb on my lips. I know what he'll be wearing – red jersey, brown tracksuit bottoms. And I know what he'll say.

Someone hurt you. I found you here like this. I want you to come with me. I know a safe place – a place close to here.

For a few quick seconds, I see her face again. Her parted lips. The little bottom teeth. The eyes bright blue and astonished.

I shut my eyes.

The building? You're taking me to the building?

I think about its wide dark spaces, terraces, corridors. The black night sky. The world turning colder. A dog barking, children laughing – a little girl waiting to find me.

I don't open my eyes. I don't have to.

I know it, I tell him. You don't have to take me. Don't you realise? I'm already there.

Acknowledgements

Frosts, Friezes And Fairs – Chronicles Of The Frozen Thames And Harsh Winters In Britain by Ian Currie partially inspired this novel and stayed on my desk throughout the writing of it. Jonathan Myerson, Gill Coleridge and Dan Franklin are – and I hope always will be – my ideal first readers. Alex Bowler gave it the kind of thorough and sensitive page-editing that most authors dream of, but rarely get. And then there were all the kind people – family and friends but also many strangers – who buoyed me up so generously through a dark year. Without you I really am not sure this book would exist.